THE
SEISMIC
SEVEN

Also by Katie Slivensky:

The Countdown Conspiracy

KATIE SLIVENSKY

HARPER
An Imprint of HarperCollinsPublishers

Library of Congress Cataloging-in-Publication Data
Names: Slivensky, Katie, author.ʹ
Title: The Seismic Seven / Katie Slivensky.
Description: First edition. | New York, NY : HarperCollins, an imprint of
    HarperCollinsPublishers, [2018] | Summary: Seven middle schoolers brought
    to Yellowstone National Park, supposedly to stop a supervolcano from
    erupting, learn that they are actually working for a brilliant scientist
    determined to destroy the world.
Identifiers: LCCN 2017034556 | ISBN 978-0-06-246318-0 (hardback)
Subjects: | CYAC: Adventure and adventurers--Fiction. | Volcanoes--Fiction. |
    Geology--Fiction. | Yellowstone National Park--Fiction. | Science fiction.
    | BISAC: JUVENILE FICTION / Action & Adventure / Survival Stories. |
    JUVENILE FICTION / Social Issues / Self-Esteem & Self-Reliance. |
    JUVENILE FICTION / Robots.
Classification: LCC PZ7.1.S5906 Sei 2018 | DDC [Fic]--dc23 LC record
    available at https://lccn.loc.gov/2017034556

Typography by Jenna Stempel-Lobell
18 19 20 21 22 CG/LSCH 10 9 8 7 6 5 4 3 2 1

First Edition

For my sister, Jeannie—my lifelong friend and the first person I'd pick to help me stop an apocalypse.

CHAPTER ONE

I check the view behind me, lining up the landscape in my camera's frame. Once I'm satisfied, I move my thumb out of the way of the shot and hit record.

"Hello, everyone! Welcome to this summer's adventures! It's sunny with a chance of mountains today here in Montana. Which kind of sounds like the word mountain, now that I'm saying it out loud." I pause and tuck some strands of dark hair behind my ear. Over my shoulder, tufts of clouds pass over the scenery, in contrast to the green of the trees and the blue of the sky. "Edit note: check if that's how Montana got its name and overlay fact bubble."

I smile extra broadly and continue, knowing later I'll cut that line and put in a video annotation to either confirm my guess or poke fun at it.

"Viewers may notice that I'm doing my own camerawork this time around, because Aunt Pauline—"

"Bri, now isn't the time," my mom interrupts me, sticking her head out from the door of our motel room. Her hair blows in front of her face, like mine keeps doing.

"Mom!" I protest.

The door opens all the way, its shadow moving along the pavement in the early morning sun, and she walks out to join me, shaking her head at my camera. "I'm sure your aunt didn't buy you this just to waste its battery in a parking lot. I thought you wanted to record Yellowstone?" Her nose wrinkles, scrunching up her freckles.

"I do." I sigh loudly, flicking the switch on the back to stop recording. "But no one is here yet, and if I want to make this a full documentary, I need a good intro. How many motels do we get to stay at with this kind of view?"

We're supposed to meet the group I'll be working with this summer at 8:00 a.m. here in the parking lot. It's only 7:45 right now, but we're up and outside already, because it's my parents, so of course we're early.

My dad cleans various beverage containers out of our sedan. "I know you're excited," he says, cramming another bottle into the bag of recyclables. "But when your professor pulls up, do you want her first impression to be you recording yourself?"

I grumble. I mean, no, but I don't want to admit that. Instead I kick a rock between my feet and watch the mountains in the distance, trying to imagine how they got their shape. Maybe that will be my next challenge in Earth Builder: replicate a real mountain range. After all, it was replicating the first eruption of the Yellowstone Supervolcano that got me this opportunity to begin with, as much as my parents dislike my obsession with that game. Their faces when they heard that I got an invitation to work with a world-famous geologist because of my *video game skills* were priceless.

"Do you think Aunt Pauline has had any luck with that building they were clearing yesterday?" I ask, checking my phone and changing the subject.

"If she has, that means she's probably too busy to text us about it," my mom replies, trying to sound reassuring for both my sake and my dad's, since it's his sister. "I know you're worried, Bri, but we'd hear if anything went wrong. We're her emergency contact, remember?"

I nod, putting my phone down and going back to the new, super fancy camera my aunt got me as a present for winning this contest to work at Yellowstone for the summer.

"Bri." My mom gives me a look.

"What?" I ask, flipping the camera around and pretending like I was just fiddling with it. "Aunt Pauline's going to want to see what I'm doing. So will my viewers."

Well, by my viewers, I mean hers, but still. Aunt Pauline and I usually take trips together for the summer, recording for her nature documentary YouTube channel. This year we had to cancel the trip, because LA had a massive earthquake—8.4 on the Richter scale—and Aunt Pauline decided to go help with the cleanup and rescue efforts. She's clearing rubble and helping build temporary shelters.

As much as I miss my aunt, I can't lie—I *am* excited for the chance to create a documentary on my own. I'll finally be able to show her that I can be more than just the kid cohost. Plus, I get to do it in Yellowstone! She and I were here last summer, and it was amazing. I have so many ideas of places to film.

"Have I mentioned how proud we are of you?" Dad says, walking over to hug me.

"Dad." I squirm. My bony elbows dig into my stomach as I push away from him.

"So proud. Even though I hate this part," he says. "I thought with your aunt away, I'd get to keep you for a summer. But you're just too talented, so I'm losing you again."

I look to Mom for help with eye-rolling, but she's welling up. That catches me off guard. Do they cry every summer when I leave?

Before I can say anything else, a blond family comes out of two of the other motel rooms. Why they were in two rooms rather than one, I don't know. One kid with them looks to be thirteen-ish—around my age. He's wearing glasses and is kind of scrawny.

The other kid with the approaching family looks maybe nine or ten, despite having her face loaded with makeup. She's much tanner than the rest of her family and walks ahead of them, her flip-flops smacking against the ground loudly.

"Hey!" she calls toward me.

"Uh, hey?" I answer.

"You waiting for Dr. Grier?" She's still yelling, even though she's close enough now that she could probably drop her voice to a normal level.

"Yes, we are," my mom says for me.

"Well, she's not coming. The park manager is picking us up instead and taking us to meet her," the girl says, pulling out a tube of bright red lipstick and reapplying it, despite definitely not needing any more. I look back at her family, trying to rein in my judgment but failing spectacularly. They all seem clean-cut and put together, pretty much the opposite of the mess in front of me. "I met her last night. Her name's Ms. MacNamary. She's okay. Kind of runs Yellowstone, so she'd better be. I'm Kenzie, by the way." She juts out her hand.

I shake it. "Brianna," I reply.

"That back there is Todd." She gestures.

"I can introduce myself." The boy frowns. Their parents look at each other, and then at Kenzie, with a mixture of sympathy and frustration.

"Todd's got some work to do on his people skills, but I bet we can make a real human out of him by the end of the summer," Kenzie says.

I laugh, despite a look from my mom.

My dad creases his forehead, adjusting the sunglasses that are pushed up into his receding hairline. "Kenzie, are you part of the crew that Dr. Grier has invited?"

"Sure am," she says. "I'm thirteen, by the way. If you're con-fused. I get that a lot."

"Oh." I blink, feeling my cheeks redden. You have to be twelve to be eligible for the contest to work with Dr. Grier, so I *way* misjudged her age. "Wow, yeah. Sorry. So, is this your brother, or . . . ?" I gesture at Todd.

I can't tell who looks more appalled. Todd, Kenzie, or the man and woman with them.

"Oh god, no!" Kenzie gags. "No way, nope."

"Definitely not," Todd says. "We just met."

The woman looks at my mom. "We're Todd's parents. Kenzie arrived last night without a legal guardian, so Laura—the park manager—asked if I wouldn't mind sharing a room with her."

"My grandma sent me on my own," Kenzie says. "I can travel by myself. I've done it before. But motel regulations or something said I had to have an adult with me." She arches an eyebrow, look-ing up at me. "Rules, am I right?"

I think I'm a whole foot taller than her. I resist the urge to reach out and fix her ponytail, which is half pulled up with a pile of waves falling out of it.

"So Dr. Grier isn't meeting the kids?" my mom asks Todd's parents.

"Dr. Grier is in a critical stage of her research, so she'll be meeting the kids on site in the park," Todd's mom explains. "Laura told us—*such* a lovely woman. So considerate with . . ." She trails off, looking at Kenzie, who smiles sweetly back at her and doesn't let her break eye contact. "Er, everything."

Kenzie continues to stare her down, her smile spreading into a grin.

"Laura said she's been working closely with Dr. Grier's team and will be supervising the kids with her this summer," Todd's dad says. "I hadn't realized that an actual member of the Yellowstone administration would be involved. An extra win for the college application forms!"

My dad squeezes my shoulder. "We couldn't be prouder."

I look away from Kenzie, embarrassment flooding through me. How awkward can parents be?

"Excuse me, are you here for the Yellowstone geology trip?" a man says from behind us. We all turn.

Next to the man is another kid. They both have darker skin. The man's hair is graying, and the boy is even skinnier than I am and wears a backpack stuffed to the point of overflowing.

"I'm Jim Cayanan. This is my son, Wyatt," the man says, when my parents confirm that we are all here to meet Dr. Grier—or now, rather, Ms. Laura MacNamary.

"Nice to meet you, I'm Todd," Todd says, immediately stepping forward.

Wyatt shakes his hand. "Hi."

"Kenzie." Kenzie jumps in next.

"Hi."

"And I'm Brianna. You can call me Bri," I say, shaking his hand last.

"Okay. Hi." He smiles at us, then steps back next to his dad, adjusting his backpack on his back. He doesn't say anything else.

With only a half moment to spare before the silence becomes totally awkward, the adults begin chatting among themselves. Meanwhile, I'm kicking myself for not filming our introductions. I'll have to do some kind of "get to know you" segments later.

"Cayanan, what is that? Indonesian?" my dad asks. I want to bury my face in my hands.

Dad!

"Filipino," Wyatt's dad answers. I risk a glance at Wyatt, but I don't know him at all and can't judge his expression.

"I thought it might be," my Dad says next even though I know he had no idea.

I'm about to check my phone again for someplace to look that isn't at or around my awkwardly prying father when a beige Dodge Caravan pulls up with the National Park Service logo on its side. It parks next to us, and a lady with curly brown hair climbs out.

"Oh!" she gasps, as a gust of wind blows by, lifting her tan ranger hat straight off her head. She grabs it, yanking it back down quickly. "It's windier than I thought!"

We've all stopped talking now, even the adults.

"Hey, it's Ms. MacNamary, everyone," Kenzie says. She jerks her thumb over her shoulder at the van.

"Yes, we know," Todd says. I see his dad nudge him, giving him a look I know all too well from my own parents.

"Well, it's great to meet you!" my mom says, stepping forward with her hand out.

Ms. MacNamary shakes my mom's hand. She looks to be around her age, I'd guess. Maybe a little older. "It's wonderful to meet *you*! You must be Dr. Dobson, Brianna's mother. And you must be Dr. Dobson, Brianna's father! And you must be Brianna!" She turns to my dad and then me, chuckling as everyone always does at my parents' twin titles. "I'm so glad you can join us."

I silently stand between my parents as they thank Ms. MacNamary for hosting us kids in the park. I feel as quiet as Wyatt now. Huh. *Quiet Wyatt.*

Ms. MacNamary introduces herself to Wyatt next and then everyone splits apart to grab luggage. I use the opportunity to turn my camera on, zooming in on my face for a moment. Glancing around to make sure no one's watching, I hit record. "And we're back! I am live on scene as me and a bunch of other young adventurers pack up into Ms. MacNamary's . . . uh, minivan."

I zoom in on the beige Dodge Caravan in the motel parking lot, deciding to put some over-the-top gritty filters on the footage later for comedic effect.

"The best known vehicle for exploring!" I bring the camera back to me. "We're about to head into Yellowstone—my *favorite* of the national parks, if you haven't been watching my aunt's series. Which, if you haven't, where have you been? Seriously, go catch up. Anyway, Mom and Dad have to go back home to Portland, and me and the other contest winners are about to head out. They're over there!" I pan the camera around to the three other kids.

"Brianna? What are you doing?" Ms. MacNamary calls over,

pulling her hat tight over her bushy hair once again.

"A video for my channel!" I reply. Is she one of those adults who will know what I'm talking about, or one of the ones who still thinks the internet is just for emailing and Facebook?

Whether she understands or not, she crosses her arms. "Well, you better get all that out of your system now, because Dr. Grier is never going to let you film in the field. She's very anti-tech out on the job."

I frown. That's unexpected. "Cut again," I say, since I'm still recording and I'll obviously want to take this section out, too. The prospect of not getting to do videos kind of tanks my summer, so I hope she's wrong about Dr. Grier's rules. Shaking my head, I go back to the mountain shot and continue. "Okay, viewers, I have no idea if or when I'll be making another of these—"

"Bri, what did Ms. MacNamary just say?" my mom interrupts.

"—since I'll be super busy helping scientists on my trip," I continue in a rush. "So I hope you all enjoyed this little intro to the summer and hopefully I'll see you again before too long!"

I hit stop.

"You're recording something? I want to be in it!" Kenzie says.

"Next one," I promise.

She grins. "I'm holding you to that. The world needs more Kenzie."

"It really doesn't," Todd says from over by the van. Wyatt looks at Kenzie, confused, and I try not to laugh as she scoffs in annoyance at Todd. Then Ms. MacNamary calls us all over, and whatever Kenzie was going to say gets cut short.

"We'll want to get going quickly, as we have a considerable drive to our campsite," Ms. MacNamary says as we gather around. "I have supplies for Dr. Grier in the back of the van, but there's room for everyone's bags on top of it all."

"So you will personally be driving the kids to meet her, correct?" Wyatt's dad asks.

"Yes. And in fact, I'll be working with Dr. Grier and your kids all summer," Ms. MacNamary tells our parents. "My contact information is in the confirmation email you got for the contest. Please, feel free to be in touch at any time. I'm probably the best person to reach out to with immediate questions, as Dr. Grier tends to get wrapped up in her work."

"I can't imagine what that's like," my dad quietly jokes to me. I laugh. My mom is awful at answering texts when she's on her hospital shifts.

"Oh, and I should mention," Ms. MacNamary continues, now turning her attention to us kids. "Cell coverage is *terrible* where we'll be in the park, but we do have a ranger laptop hardwired to the internet at the campsite, so emailing is fairly reliable. You're welcome to write to your friends and families as often as you'd like."

"Every day," Todd's mom insists. Todd blushes at that.

"When I get bored," I tease my own parents.

"You? Bored, in Yellowstone?" My mom shakes her head. "I won't hold my breath."

"Does anyone else have any other questions?" Ms. MacNamary

asks. She only waits a half second, checking her watch, clearly hoping to keep us on schedule. "If not, we can pack up and get going."

"I'm ready to hit the road," Todd says. "Thank you for driving us, Ms. MacNamary."

"Suck-up," I hear Kenzie whisper in Todd's general direction, as his parents hug him goodbye. Mine do the same with me.

"Be good," my mom says, holding me tightly. "Don't spend all your time with that camera. I already told Ms. MacNamary that it's a privilege, not a right, and she can take it away if she needs to."

"Mom!" I exclaim. Our hug just got way less sentimental.

"I'm just saying, I know you want to be a filmmaker-type person like your aunt, but maybe this summer try focusing more on the science side of things? You're so good at it."

"Yeah, okay," I say.

"I'm serious, Brianna Marie," she says. "Look what you did with that video game! Look where it got you!"

"Yes, got it." I pull back, trying to ignore my mom's pained expression as I disentangle us. "Dad? Any parting instructions?"

My dad smiles down at me, pulling me in for a huge hug. "Take advantage of this opportunity."

"Right," I say, sighing.

"I love you," he says next.

"Love you, too," I say.

"And I love you," my mom says, as I pull back from my dad.

My eyes land on Wyatt, who is getting a pat on the back from his dad, then on Kenzie, who is weirdly watching me with laser focus.

"Can I help you?" I ask her.

She shrugs. "Are we videoing now or later?"

"Later," my mom answers for me. "You're supposed to be packing the van now, remember, Bri?"

I nod. "Yeah, I know. I—"

Just then, the ground moves below my feet.

"What the—?" Kenzie starts.

Todd yelps, grabbing for his parents. My dad reaches for me, clutching my arm to steady me, but just as quickly as the shaking started, it stops. The fading motel sign swings on its hooks—the only indication anything out of the ordinary just happened.

"Whoa!" Kenzie exclaims. "What was that, a buffalo stampede nearby or something?"

"Bison," I correct.

"Earthquake," Wyatt says. "That was an earthquake."

"I believe it was," Ms. MacNamary says. "Wow, what timing! A little taste of the seismic activity that this region can bring, right before we all head off to explore it."

I chance a wary glance at my parents.

"How cool!" my mom says, actually smiling. My shoulders drop in relief—I wasn't sure if we were going with "cool" or "no way, you're coming straight home!", despite home being Oregon, where we get little quakes like that all the time.

We share a laugh, and then a thought hits me. "I should've been recording!" I lament.

"We can reenact it," Kenzie says. She gives Todd a shove next to her, and then fake wobbles on her own feet. Todd straightens his shirt, recovering as smoothly as one can after being earthquaked by a surprisingly strong ninety-pound girl.

This is going to be an interesting summer.

CHAPTER TWO

I film my parents' car leaving the motel parking lot, panning to the backdrop of the mountains and blinking away some unexpected tears.

It took two days for us to drive here, and will take two days for them to drive back. They both had to call out of work to make this happen, and I know that means they'll have to take on some long shifts in the coming weeks. My friends often tell me how awesome my parents are. It's in moments like these that I see what they mean.

A shout from Todd pulls my attention away. "Hey, leave my stuff alone!"

Kenzie drags a suitcase toward the minivan. "Buddy, if you want to get moving *ASAP* like you said you did, you're going to need to pick up the pace. Like Wyatt, here." Kenzie gestures at the other boy. "He packed light. One backpack, and he's in!"

"Where's your stuff?" Todd asks, taking his suitcase from Kenzie and hefting it into the back of the van.

"Already loaded last night," Kenzie says.

Quiet Wyatt sidesteps around Kenzie to get out of the way. I wonder if he's really deserving of the nickname Quiet Wyatt, or if it's more that Todd and Kenzie are just that loud. I guess time will tell.

Behind me, Ms. MacNamary coughs slightly. "You're welcome to do a video up at the top of Beartooth Pass once we get there," she tells me. "I don't want to rob you of your fun. Didn't mean to scare you earlier about the anti-tech thing."

"Thanks," I say, somewhat surprised. She nods pleasantly, then goes to shut the back of the van now that we're loaded up.

"So what did you do for your project?" Todd asks me, clearly looking to escape from Kenzie's attention.

"I did simulations of volcanic activity in Earth Builder," I say. His face goes blank, so I realize he must not know what that is. "The video game?"

"Oh, right." Todd nods, even though I'm pretty sure he still has no idea what I'm talking about. "Well, mine was about variable pressures for geyser eruption. I used R to run my stats. What software did you use?"

"Earth Builder," I repeat.

"That's a video game," he says.

"Yeah, and it keeps track of statistics. Percent successes, failures, catastrophes—those are the best of course."

"No, I meant what *scientific* software did you use?" Todd asks.

"What, like a real scientist?" I stare at him. "I'm thirteen."

Todd stares back until Kenzie jumps in. "You did your project using a video game and *still* got in to this program? You must've really blown the socks off Dr. Grier!"

I flush. Honestly, when I first found out, I was just as shocked as Todd. I've always done well in school, but I've never won anything before. I'm constantly being lectured at to apply myself. My fifth grade teacher in particular had quite the conniption a couple of years back when I turned in my math test and had transformed all the word problems into comic strips.

"You have so much potential and your creativity is wonderful, Bri, it really is, but there is a time and place for it and you just haven't found it yet."

I scan the mountains beyond Ms. MacNamary's van. I wonder what Mrs. Thriftly would think of me now. About to head off to join Dr. Samantha Grier, world-famous geologist, for a summer of official science research.

In your face, Mrs. Thriftly.

"Honestly? You're lucky you got in the way you did," Kenzie says. "I got stuck going to a geology conference to present my project at a poster session with a bunch of lame-butt nerds and science fair trophy kids."

"Hey," Todd pouts. "Dr. Grier picked me because I won my state science fair." He looks genuinely hurt. I can't help but shake my head at him. Pale, skinny, glasses, and a science fair winner on top of it all. It's like Todd is living his life according to some sort of nerdy stereotype manual—with the one exception that he isn't addicted to Earth Builder, like every good nerd should be.

"My point stands," Kenzie says.

I cover up a laugh. "What about you, Wyatt?"

He looks up from his phone. "My project was about lava flow patterns. I used to live in Hawaii. My mom worked as a ranger at Volcanoes National Park until she died. Then I moved to Texas to live with my dad. I missed volcanic places, found out about this opportunity, and wrote something up going off of all the pictures I had from back home."

I blink, not really sure what to do with that sudden influx of personal information.

"Your mom died?" Kenzie asks. "That *sucks*."

"Kenzie!" Todd chastises.

"Tell me about it," Wyatt says, looking super unfazed by Kenzie's bluntness. "So yeah, that's what my project was."

"Cool, cool," Kenzie says. "I'm all about plate tectonics. They move the world, and that's what I plan on doing."

"You're each very impressive," Ms. MacNamary calls out the window from the driver's seat. She's already got the van started. "It's why Dr. Grier selected you. So how about we get this show on the road and drive in to meet her?"

"Right! Coming!" Kenzie replies for all of us.

Todd calls shotgun. Kenzie and I climb in and take the middle seats. Wyatt squeezes into the back, awkwardly sandwiching himself next to a bunch of our bags that spilled over from the rear of the van.

We pull out of the parking lot in the opposite direction that my parents did. Todd and Kenzie start speculating loudly about what kind of classification we're going to be doing in the next weeks, and my mind drifts to a series of videos I want to make interviewing everyone about their projects. I'll call the segments "Nerd Time." I want to get everyone a hat to wear during their interviews that says "Nerd in Charge," though where I'll find one of those out in the park, I have no idea. But I smile thinking of how Aunt Pauline will react to the clips if I pull off their editing well.

"We all knew the quake was coming," Todd says. Apparently, they've moved on from talking about classification to talking about the LA earthquake.

"We didn't know it was going to be *that* big," Kenzie replies.

"The San Andreas fault has been—"

"The San Andreas fault has been dangerous for, like, ever, so yes, people should have been somewhat prepared, but you don't get to say the ones who weren't were idiots."

"Mother Nature is a force to be reckoned with," Ms. MacNamary intones from the driver's seat.

"See? Mother Nature. Force to be reckoned with." Kenzie puts on more lipstick.

"My aunt is actually helping with the cleanup." I hop into the conversation.

"That's amazing!" Kenzie exclaims, folding her tiny legs up underneath her on the seat. "What's she doing?"

"Last I heard from her, she was clearing rubble to get more streets reopened," I say. "She started by doing search and rescue for all the missing people." I don't bring up the fact that they never *found* a lot of the missing people, because that was really tough on my aunt. "Then she spent a couple months building new shelters for everyone who lost their homes. She's been there since January."

"God, that is awesome," Kenzie says. "Can I join your family?"

I laugh. "My parents already don't know what to do with me."

Kenzie's phone buzzes and she pulls it out. I take the chance to check my own phone, looking up my Earth Builder rankings after scrolling through some messages from my friends. I'm in the middle of the pack on the EB live stats page, which I guess is okay since I haven't played in days. I know I'm going to drop lower and lower all summer. Just something I have to accept.

Next, I pull up my aunt's YouTube channel to see if she's updated at all.

Nothing. She really must be busy. I lower my phone and lean my head against the van window, trying to squish away the feelings of wishing she was on *my* adventure with *me*.

Ms. MacNamary begins heading up the switchbacks. The roads get steeper, cutting back and forth along the mountainside. Forests extend as far as I can see. I pull my camera out to start getting some B-roll footage, especially as we make the hairpin turns to reverse and head up the next switchback. I try not to laugh as Todd grips his armrest in front of me tighter and tighter. I zoom in on his paling knuckles for a few shots and then go back out the window.

From the height of my seat—which isn't that tall, since this is a minivan—it almost looks like there is no ground between me and falling to my death. These roads are super narrow, and we're basically on the edge of a cliff the entire way. Aunt Pauline would love this. Mom and Dad would not.

We finally get above the tree line, where everything becomes bare rock. I decide a fact bubble here would be useful to talk about altitude and how high up mountains trees can grow. There are even patches of snow to emphasize the drop in temperature. When we reach the top of the pass, Ms. MacNamary pulls into a makeshift parking lot, and I immediately unbuckle and get out of the van.

A few cars are already up here. Some burly guys hang out by the edge of the overlook. A family walks by speaking in what I think is German, though I'm not entirely sure because the only other language I know any small bit of is Spanish. A group of college-aged people point at something on a bronze plaque. Kenzie shoves her way out of the van, whooping loudly at how fantastic the view is, and I fire up my camera. Spinning it at myself, I hit record as quick as I can so I can get my most natural reaction shot.

"Oh my god. This place is *gorgeous*," I say, staring out over the edge of the mountaintop. Below are rolling hills of green, speckled with big gray boulders, clumps of snow, and random pine trees. The contrasting colors, especially with the blue sky overhead, make for a scene I know my camera will never properly capture. So I'll need to ramble.

"Guys, I wish you were all here. Everyone should visit the

Beartooth Pass. Spoiler alert: no bear teeth in sight yet, but I don't even care. This is hands-down the best entrance to Yellowstone! Seriously, are you *seeing this*?" I pan the camera around. I'll throw a bubble up here to explain that it's the shape of the mountains that give the pass its name, not because there are actual bear teeth. But in the meantime, as promised, I turn the camera on Kenzie. "Kenzie, please tell the audience how you're enjoying our pit stop at the edge of paradise."

"Well, Bri, I have to say it's beautiful beyond belief. Ten out of ten; would beartooth again." Kenzie looks straight into the camera, giving a solid nod. I can already tell she's going to be a great filming partner. I've decided her mop of hair doesn't need to be fixed; it adds charm.

Then I remember what Ms. MacNamary said about Dr. Grier's lack of love for technology and how this might be my last chance for a video.

I look down over the landscape once more.

Worth it.

I close up shop, turn my camera off, and head back to the van where Ms. MacNamary waits patiently.

"Enjoying the view?" she asks me, wistfully gazing out over the scenery.

I nod. "It's amazing."

"I love driving in this way. I just had to let us stop here before we continued." Ms. MacNamary adjusts her hat on her head. "But it is time to get moving, so would you mind helping me get everyone back together?"

"Sure," I say. I wave Kenzie over, and Ms. MacNamary goes off to gather the boys.

"Hey, is this you?" Kenzie asks, watching her phone. I check out what she's looking at. It's one of my aunt's videos.

"Yeah," I say, both embarrassed and proud all at once.

"That's so awesome," Kenzie says. The video is from last summer, when Aunt Pauline and I were at Old Faithful. We spent hours there, timing it just right so we could have shots of the geyser going off at different angles, including one where we did forced perspective to make it look like it was exploding right out of the top of my head. Kenzie laughs when we get to that part.

"Oh, is that your video game simulation?" Todd asks, joining us.

"No," I answer. I pull out my own phone, going onto the Earth Builder Featured Users page to bring up that video next.

The pixelated gameplay takes us frame by frame through simulated geological history of the Yellowstone area. After visiting the park last year, I became kind of obsessed with the idea of the Yellowstone Supervolcano. I mean, who wouldn't? A volcano that is thousands of times bigger and more powerful than regular volcanoes, lying dormant under a National Park? Which explains why so much cool stuff happens here, like hot springs and geysers? Freaking amazing. The first thing I did when I got home was fire up Earth Builder and try to see if I could make a supervolcano of my own.

I spent months putting the pieces in place, attempting to set up an event just like the Lava Creek supervolcanic eruption, which was about 630,000 years ago. Eventually, I got the conditions just right and it exploded in the exact—well, almost exact, I suppose—same way the supervolcano fired in real history. I don't know why I put so much time into making it so precise. I think I just wanted to see if I could mimic an actual event and not just set up new volcanoes like most people do in Earth Builder. I had to construct the magma chamber, the type of rock overhead, the fault lines, and the mineral content perfectly. Then, release the pressure, and voila.

On the video, the volcano hisses for a moment, and then comes the catastrophic explosion. Ash skyrockets miles into the air. Lava spews out without end, turning to rock in the sky and raining down across ancient North America.

Todd whistles. "Epic."

Wyatt, who I hadn't noticed join us, agrees. "Well done. Did you do the other two?"

"No," I answer. "Haven't had time yet." The supervolcano under Yellowstone has exploded at least two other times in history. Probably more.

"Hate to say it," Ms. MacNamary interrupts us, "but we're going to head into the park now to meet Dr. Grier, and she won't want to see phones. So I'm going to have to take all those from you."

"What?" Kenzie stares at Ms. MacNamary like she just asked if she could have Kenzie's liver. "Can't we just put them in our bags and promise not to take them out?"

"What about my camera?" I ask.

"I know how hard it is for your generation not to look at your screens—it's not your fault, it's autopilot for you," Ms. MacNamary says sympathetically. "So for now, I'll take all tech. To help you. I'm sure you won't see it that way, though." Her eyes twinkle as Kenzie flails and sputters. "We can try to make arrangements once we're at camp for you to have your phones back, but it's better if we don't upset Dr. Grier right from the get-go. She can be temperamental."

Even though I'd been mentally preparing for this moment, it pains me to put my phone and camera in the bag Ms. MacNamary holds. I hope Dr. Grier turns out to be more reasonable than Ms. MacNamary is implying. Not going to lie, the more I hear about her the more nervous I am about working with her.

Ms. MacNamary puts the bag in the back with our luggage, and we all climb into the van, the atmosphere a touch grumpier than before. Once settled in, we head down the other side of the mountain, straight through the beautiful scenery. I'm glued to the landscape outside and want to scream internally that I can't get any footage. How am I supposed to show Aunt Pauline what I can do if I'm not allowed to do it?

When we reach flatter ground, I spy an elk near the side of the road. She looks up at us, and for a second, I feel like she's staring straight at me. I press a hand to the window as we drive by.

Capture the image in your heart, I hear my mom's advice. It's what she says every time she gets annoyed with me for recording with my phone. I strain to watch the elk as she gets farther and farther away. Another little head pops up when she's almost out of sight, and I realize she's a mother. I could've gotten footage of an adorable baby elk. Dangit!

A few minutes later, we pull up to the park gates. Ms. MacNamary chats for a moment with the ranger at the entrance, and he waves her through with a big smile. Then we turn off the main road onto a small dirt path that I wouldn't have otherwise noticed. From there, we drive deeper into the forest, past a burnt section, and into much older growth.

Last year, Aunt Pauline and I focused on these burnt sections for her documentary, talking about how forest fires can result in life later on. Some trees can't sprout from their seeds until they're heated up by fire and need everything else burned away so they'll have the most access to sunshine and nutrients without competing with other plants. It's really weird to think about, but totally natural. A lot of fires unfortunately aren't natural, though, so another part of Aunt Pauline's documentary was interviewing firefighters and rescue workers in the area about how they go about stopping those.

Eventually, we leave the forest and reach the base of a huge hill—which could be a mountain in its own right, honestly, but since there are so many larger ones in the area, I don't know if I'd call it one. We stop here, despite there being no visible camp. In fact, all I can see are signs everywhere warning tourists that this area is off-limits because of rockslides and grizzly bears.

"Okay, everybody out." Ms. MacNamary's voice takes on a serious tone. "Make yourselves presentable."

The sound of unbuckling belts fills the van, and I slide the side door wide open. Hopping out into the field of grass and wildflowers, I notice there are piles of rock rubble at the hill's base—maybe from the rockslides the signs were warning people about.

I'm about to ask if it's safe for us to be here, when I notice a person waiting by one of the giant piles of rock.

"Dr. Grier, these are our summer volunteers," Ms. MacNamary says, motioning at us.

Dr. Grier is even paler than Ms. MacNamary and taller than her, too. She's wearing a long-sleeved blue shirt tucked into her cargo pants. She's definitely older than my mom, but not quite grandma aged.

"Have they been briefed?" she asks Ms. MacNamary, not even acknowledging us.

"No," she says. "I thought it'd be best if you did it."

"Hmm," Dr. Grier replies. "Well, then. I'll get right to the point." She finally turns to face us.

A few birds fly by, soaring into the blue sky above. Other than their chirps and the sound of the wind, there's no noise. None of us dare to move, even as I notice some ants crawling over my shoe. Something about Dr. Grier makes me feel like I need to stand at attention, like I'm in the military.

"You four weren't invited here to help me with my research." She sniffs, as if the idea of kids helping her do research was laughable, save for the fact that this woman clearly has never laughed once in her life.

We . . . weren't?

"Say what now?" Kenzie asks, speaking for all of us.

Dr. Grier continues. "You were invited here because you seem knowledgeable, capable, and have the right physical features in common to help me do something much more important."

Physical features in common? I glance down our lineup. I guess we are all on the thin and gangly side. That's about all I can see that she could mean. But what the heck is she *talking* about? Why are we really here?

"What could be more important than your research?" Todd asks.

Kenzie coughs. *"Teacher's pet."* She coughs some more as Wyatt lets out a small laugh.

Dr. Grier clears her throat, and we get ourselves under control. Ms. MacNamary nods reassuringly at her, and I imagine she's trying to tell Dr. Grier that it's okay to trust us. The geologist really does *not* look impressed, but once she is certain she has all of our attention, she continues.

"Okay. Thank you," Dr. Grier says. "Now, as to why you're here: I presume you all have heard about the supervolcano under Yellowstone?"

"Of course we have," Todd says.

"Duh, who hasn't?" Kenzie adds.

Wyatt and I nod. Dr. Grier should *know* I have, since that's what my project was on. I debate whether or not to mention that. But the next thing Dr. Grier says derails that train of thought completely.

"It's about to erupt again. And we need your help to stop it."

CHAPTER THREE

"What?!" I gape at the lady in front of us. No. No way. I could *not* have just heard that right. She can't possibly mean that! I glance around, looking for the hidden cameras. "We're on a prank show, aren't we?" I ask. "You can't be serious!"

"You want us to stop the Yellowstone *Supervolcano?"* Kenzie asks.

"No, you're not on a prank show. And yes," Dr. Grier confirms, nodding at Kenzie. "That's exactly what I want you to do."

"But, but—it can't erupt!" Kenzie exclaims. Wind blows her blond hair in front of her face, and she rapidly smacks it out of the way. "It's dormant; there are no signs! There's been loads of research done. I mean, the magma is down there, sure, but there's no reason for it to come up right now!"

"We are past our due date for an eruption," Dr. Grier begins.

"That's ridiculous, that has no real meaning," Kenzie interrupts. "If it was really about to blow, there would be—"

"Signals of increased geological activity?" Dr. Grier interrupts her in return. "There have been. Worldwide."

I run a hand over my face. My cheeks feel numb. Holy mackerel. A Yellowstone eruption would be catastrophic. Dr. Grier has to be wrong. She *has* to be.

"Bolivia, New Zealand, LA," Ms. MacNamary begins to list the biggest quakes of the past few years. "These aren't coincidental. I know this sounds improbable—in fact, that's why so many people aren't doing anything about it. But Yellowstone *is* on the verge of erupting, and Dr. Grier is the only one who has taken it seriously and found a way to stop it."

"You knew this was what she wanted us for?" Kenzie spins toward Ms. MacNamary. Her question reminds me of the other ridiculous part of all this—they want *us* to help them stop this disaster. I almost laugh.

Ms. MacNamary meets her accusing glare with a soft sigh. "Yes. Please, hear her out before you jump to conclusions."

"Excuse me," Todd cuts in. "Not to undermine Dr. Grier, but how can humans possibly stop a volcano? Much less a supervolcano?"

"If a supervolcano the size of Yellowstone erupts, it would be like a thousand nukes going off," Wyatt says.

I shake my head at all of them, since they're clearly missing the biggest point of all. "Why do you think *we* of all people can help?"

Kenzie nods at me. "Exactly! Even if what you're saying is true—which would be ludicrous—how are we supposed to stop it?"

"Maybe if you all would just listen to Dr. Grier for a minute before arguing, you might understand," a new voice says.

I turn to see several large men behind us and a parked blue truck. I recognize them as the men we saw at the overlook. Did they follow us here?

"I work for Dr. Grier," one of them says. "So do my men. We're not interested in the world going to hell."

I notice all three of them have some serious muscles, and I'm not sure any of them are people I'd want to debate with. Kenzie, however, has no qualms. She makes a frustrated *guh* noise and rolls her eyes dramatically.

"Well, I'm not interested in that either, obviously," she says. "But I'm not hearing anyone offer up any proof of what you guys are claiming is true."

"I am happy to provide you with my research once we get to camp," Dr. Grier says. "Think of it as a thought experiment until then. Regardless, Yellowstone isn't going to wait until everyone on the planet believes it's happening."

We fall silent. I picture my Earth Builder simulation and imagine the explosion in real life—half of the park blown away at once. Lava spewing everywhere. Clouds of pyroclastic dust filling the sky, blotting out the sun. Ash and rock raining down from the Pacific to the Atlantic. North America essentially wiped off the map as the shock wave and the poisonous gases spread. An endless winter descending on the entire planet . . .

"This is a lot to take in," Ms. MacNamary says next. "But it's all true, and our work must be kept secret. Even my park rangers have no idea what's going on here. We don't have a perfect solution to stop the volcano, but we can settle it down. To do that, though, we need you. You've all proven how smart and capable you are."

"And—importantly—you're the only ones who will fit," Dr. Grier adds.

"Fit?" Wyatt asks.

"Through the tunnels," Dr. Grier goes on. "We're drilling down to the magma chamber to release the built-up pressure in timed, controlled intervals."

"Release the pressure?" I stare, thinking back to Earth Builder again. "But that's what I did to *cause* the eruption in my simulation."

"If we control the release, we can let out a small amount of gas and magma from the chamber," Dr. Grier explains. "This would reduce the risk of a major pressure release later on that would evacuate the upper rhyolitic magma and reach the basaltic partial melt below, creating a sustained explosion and ejection."

I guess we don't immediately respond the way she thinks we should, so in a much slower tone, she adds:

"That would be bad. That would be the supervolcanic part."

"Allow me, Samantha," Ms. MacNamary says, gently cutting in. She pulls out a bottle of soda from her bag. "This is what helped me first understand." She shakes up the bottle, making sure we're all watching. "If I open this, what happens?"

"It explodes," Kenzie says.

"Yes, but if I only open it a little bit, and then shut it, and then open it, and then shut it—" Ms. MacNamary demonstrates, opening the bottle quickly, and then twisting the cap shut. A hiss escapes, but it doesn't explode. She repeats the movement. "I can lower the pressure inside, safely and with control."

The wheels turn in my head. In Earth Builder, when I built up the pressure but didn't release enough of it, it totally ruined my experiment because then the volcano would settle and I'd have to set it up all over again. This . . . actually makes sense.

"We're at the point where the top of Yellowstone's soda bottle is ready to blow," Ms. MacNamary says. "We either do something to calm it down, or wait for catastrophe."

"Unfortunately," Dr. Grier continues, "we can't do this alone. The pods we built to drill underground ended up far more tightly packed than we had anticipated." She shoots a glare at the men behind us, as if it is all their fault somehow. "We can't widen them if we want the correct rate of pressure release. Therefore, we must rely on kids such as yourselves to squeeze into the drilling pods, tunnel down to the magma chamber, and set some carefully controlled charges."

I look to the others to gauge their reactions.

"If all of this is really true, and you've found a way to control an upcoming eruption of nightmarish proportions, why keep it secret? Why not get the world involved?" Wyatt asks.

"The world doesn't care," Dr. Grier snaps.

"Maybe not if you talk to them like *that*." Kenzie snorts.

"We've tried to ask for help many, many times," Ms. MacNamary says. Her eyes land on Kenzie, and the ghost of a smile plays on her lips. "Nicely, even. But no one listens. We've only found a few people who are willing to put in the time and money, and most of them are here on site with us. Others would rather take their chances that this won't impact them during their lifetimes, even though it's already starting. Denial is a powerful thing."

Already starting? I suck in a breath. That doesn't sound good.

"What?" Todd asks. "That's ridiculous! They *have* to care. And the government could help if—"

"You obviously aren't old enough yet to know how the government works," Ms. MacNamary replies with an unamused laugh.

"And you obviously have no idea how to ask people for help!" Kenzie responds. "You just met us. How can you possibly trust us with this?"

"We don't have a choice," Dr. Grier says. "What we're doing sounds unbelievable to people who can't be bothered to understand the science, and if we go public with our plans, the government will stop us. Think: if we had been honest and told your families that we needed your help to drill down to one of the biggest magma chambers Earth has to offer, would your parents have allowed you to join us?"

My eyes widen even more. Abso-*lutely* not.

"This is our only chance," Ms. MacNamary says, apology

written all over her face. "I'm so sorry I couldn't tell you sooner. You have no idea how hard Samantha and I have tried to protect our planet from disaster, just to have officials slam the door in the face of our efforts. If we don't operate independently, and in secret, this is never going to happen." She sighs. "Listen, I'm almost fifty years old. I can tell you right now, there will never be another time in your life where you will literally be asked to save our planet. Yes, it will be dangerous. This is asking everything of you—but if you do this, you will be heroes."

I straighten a little where I sit and see Todd do the same. However, none of us speak up just yet. I think we're all still trying to process everything.

Dr. Grier scoffs at our lack of answers. "I told you they wouldn't agree," she says to Ms. MacNamary. "I told you they wouldn't—"

"How about we walk to our camp while you think about it?" Ms. MacNamary proposes, interrupting Dr. Grier. "You can read the research once we're there."

A wave of gratefulness washes over me at her suggestion, on the heels of the wave of guilt from Dr. Grier's accusation that we don't want to help.

"Yeah, sure." Kenzie throws her hands up. "Not like we have anything better to do, right?" I wince at her attitude, even if I do understand it. This is . . . so *much*.

I wonder what Aunt Pauline would do.

Actually, no I don't. I know what she would do.

"Which way?" Todd asks. The men from the car gesture up

the mountainside. Tucked away in a dark shadow amid slabs of dirty rock is a path. And in front of that path, there's a person watching us—a person with three heads.

I can't be seeing that correctly.

"Come on, everyone grab your things," Ms. MacNamary says. She's back by the van, popping open the hatch.

I glance up the cliff again, but the person is gone.

Ms. MacNamary hoists our bags out, and we each retrieve them. Meanwhile, the men begin unpacking loads of supplies out of their car. I don't even consider asking for my camera when the bag of tech is dug out of the back of the minivan. My mind is elsewhere as I swing my duffel over my shoulder, stumbling as it lands with a *fwump* on my back. The straps press against my skin and pinch it painfully.

Saving the world . . . someone is actually asking me to save the world. . . .

I start walking, trying to catch up to everyone who has already gotten ahead of me. Only Ms. MacNamary is left behind, closing up the van. I put one foot in front of the other as we ascend higher and higher.

Getting up the mountain is tougher than I'd first thought it would be. Todd and Kenzie started with an unspoken foot race, but they're both huffing and puffing with the rest of us by now. Wyatt has a slight limp going on. Dr. Grier is the only one of us who seems to handle the climb without issue, and she's carrying most of our excess supplies. It's a little embarrassing.

When we finally reach the ledge where I saw the mysterious

three-headed person, I realize we weren't climbing to meet some-body. We were climbing to reach the entrance to a cave. It's not a large opening—just big enough for a small car to drive into if it somehow could get up here. The four of us drop our luggage in the dirt, groaning, gasping for breath, and definitely not ready to continue the trek just yet.

"Wait here while we load in supplies," Dr. Grier tells us.

"We'll be back in just a few minutes," Ms. MacNamary adds, smiling. "Good job getting up the path!"

Kenzie gives her an exhausted thumbs-up, then dramatically collapses onto her duffel bag.

The adults take turns lugging things into the cave, always leaving at least one person out to watch us, I notice. That raises the hair on the back of my neck. Dr. Grier and Ms. MacNamary stressed how secret this was—if we don't agree to help, how can they trust us to go home and not tell others about what they're doing? Or are they just going to make sure we *don't* go home?

Wyatt and Todd wander to the edge of the flat overlook we're on, each seeming lost in his own thoughts. Kenzie walks over to join me.

"You've been to Yellowstone before. Which direction to the caldera and civilization's certain, inevitable doom?" Kenzie asks, holding a hand over her eyes to peer out over the park.

I point south and pan west. "We're in it. Most of the rest of it is that way."

From here, it's barely possible to tell where the earth swells up in the middle of the wider caldera depression that Yellowstone sits in. We're closer to Sour Creek Dome than Mallard Lake Dome. Both of which are places where magma underground is pushing at the surface—obvious indications that something's going on down there.

"What do you think Professor Grumpy-pants would do if we said no?" Kenzie asks next, more quietly this time.

"Can we even *say* no?" I glance at the man currently standing at the edge of the cave entrance, casually leaning against the rocky wall.

"Kind of hard to when someone is literally asking you to save the world," Wyatt says, joining us. "But I would like some real proof before we start."

That wasn't entirely what I meant, but I nod. The wind blows past us, bending the tops of the spruce trees that dot the meadow below.

Kenzie nods thoughtfully at Wyatt. "Yeah. Not to quote my obnoxious chem professor grandmother, but where's the peer review?"

"Guys, this is Dr. *Grier*," Todd says, joining our little huddle. "She wrote the book on volcanology. Literally! I'm certain her research is spot on."

"Todd, you just want to be the hero that saves the world," Kenzie says.

"Don't you?" Todd says right back.

Kenzie goes to retort, but as the full meaning hits her, she shuts up.

I fidget with my jacket sleeves, trying to tug them tighter.

I'm shivering, and wish I could blame it on the wind, but frankly it's hard not to shiver when you've just been informed that death might be waiting below your feet. There's an unbelievably picturesque view of Yellowstone in front of me, but my mind overlays it with images of churning lava and volcanic ash billowing up to block the sun. I don't think anyone could make fun of me for being jittery.

Before we can continue our conversation, Dr. Grier walks out of the cave.

"Let's go," is all she says, before heading back in.

Everyone hesitates at the mouth of the cave. Going in seems like we're committing to the job, and I don't think any of us want to be the first to do that. But it doesn't look like Dr. Grier is going to wait for us to debate. And they did say we'd get to see Dr. Grier's research at the campsite, so I guess if we want to figure out how legitimate this is, we should follow her. . . .

"Come on," Todd says, grabbing his suitcase. "Even if this doesn't work out, I'm not lugging all my stuff back down this mountain today. At least we can sleep here for a night."

With one last glance around, we pick our remaining bags back up and head inside. One of the men follows us, and I pull my jacket even tighter as the cool cave air hits me full blast.

CHAPTER FOUR

My stomach rumbles, and I worry that it's going to echo around the dark hall.

Ms. MacNamary leads the way now. Dr. Grier dropped back to walk with the men from the truck. A string of lights next to us illuminates our path, but it's impossible to see anything beyond their reach. I've never been in a cave like this before, with square walls reinforced by old wooden beams. Did someone cut through here on purpose?

"This was a failed attempt at a coal mine once upon a time." Ms. MacNamary gestures around.

Oh.

"They tried a few of these throughout the region, but most didn't end up going anywhere," Ms. MacNamary continues. "This one isn't on any map we've ever come across in any of our park history. Dr. Grier has modified it for our purposes and blasted some tunnels deeper down for access to the natural cracks in the Earth at the edge of the caldera."

"Is that where you're drilling?" I ask. Around us, there are veins of what I think is gypsum flickering in the dim light. Not many stalactites, though, for there being this many mineral deposits. In Earth Builder, whenever there were a ton of mineral deposits, usually stalactites would form from water dripping down in caves.

"Yes, very good," Ms. MacNamary says.

"Why did you pick this side of the caldera?" I ask next. The caldera runs in a full ring around Yellowstone, and there are underground cracks along its entire edge, all heading down to the magma below.

"The western edge has its magma chamber far deeper down underground, by our calculations," Dr. Grier explains from behind me. "We are concentrating our efforts first on the northeast, where the magma is closest to the surface and has the greatest chance of erupting."

"I think that makes perfect sense," Todd says.

Kenzie rolls her eyes my way.

"Okay, now watch your step." Ms. MacNamary's voice echoes around us. "This is where the main path ends. It's a short journey to the stairs, but these stones are loose, so be careful."

I step gingerly off the trodden down path and onto a bunch of rocks ranging in size from golf balls to basketballs. It's too dark to see what kind of rocks they are, and also unfortunately too dark to walk across them without tripping and slipping. I feel super foolish every time I lose my footing and hope no one is watching me fail my way across the cave floor.

"Keep up." One of the men prods Wyatt forward. He wobbles a bit, but then picks his way across the rocks to join us. The man shakes his head at Dr. Grier, who shuts him up with one look.

I really don't like these guys following us. Okay, sure they might work here trying to save us all from the apocalypse, but they also make me feel like I can't back out of this. Mustering up my courage, I decide I need to ask, right now, what our options are. Because I did *not* sign up for a summer of tunneling underground to a magma pit.

"Hey, Ms. MacNamary?" I hop from one big rock to another to get closer to her.

"Yes?"

"Just out of curiosity, uh, what would you guys do if we said we didn't want to help?" I can taste the guilt in my mouth as I ask.

Ms. MacNamary glances back at Dr. Grier. "Well . . . we're really hoping you'll say yes. But if you said no, we'd ask that you stay here with us for the summer until it's all wrapped up."

I stumble at that. "Oh."

"Of course, if you want to leave, we can't stop you," she continues quickly. "But ideally, if you decided not to help us, you would work with me in other areas of the park, doing more of my normal duties for the next couple of months, so we don't risk things leaking out."

I nod, pulling my jacket tighter again. I'm not sure if this makes me feel better or worse.

"We wouldn't dream of forcing you to do anything that made you uncomfortable," Ms. MacNamary says. "But we *are* talking about the fate of our world. If that sounds dramatic, that's because it is. Time is running out. We need you, Bri."

I try to nod again, but find I can't. I want to be brave enough for this, but I keep thinking how Aunt Pauline would be way better at this than me. I mean, she's off in LA, risking her life cleaning up collapsed buildings, and here I am, barely walking across a cave without tripping.

I take a deep breath and imagine Aunt Pauline here, filming me. *The intrepid explorer, Brianna Marie Dobson, has been asked to join an operation to save the planet Earth. Will she agree, even if it puts her own life at risk?*

I don't have an answer to that. But I do know that video would get a heck of a lot of views. A thought hits me: If I agree to help, could I get my camera back? What would be more epic than a documentary about drilling through our planet to save the world? My mind threatens to run away with the idea, and I have to pinch my nails into my palms to bring myself back.

We reach a spiral wooden staircase. Some of the steps have been replaced by metal, and I wonder if it's because they had rotted too badly to be safe.

"Our base of operations is just down here." Ms. MacNamary turns to address the group. "There, we'll get you four settled in and fed, and we will pass out some of your gear."

"Gear?" Wyatt asks.

"To go underground," Todd answers. "Obviously."

I frown in his direction. I'd wanted more specifics than that, but the adults seem content to let that answer sit as it is. I look back at Kenzie for some help, but her eyes are glittering outward to the next section of cave, and I soon see why.

An absolutely *massive* cavern lies ahead of us. Holy moly. The space below and ahead of us puts the car-sized cave entrance to shame. If you shaved off the sides, you could probably fit my entire school in here.

I really wish I had my camera now.

Several small buildings sit below us in an open camp-like area. Hanging lamps illuminate the paths between the structures like streetlights. I can see half a dozen other adults already from my vantage point on the stairs, and even some pickup trucks, shuttling stuff around. *Wow.* This big of an operation must have taken ages to put together and must be super hard to keep secret.

We start our descent down the winding stairwell, each silently taking in the idea of a tiny town inside a mountain.

"Who are they?" Wyatt asks, pointing to the edge of the cave town from a couple steps higher than me. I peer out but don't see anyone.

"Who?" Kenzie asks, hopping where she stands to look over the buildings.

"I thought I just saw some other kids," Wyatt says.

"Oh! Well, we've needed people your size to help for a while now," Ms. MacNamary explains. "You're not the first kids we've invited here, but you are the first who will help with the next phase of this whole operation."

"Really?" I ask, honestly a little hurt. Despite not being sure I want to be here at all, learning we weren't Dr. Grier's first choices stings. Todd, perhaps feeling similarly, shoves his hands in his pockets and continues down the steps.

I shake my head. I need to get my ego under control. I'm sure the other kids are nice, and we'll be able to work together just fine.

. . . *If we decide to do the work at all*, I remind myself. None of us have agreed to help yet, and I can't start thinking like I have when I haven't.

Kenzie huffs next to me, crossing her arms. I mimic her, and together we follow Todd and Ms. MacNamary down. Wyatt trails us with Dr. Grier and the unnamed men.

After we reach the bottom, they lead us to one of the buildings. It's windowless and made out of wood, with a small metal chimney at one end, like a strange variation on a log cabin. Ms. MacNamary opens the door to reveal a room warmed and lit by a small stove. Sleeping bags line the floor.

"You'll be staying here," she says. "I trust you girls and boys can behave together?" She grins, and I think all four of us must be blushing, but I can't know for sure because I refuse to look at anyone else.

"Oh god, I don't know. Somehow, I think we'll manage to

keep our hands to ourselves," Kenzie says, breaking the awkward silence.

Our laughter stops when the adults dump our stuff onto the wooden floorboards—all except for our phones and my camera, I notice. Those remain in the bag Ms. MacNamary collected them in, which is still in her possession.

"We'll be back to get you for dinner," Dr. Grier says. She hands out piles of papers. "For now, read these. They'll give you all the information you need."

"What about our phones?" Todd asks.

"No tech," Dr. Grier says. "I can't have any of you bringing attention to this place."

We immediately launch into protest.

"What?!"

"But what about—"

"For the whole *summer*?!"

"We all have to make sacrifices!" Dr. Grier snaps.

"Samantha," Ms. MacNamary cuts in gently. "We're asking so much of these kids, I think we can trust them—especially seeing as there's basically no service here." She turns to us. "But if any of you do get a signal, you just have to promise to keep what we're doing on the down low. Can you do that?"

Kenzie's already grabbing the bag from Ms. MacNamary's hands. She pulls her phone out, then passes the knapsack around to each of us as Dr. Grier's eyes narrow. Ms. MacNamary gives the woman a sheepish shrug.

Like Dr. Grier, I can't help but stare at Ms. MacNamary and

think of her apparent faith in the honor system as I take my phone and camera out. It's kind of sweet, but also really, really naive.

But then I unlock my phone, and to my dismay, quickly find out that just like Ms. MacNamary predicted, I can't get any service, at *all*. No Wi-Fi, no data, nothing.

"Maybe if we go outside." Todd holds his phone up and walks the cabin trying to get signal. I'm right there with him.

Come on . . . come on! I raise my phone all the way up to the wooden rafters.

"I've never managed to get service out in this region of the park," Ms. MacNamary says. "It's not one of the areas visitors frequent, so coverage is poor."

"No tech." Dr. Grier repeats herself, more firmly. One of the men takes the bag from Kenzie and holds it out in front of her, insisting she put her phone back in it.

"I'm not giving you my phone," Kenzie says. "I haven't even agreed to help you yet!"

Behind her, Wyatt leafs through some of the papers Dr. Grier handed out.

"You will agree," Dr. Grier says. "Once you see the data. At least, you should." She stares down Ms. MacNamary, something akin to anger flashing in her eyes. "You four were chosen because you would *understand*."

Ms. MacNamary actually laughs at that. "Oh, Samantha, they will," she says. "Honestly, I think you made excellent selections for student participants. Isn't skepticism the hallmark of good scientists?"

"So is open-mindedness." Dr. Grier nods at Wyatt, who is already reading.

Kenzie grumbles.

"I've got nexts after Wyatt," Todd says, eagerly eyeing the pile of research.

"*BS*, I called firsts on our way in here," Kenzie says. I don't remember her saying that, but watching Todd's face screw up is worth keeping my mouth shut.

Ms. MacNamary laughs once again. "My goodness. Language, Kenzie!"

"Bachelor of Science, my future degree." Kenzie sniffs. Out comes the lipstick again.

"Here." Wyatt hands Kenzie half the stack.

"Hey, I said nexts!" Todd protests.

"Phones," Dr. Grier insists. The man next to her holds out the bag once again.

Ms. MacNamary shakes her head from the cabin doorway, and I crumple inside, realizing she's about to give in and stop fighting for us to keep our stuff. "It'll be easier for everyone if you just do as she says right now," she tells us. "If you really want your phones, we can figure something out later."

"What about my camera?" I ask, clinging to it.

Ms. MacNamary sighs. "I'll work on that, too. For now, just turn in all tech and let me worry about getting it back for you."

Todd sighs and grudgingly hands his phone in.

"This is just a precaution," Ms. MacNamary goes on to say. "Dr. Grier is right—we can't accidentally have any information get out about our operation."

Wyatt hands his phone in next, and I part with mine after him.

"Camera, too," the man holding the bag says.

I chance a glance at Dr. Grier. For someone who wants to save the planet, she certainly isn't that nice. She nods at me, and I reluctantly put my camera into the bag.

"Please be careful with it," I tell the man. "My aunt gave it to me."

"I will," he promises. Then he goes back to Kenzie. "Okay, little lady. Your turn."

Kenzie clutches her phone like a feral cat guarding a kitten.

"Kenzie, please," Ms. MacNamary says. "The sooner you turn it in, the sooner I can get it back to you."

I glance at Dr. Grier again to see her reaction to that, but her face is expressionless.

Kenzie eventually does hand it in, her fist tightening around the papers Wyatt gave her. The adults begin to exit, and I head over to the water cooler in the corner of the cabin, pulling out my bottle from my duffel to refill.

"There's a box of games over by the stove for when you're done," Ms. MacNamary says. I glance back at a trunk at the rear of the room. "I'm sorry that's all we have at the moment for entertainment. Please, settle in, read the research if you'd like, and feel free to relax until we come to find you."

"Games? Really?" one of the men asks on his way out.

Ms. MacNamary gives us a sympathetic smile. "It's the least we can do. They deserve a chance for fun while they're here."

"Saving the world isn't about fun." Dr. Grier snorts.

Whatever else the adults say gets cut off as the door shuts, leaving the four of us in the weird, windowless cabin.

"*Ugh.*" Kenzie swears loudly, kicking her duffel bag and quickly contradicting her earlier claim that BS actually stood for a degree. "No phones? What are we, living in the stone age?"

"We probably need to prove to Dr. Grier first that we're serious," Wyatt says. "And if we have to lie to our parents about this, it'll be easier to do that over email. At least we have a good excuse not to call home."

I squirm, still not sure how I can lie to my parents for months. But Todd probably has it worse—his mom did tell him to write every single day. That's a lot of lies to keep up with.

"Are you seriously trying to find something good about not having our phones?" Kenzie gawks at Wyatt. "I mean, it's not like I was planning on texting my grandma this summer, but how am I supposed to keep up with any of my friends? By *daily emails*? I don't think so."

"I doubt Dr. Grier or Ms. MacNamary are going to be on board with us talking to our friends, even if we did want to do it over email," I say. "This is a pretty massive secret they're trusting us with."

We're all silent for a moment. Then Todd grunts, walking into the center.

"Okay, this is the boys' side," Todd proclaims, grabbing a red-and-blue sleeping bag and pulling it over to the right half of the cabin. "You two stay on the other half."

"Real mature, Todd," Kenzie says. "But at least your guy stink will be contained."

I feel bad as I see Wyatt flush.

"So are we going to read any of the research, or . . . ?" I ask, refocusing us.

Kenzie splits her wrinkled pile of papers with me, and Wyatt splits the remainder of his with Todd. We all sit down and begin reading.

After taking a long swig of water, I start with a paper called "Analyzing Seismic Signals in the Yellowstone Sour Creek Dome." The graphs in the paper look . . . well, they don't look good. Dr. Grier has side-by-side comparisons with graphs that have come out in previous studies, and hers are much more terrifying.

Kenzie's eyebrows are furrowed, creasing her forehead more and more the longer she reads. I suspect she's skimming more than she's letting on. Especially since she keeps pausing to flip back to previous pages. I feel a little better—I don't think Kenzie is absorbing any more of the scientific language than I am.

The gist of it, however, both of us get. According to these papers, seismic activity has been on the rise, and the odds of Yellowstone blowing up aren't the miniscule ones we'd been led to believe. There's a 98% chance of it going *kablooey* within the next five years. Before I even graduate high school, my home state could be buried under rock and ash.

Like swallowing an ice cube, the spine-tingling reality of what we're dealing with sinks in.

People are going to die. Our country . . . our whole

continent . . . the *world* will never be the same. Entire states will be wiped off the map. Crops won't grow anywhere. There will be starvation. There will be disease. Summer will be a thing of the past. Our atmosphere will flood with dust and aerosols, blocking the sun.

My hands tremble, clutching the paper I'm holding. I can't think of a single disaster in history bigger than this.

"Why hasn't anyone published these findings?" Todd asks. It's like someone dropped a plate in a restaurant—we all startle, looking over at the sound of his voice.

"I have that here," Wyatt says, waving around some papers that look very different from any we're holding. "A bunch of emails between Dr. Grier and other scientists. Lots of rejections from scientific journals. But none because her science is bad. They're all because her methods weren't sanctioned and she collected data without permits." He looks at each of us in turn, swallowing. "No one actually disagreed with her findings."

I let that sink in next. Dr. Grier found out the world was in danger, and people told her she couldn't share her findings because she cheated in how she got her information? What is *wrong* with people?

Kenzie starts to say something, but whatever it is gets cut off as we're jolted to one side. Sawdust falls from the rafters. A dull rumble starts up and we all jump to our feet.

"*Earthquake!*" Todd yells.

The ground jerks below us. I trip over my bag, flailing, as we scramble like rats. The water cooler topples over, splashing water all over the floor.

This is way worse than any quake I've ever felt before. Worse than the ones back home, worse than the one from the motel parking lot. Everyone's yelling. The shaking makes it impossible to keep my footing. As I stumble left and right, all I can think about is how we're underground, and this cave could collapse on us at any moment, crushing us to death. . . .

But then, just as quickly as it started, everything settles down.

The ground steadies. The water cooler rolls to a stop, hitting the stove. All of us stare at one another, wide-eyed. I've got a hand on the wall, my nails digging into the wood. We wait.

Nothing more happens.

"Oh my god, I had a heart attack. I'm dead. I died." Kenzie clutches at her chest. She looks exactly how I feel. I honestly had thought for a moment that we were about to be blasted to smithereens by the supervolcano. Holy cow. If that could never happen again, that would be fantastic.

"It's okay," I say to myself and to everyone. "It's okay, it stopped."

Wyatt slowly moves to go set the water cooler back upright. Todd is frozen by the door, a hand on each side of its frame.

"Everyone all right?" Ms. MacNamary flings the door open, bursting into the cabin.

Todd yelps, jumping back.

"We're fine," I answer, prying my nails out of the wood and wincing as I feel a splinter in the tip of my ring finger.

"Good," Dr. Grier says, pushing her way in with Ms. MacNamary. They must have rushed over here together to check on us. My opinion of Dr. Grier warms slightly. "How's the cabin?" She looks around, inspecting it for damage.

"It held up," Wyatt says, finishing propping up the cooler. "Also, Dr. Grier?" He sets his shoulders, looking directly at the geologist. "I'm in."

I gawk at his sudden decision. "You are?"

He nods. "I'm ready to help."

Kenzie blinks. "*What?*"

Wyatt has been impossible for me to get a read on, but in this moment, one thing's for sure: he's the bravest of us all. "I don't know if your research on this is right, but having a safety plan in place to stop a supervolcanic eruption can't be a bad thing. Obviously, this place isn't exactly geologically stable right now."

Wyatt glances toward me for some reason. I'm still a frazzled mess from what just happened, and half expect the ground to start shaking again any second, but I give him a nod. I get it. This is bigger than all of us. *Something* is clearly happening to Yellowstone. Wyatt's right—a safety plan can't be bad. "I think I'm in, too."

"What?!" Kenzie repeats, spinning toward me now.

"Todd?" I turn, trying to ignore the leaping sensations my stomach is still experiencing.

Todd's blond eyebrows are furrowed, making his glasses ride

up on his nose. "I didn't think you'd say yes, Wyatt," he admits.

"Are you in?" Wyatt asks.

Ms. MacNamary watches us from the entrance to the cabin. Dr. Grier stands by a wall, arms crossed.

"Of course," Todd says. There may have been the barest hint of a moment's hesitation, but he covers it well. "If we have a chance to save millions of people, it's our duty to do so."

"You said 'doody.'" Kenzie grins.

"Really? That's your response?" Todd's voice sounds pained.

"Nah," Kenzie says. "I'd just rather stay here than go back to my grandma's prissy apartment in Miami, so I'm in, too. For now. Obviously you all need someone of my genius to make this work. I'd be a jerk to say no."

Dr. Grier taps her arm with one of her stern fingers. "I suppose that's all I can ask," she says, her eyes trained on Kenzie.

"I expect my phone back at some point, though." Kenzie leans back to better look up at the geologist, defiance blatant all over her overly made-up face.

Dr. Grier nods. Her eyes have moved past Kenzie now, though. Thoughtful. Distant. "We'll see," she says.

Todd tries to stand as straight as Wyatt, clearly less comfortable with his choice than he's letting on. I'm a ball of nerves, but I'm also weirdly . . . excited.

"So, what now?" I ask, cutting my brain off from imagining the medals we're going to get when we save the planet.

"Now we make preparations!" Ms. MacNamary beams. "I'm so glad you all agreed. We'll come and get you for dinner soon."

"Aww, we still have to sit in here?" Kenzie says.

"What if another quake happens?" Todd asks.

"You better get used to those," Dr. Grier says.

"And hope the worst one waits until we're ready for it," Ms. MacNamary adds.

The Summer I Saved the World. That's what I'll call my documentary, whenever I get to make it. That is, if I'm allowed to have my camera back.

And if I don't get blown up by a volcano first.

CHAPTER FIVE

"Dinner," a man announces, rapping on the door.

The four of us look up from our game of Scrabble, which Kenzie found in the chest Ms. MacNamary had talked about. I held my own in the game, despite being stuck with a *J* for what felt like an eternity. All around us, the wooden walls dance in the light and shadows from our stove's front grate. We could barely see the Scrabble tiles, which Todd decided was perfect, because we voted to play it as Apocalypse edition, only using words that spelled out the End of Times for All Humanity.

"Coming!" Kenzie shouts, slamming a letter *S* onto *KABOOM* for a double word score and declaring herself a winner, even though she started the game so it wasn't really fair she got an extra turn.

We all get up. One of the men from earlier waits for us just outside of our cabin, looking grumpy about being on Kid Duty.

"So what's your name, anyway?" Kenzie asks. Wyatt shuts the door behind us as we start to walk across the cavern.

"Jerry," the man says. "Jerry Stiles. You can call me Mr. Stiles."

"How long have you worked here, Mr. Stiles?" Todd asks.

"Mr. Stiles sounds like a bad DJ name," I lean down to whisper to Kenzie, who snorts.

"I've been working with Dr. Grier for many years," he answers. "I'm the team's lead engineer. Most of the equipment you'll be using has been designed by me or Dan Fee." He nods toward another man with dark hair heading in our direction.

We round a corner to a tarped area, and Mr. Fee joins us. There are two buildings here. One has a couple of people darting in and out, carrying big dishes of food. Around the tarp are a bunch of camping chairs.

"We're having curry tonight!" Ms. MacNamary says, smiling as she walks up to join us. "My favorite, so I'm sticking around for dinner before heading back to my office."

Wyatt looks around. "What about the other kids?"

"You might meet them tomorrow," she replies. "They had dinner on the early shift. They need to tackle some evening work and take care of some things that can't happen when the park is crawling with visitors. I can keep *most* people away from this area through some basic park management, but even so—we'd rather not take risks."

Dr. Grier is lucky she was able to talk Ms. MacNamary into helping her. I can't imagine this operation working without someone from the National Park Service on the team.

The four of us line up to get bowls of curry. There's no table, so everyone holds their bowls on their laps when they sit down to eat. Wyatt scoots himself closer to the space heater that's plugged into a generator on one side. I end up in a different circle of camp chairs than the other kids, because Ms. MacNamary asks me to sit by her and I can't think fast enough to say no. Unlike her, curry isn't my favorite, but it *is* my dinner, so I begin picking at it.

Ms. MacNamary watches me for a moment. "You know, I think I know a way to let you use your camera here," she eventually says.

I drop my fork in my bowl. "Really?!"

Ms. MacNamary stretches in her camp chair. "Yep. Our biggest concern is obviously people finding out what we're doing and shutting us down, but I've looked at your camera. It doesn't have a Wi-Fi card. There's no way it can connect to the internet."

I nod, trying not to get my hopes up too high.

"Seeing as recording work is a major part of the scientific process, I think Samantha would be open to letting you use your camera to document your daily progress," Ms. MacNamary says. "As long as you phrase it the right way, we can get her on board. I've had decades of practice getting her to do things she doesn't initially like. She can be stubborn, but she's logical. A good argument can persuade her."

At that, I wonder how long Dr. Grier and Ms. MacNamary have known each other—decades sounds like *forever*—but mostly I'm concentrating on not squealing out loud at the prospect of getting my camera back. "That sounds amazing," I manage to say. "Will it really work?"

"Give it a try," Ms. MacNamary says, winking as she stands up and leaves.

Dr. Grier moves in to sit in her vacant seat. *Oh. She meant give it a try right* now.

"Uh, hi, Dr. Grier," I say.

"Hello, Brianna."

A good argument. I straighten up and try to channel my inner professional adult. "So, I was thinking—I'd like to record my work each day," I start. So far, so good. "My camera doesn't connect to the internet, so it won't be any risk. But it would give you tons of footage to use if you want to analyze it for any research. I think, scientifically speaking, it's good to have as much data as possible. And this is a kind of data—like, visual data. Right?"

I feel like I lost some of my momentum near the end there. Dr. Grier says nothing, and I begin to panic.

"My science teacher last year was really intense about recording our methods in every experiment. She would go on and on about how that made experiments replicable," I ramble. "I understand being scared of anyone finding out what you're doing and getting it wrong and shutting you down and all that, but maybe with video you could show them that you're doing the right thing and that your methods are safe." I shut up after that, not trusting myself to say anything more.

To my surprise, after a moment's silence, Dr. Grier nods.

"Fair points," she says. "Recordings could be useful for training purposes."

My heart leaps, even though that wasn't one of the reasons I'd given her. Whatever convinces her is fine by me.

"But how can I trust that you won't leak the video somehow?" she asks me.

"I'll give you my camera every night," I say, kicking myself the second the words come out of my mouth. *Why did I suggest that? Come on!* But Dr. Grier's eyebrows twitch up in interest, so I continue. "That way you'll know I'm not doing anything against the rules. And the footage can be like a daily report for you to review. And you can tell me if there's anything you want me to change." I await her response, my breath held, squeezing against my chest.

Eventually, she nods once again. "Not a bad plan. Okay. You've convinced me."

My mouth falls open. "I did?" I ask, then immediately wince. *Not the professional way to respond!* "I mean—thank you."

Dr. Grier studies me for a moment, and it is impossible to read her expression. "You're welcome."

I'm going to get my camera back! Yes! I shovel several bites of curry into my mouth so I don't say or do anything else embarrassing.

"Congratulations." Ms. MacNamary rejoins us, smiling at me and putting on her park ranger hat. "You managed to talk Dr. Grier into something faster than even I usually can."

"She's a smart girl," Dr. Grier says. "Logical. I respect that. You could go far in the sciences." She nods at me, and a bubble of pride swells up inside. Maybe Dr. Grier isn't so bad.

"Bri, are you going to eat your whole dinner with the adults and ignore us? Get over here!" Kenzie demands from her camp chair on the other side of the tarped area.

"What if I like the adults better?" I reply, settling farther into my own chair.

"Sucking up is Todd's job," Kenzie calls back.

"Hey!" Todd objects.

"All right, you kids have a good night," Ms. MacNamary says to the full group. "I have to head back to my office, but Mr. Stiles and Mr. Fee will begin the introductions to your gear after dinner."

We all wave goodbye to Ms. MacNamary and finish eating our meals. The moment the last forkful of rice reaches my mouth, Dr. Grier speaks up once again.

"First on the gear list: boots," she says. "We've ordered the boot sizes your parents requested for you on your applications, but we need to confirm those are correct."

The sound of a pulled tape measure whooshing into its case snaps my attention behind us. There, the two men from earlier stand. Mr. Fee holds several large bags. "Shoes off," Mr. Stiles says, impatiently tapping the tape measure on his palm.

A man in big rubber gloves comes out with a dish tub for utensils and bowls, and Kenzie drops her bowl into it from a height that ensures maximum clattering. Then she drops her fork from an even greater height. Dr. Grier puts one hand to the side of her head to rub her temple. "I'll let Mr. Stiles and Mr. Fee take it from here."

Dr. Grier leaves us, as we all kick our shoes off onto the tarp on the ground. Even with the lights strung up around here, the darkness of the cave quickly envelops her as she heads away toward a cabin at the far edge of camp.

"We're going to measure you all to make sure you've got the right fit," Mr. Fee explains, holding up the tape measure and jiggling it back and forth for emphasis. "Now which one of you is the amputee?"

I blink at that.

"Say what?" Kenzie asks.

Wyatt puts a hand up. "I guess that's me? But—I'm not an amputee. I was born like this." He hikes up his left pant leg to the knee.

"What?!" Kenzie spins. "Whoa!"

I can't help but move to get a closer look, even though I immediately realize that's an inappropriate reaction. Halfway down Wyatt's left leg, a few inches after his knee, there's a plastic cap and then something that looks like rubber, but is much sturdier. I'm guessing there's metal under it. The end of it goes straight into a sneaker, tied up just like mine.

"All right, buddy, we've got a special boot, just for you." Mr. Stiles's voice changes. He sounds like he's talking to a five-year-old.

"Stay right where you are," Mr. Fee says, fishing through his bag. "We'll bring it to you."

"Um, I can walk," Wyatt says. "That's the entire point of my prosthetic." To emphasize that, he stands up from his camp chair, walks over, and takes the boot Mr. Fee is holding.

"Hey now, calm down, we're not trying to be insulting," Mr. Stiles says.

"We just don't want you to hurt yourself," Mr. Fee says. "You've got some difficult work ahead of you."

Wyatt sits back down with the boot in hand, undoing the laces off his prosthetic. "What makes you think I'm going to hurt myself? I've been walking around here just fine, haven't I?"

"Walking the camp and scaling the tunnels are totally different things," Mr. Stiles says. He turns to Mr. Fee. "Maybe it'd be better if he didn't do the tunnel work. He could help Nolan—"

"I won't slow anything down," Wyatt states firmly.

"Who's Nolan?" Todd asks.

"Hrm." Mr. Stiles grunts, ignoring Todd and warily eyeing Wyatt.

"Geeze Louise, he said he'll be fine!" Kenzie butts in, glaring at the two men. "Stop being insensitive jerkfaces."

They fall awkwardly silent. I want to applaud Kenzie and hug Wyatt, but I can tell he wouldn't be happy about that attention.

After Mr. Fee finishes with Todd's boots, Todd scoots over to Wyatt. "Okay, but for real, do you think it'll *actually* be hard for you to do the work we have to do?" I hear him ask.

Wyatt shrugs. "I've never been spelunking for supervolcanoes before. Maybe? Maybe not? Will it be for you?"

Todd sits back, silenced. I smirk a little.

"Well, *those* are the ugliest things I've ever seen," Kenzie says at the sight of our dark blue jumpsuits, distracting all of us. Which was perhaps her goal, so Wyatt could catch a break.

Mr. Stiles hands me my jumpsuit from a bag. I poke at the reflective tape running down it. "What are you talking about, Kenzie? These are most definitely the *height* of fashion."

After we finish trying on our tunneling uniforms, we're sent back to our cabin for the night. Once inside, Kenzie tosses her boots and jumpsuit onto the floor and kicks them against the wooden wall. "What a weird, weird day," she says.

"I don't know if I'm going to sleep like a log or not sleep at all," I agree, folding up my jumpsuit and placing it on my duffel bag.

"I can't stress this enough. You might see this as an imaginary line, but it is a very real line across the room," Todd says from the "boys" side.

"Actually . . ." I trail off, looking around. "We could probably do with a changing wall. I don't want to have to get dressed in those little porta-potty bathrooms each day."

"Good call, Bri," Kenzie says. She goes to the corner where there's a pile of blankets. "How about these?"

I glance at the open rafters on the ceiling. "Perfect."

After twenty minutes of climbing up on boxes and draping blankets to divide the cabin down the middle, we all step back to examine our handiwork. Satisfied that things are sufficiently blocked off, we call it a night.

I curl up in my sleeping bag, pulling it tight around me. Tomorrow we start our work to save the planet. Because, yep, that's a thing we're doing.

CHAPTER SIX

I wake up to the sound of someone knocking. It's Dr. Grier.

"Up and at 'em in there," she says. "Breakfast is in fifteen minutes."

Next to me, Kenzie groans from her sleeping bag, rolling over and shoving a pillow on top of her head. I can hear quiet shuffling from the other side of the room, which I'm guessing is Wyatt, because Todd does not strike me as the sort to get up early, either.

I stretch, blinking blearily. I didn't sleep great on the floor, but I signed up to do that for a whole summer, so I have to at least act like I'm okay with roughing it. Sitting up, I stifle a yawn. "Morning, everyone," I say.

"You shut your mouth," Kenzie responds, her voice muffled by her pillow.

"How is it already morning?" Todd groans from the other side of the room.

"It's our first day on the job," Wyatt says. "Let's not waste any time."

That seems to get Todd moving, because I can hear a lot more shuffling from their side now.

We all get ready, even Kenzie eventually. Before eating, we make our way over to the makeshift bathroom facilities. I decide a shower can wait until after the day's activities, because it sounds like I will probably work up a sweat.

At the food tarp area, we settle into camp chairs, waiting to see what's for breakfast. Turns out it's a giant vat of oatmeal.

. . . Yum.

The cook drops a glop into a bowl for me, and I smile weakly. "Thanks."

"No problem," he says. I don't know his name, but there's at least a dozen adults here I haven't caught the names of yet.

I lean back, waiting for the person passing the sugar to hurry it up. I'm not eating this stuff plain. Glancing around, I don't see Ms. MacNamary anywhere today. I guess she's off doing her normal work in the park.

"We will do all training this morning so we can get you officially started midday," Dr. Grier says, without any prior announcement that we should be listening or paying attention to her.

One by one, we stop talking and turn to face her. Quietly, I take the sugar from Wyatt and pour it into my bowl, stirring.

"As explained yesterday, your job will be to follow a tunnel down into the ground, to a pocket of cracks on the caldera's edge." She holds up a tablet with a diagram on it. "We call this tunnel the alpha tunnel. It curves from vertical to horizontal about a mile in, thanks to the fracking drill equipment we used to make it." Dr. Grier snorts. "At least that equipment has served *one* useful purpose for the world."

She waits for our reaction, but we all are silent, so she continues.

"Once the tunnel goes horizontal, you'll find it passes by a series of natural cracks that need to be extended down." She points on her diagram. "Those will become the beta tunnels. You will be making those yourselves. We've modified our fracking drill bits to attach to the front end of some specialized pods that run on tracks—tracks you will need to install inside your beta tunnels as you go. Your primary job will be to drill into the natural crevasses, make the beta tunnels, and extend them deep into the Earth's crust until you reach a critical point just above the magma chamber—a point which you *will* need to determine for yourselves. Trust me, it is not a place you want to make mistakes."

Drilling to just above the magma chamber definitely sounds like somewhere I wouldn't want to make mistakes. Can't argue with that.

"There, you will deposit small explosives, which can be remotely detonated, so we can trigger them from a safe distance. Upon detonation, a beta tunnel will crack and reach the magma, releasing pressure. This shake-up will melt a manageable portion of the magma, which will rise through the tunnels, into our cave, before calming and cooling. We can then re-drill through the alpha tunnel and repeat with the next beta tunnel as needed."

I gulp. This sounds incredibly risky. But it's not like I'd be able to come up with a way to stop a supervolcano, so I guess I need to trust in the professionals. Next to me, Wyatt crosses his arms, drumming his fingers.

"It's crucial to keep all drilled areas at the exact sizes I tell you, so that the pressure will be just right. Each crevasse you work in will be different. Each will have its own risks. Nature is not neat and tidy. And the magma chamber is not at even levels throughout," Dr. Grier concludes. "Does everyone understand what they need to do?"

We nod.

"Wrong answer. You don't understand yet. You have no details." Dr. Grier shakes her head at us, then begins to list stuff on her fingers. "What kind of mineral veins should you watch out for to avoid coming face-to-face with a pocket of superheated water?" One finger goes up. "At what distances apart are you drilling for the tracks?" Another. "How close is too close to the magma chamber? What temperatures should you monitor in the tunnels to be assured you're in a safe zone? What kinds of rock can you drill through and what would crumble, possibly triggering a pressure drop or a hydrothermal fluid release too early?"

"Gypsum, calcite, sulfur, iron," Kenzie answers Dr. Grier's first question, imitating her by ticking each mineral off on her fingers.

"The distances to drill for the tracks will likely vary depending on numerous factors, which I'm sure we'll have to calculate ourselves on the job," Todd says.

"The density and composition of the rock above the magma chamber will determine how close we can get," I jump in, excited that I can answer one of her questions.

"We should note temperature increases if they rise, but if they're stable, even if they're warm, we should be safe," Wyatt says.

"And as for the rocks we can drill through—granite will be the safest, rhyolite is probably fine—" Kenzie starts.

"Nonlayered metamorphic rock should also be okay—" Todd says.

"I don't think we'll find any, but if we do, we should avoid sedimentary rock unless the grain size is next to nothing," I say.

"And it'd also need to be cemented strongly together already," Wyatt adds. "Small grain size and strong cementation."

Dr. Grier doesn't smile, but she does raise her chin slightly and her cheek twitches. "Show-offs. You're all close. But you're still going to have to do the official training. I can see Ms. MacNamary picked candidates wisely, after all. I will have to thank her."

That startles me—I thought Dr. Grier had chosen us herself. Ms. MacNamary did? But how would a park ranger be a better judge of geology candidates than an actual geologist? Just one more thing to add to the list of weird stuff we've learned in the past twenty-four hours.

"Okay, gather around," Dr. Grier says. She brings up more slides on her tablet. "Stopping the Yellowstone Supervolcano 101."

She pauses for a moment, and I wonder if she was expecting us to chuckle or something, like earlier. But the moment passes fast, and she continues, diving straight into her slides.

"This will be your home away from home down in the tunnels," Dr. Grier says, pointing at a picture of a contraption that looks like a cylindrical cage with giant hunks of metal on the top and bottom. "Your drilling pod. On the bottom is the fracking drill." She expands the image size.

The drill looks almost like a giant metal flower. I expected a drill to be . . . well . . . *pointier.*

"It will churn the rock up and through the pipe that runs up the side of your pod. This pipe goes all the way to the surface, along with your power cables and safety lines." She points at a series of tubes and cabling that sticks out the top of the pod in the picture. Next, she points to the top of the pod. "On the other end of your pod is a motor. This motor runs on the tracks I mentioned before."

She shows us a picture of the outer edge of our pod. On the opposite side from the pipes, the pod attaches to some long metal two-by-four-looking things that go down the tunnel in a straight line. The motor at the top of the pod hooks directly onto these tracks. It pushes the pod along, kind of like a toy train diving directly down into planet Earth.

Dr. Grier continues to talk, and I can't help but start to shake at the thought of us really doing everything she's outlining. Mom doesn't let me use the *blender* by myself, and here I am, about to be in control of a machine that can cut through our planet. All while carrying a poisonous gas detector in case the air turns bad. And a tank of oxygen to breathe for such emergencies. Which we have to safeguard from sparks, because we're going to be operating a giant drill *and* operating a hand drill to install metal tracks. *What?!*

Bri. I shake my head at myself. *You agreed to help stop a super-volcano. You probably should have expected it to be difficult and scary. Get over yourself.*

After her slides, Dr. Grier waves Mr. Stiles over. He opens up a briefcase filled with measuring instruments.

"This one here is what will detect if there is water in the region." Mr. Stiles hefts a rectangular-shaped thing out of the case. "You'll want to take measurements thoroughly around an area before installing tracks. Hidden seams of H_2O will likely be superheated from convection. Which means scalding steam. So you really don't want to pin a track into one."

Mr. Stiles shows us how to use all the equipment, one item at a time. He makes each of us test everything out before he hooks it onto a tool belt on the table. The only thing he demonstrates that I feel confident being able to operate is the headlamp.

Once Mr. Stiles finally finishes showing us everything in his Scary Case of Important Tools, he gives each of us a completed belt.

"Width of the holes for track installation?" Dr. Grier quizzes us.

"One point two seven centimeters," Todd replies.

"Distance between?"

"Half a meter, unless unsafe," I say. "Then we adjust according to the surrounding rock."

"Dangerous humidity level?"

"Anything over eighty seven percent," Wyatt says.

Dr. Grier nods. "Keep an eye on your barometers."

"Trust me, my eyes are going to be *glued* to my thermometer, barometer, all the 'ometers," Kenzie says. She shakes like a tiny leaf, hooking her belt on. "You're going to have to make sure I pay attention to anything *else*."

I try my own belt on, flipping some of the equipment so I can read it more naturally and testing to see how hard it is to unhook and rehook the tools.

Dr. Grier looks at each of us for several moments, then turns to Mr. Stiles. "If they find suitable crevasses, we'll try them with five meters of drilling and track laying to start today. If they get that done safely, we'll advance them to as much as they can do before dinner."

I try to ignore that she said the word "safely."

"Will the alpha tunnel be ready for them by now?" Mr. Stiles asks.

"It should be." Dr. Grier's eyes flash.

"Right, of course, I just hadn't checked with—"

"Then *check*."

"Right."

Dr. Grier turns back to us as Mr. Stiles scampers off. I feel like scampering, too. Instead, I adjust the headlamp I'm wearing so the strap is tight enough. Then I put on my seriously sci-fi-looking dust mask, with two filters on each side, and a pair of goggles.

And then, like a grumpy Santa Claus, Mr. Fee shows up and hands me my camera.

"Hah, *yes*!" I take it from him, my cheeks pinching against my face mask as I smile extra wide.

"Aww, what? No fair!" Kenzie pouts. "Where's my phone?"

"No tech with internet," Mr. Fee says. "Dr. Grier has given Brianna here special permission to record the drilling process with her camera because it can't get online."

Immediately, I turn my camera on, a rush flooding me as the screen powers up. My courage boosts and my nerves disappear in an instant. It's like magic having my camera back in my hands.

"Hello, world!—And by world, I mean Dr. Grier," I say quickly. I can see my face on the flipped selfie screen and have to laugh at my goggles and mask. "I am suited up, about to descend into the depths of the Earth to put a stop to a supervolcano. Yes, you heard that right. A *supervolcano*. Meet our team!"

I flip the screen back and pan around. Kenzie lets out a whoop, making muscle-arms at the camera. Todd nods seriously, doing his best to ignore Kenzie. Wyatt waves.

"Okay, okay, enough." Mr. Stiles pushes my camera down.

"You're no fun," Kenzie says. I turn the camera off, my courage still flying high. This has all been so weird and unfamiliar. It's beyond comforting to have something from my normal life back.

For the next few hours, Mr. Stiles and Mr. Fee run us through several practice sessions with our sensors, our hand drills, and the controls for the *big* drills. After we start to consistently pass their tests, they march us over to the worksite, down several flights of stairs in the cave, and across a few narrow patches of cleared ground.

Ahead of me, Kenzie keeps punching one hand into her other, clearly psyching herself up. She bobs from toe to toe, her headlamp dancing along the ground as she does so, and I smile. Next to her, I notice that Wyatt has no problem moving in the boots he was given and want to rub that in the adults' faces. Now that I have the ability to record stuff again, I feel like I could take on the world. *Let's do this!*

But then we reach our actual starting point, and everything inside me turns back into pitifully trembling goo.

This new cavern is even bigger than the main camping area. Giant lights illuminate massive pieces of equipment. Huge pipes stick straight into the walls, as if they lead directly out of the hill we're under. A big yellow cube-shaped machine is hooked up to some smaller pipes and hoses. Beyond that, there's a massive orange contraption with chains and a crank that latches to cabling running across the floor. The cabling itself is hooked through two of the pod things that Dr. Grier told us about. To the left of all that is a vat that's too big to see into, so I have no idea what's in it. And next to the vat is a giant cement mixer. Past all the equipment, there are piles and piles of rock and debris.

But my eyes don't linger on any of that stuff, as impressive as it all is. Because directly in front of us, where the cables and smaller pipes run, there is a pitch-black hole in the ground, not more than a foot and a half in diameter.

"*That's* what we have to go into?" I ask, meekly.

"Yeah . . . um, that's going to be a tight fit," Todd says. We sidestep next to each other as our headlamps wash beams of light over the opening.

I have *no* idea how they expect us to manipulate tools and drill in such tight quarters. Holy mackerel. I don't have claustrophobia, but I might in about, oh, two minutes. I can feel my legs wobbling beneath me and it takes all my willpower to stay steady.

"Okay, it's going to be one after the other, as soon as the alpha tunnel is clear," Mr. Stiles says. "I don't care who goes in first, but whoever does has to go to the farthest location to work, so we're going to need a brave volunteer."

Just as he's explaining, and just as I'm about to raise a weak arm to ask if I could be one of the ones who *doesn't* go in as far, a buzzer sounds, and a couple of other pods get raised up and out of the tunnel. Two people shimmy out of them. We all gawk.

They're kids, like us. Maybe they're the ones Wyatt saw yesterday!

I can't make out facial features, because they're wearing dust masks and tight goggles, but their hair is filled with gray stuff and their jumpsuits are trashed. They smell like fireworks, the stench reaching my nose even through my face mask. One of them looks at us and pauses for a moment.

"Hi!" Kenzie says, waving.

The taller one pulls the shorter one away, and some of the men with Mr. Stiles immediately flock to the kids, blocking them from our view and whisking them off into the cavern.

"Friendly," Todd notes.

"They're probably just tired," I say, imagining how I'm going to feel in a couple hours.

"Yeah, and obviously need a shower," Kenzie adds. She looks thoughtful through her goggles. "Hey, we *do* get to shower after this, right? Because I'm not sharing a cabin with gross sweaty people."

"That's enough time wasting," Mr. Stiles says, nodding toward the tunnel. "It's your turn to head in."

I swallow behind my dust mask. The narrow darkness seems to grow in front of me, taking over my vision. Wyatt takes the first step forward, and mentally, I thank him. Todd moves away from me to follow him. I punch my hand with my fist the way Kenzie did earlier.

Okay. I force one foot in front of the other. *I guess we're really doing this.*

I end up right behind Kenzie. Mr. Stiles directs each of us to step into a pod. Wyatt and Todd take the pods just used by the other two kids, while Kenzie and I end up with the ones farther back down the cable.

A man I don't know holds a pod upright for me. I step into it, hugging the cable in the center and standing on top of the giant fracking drill, as instructed. Other than the main central line, all other pipes and wires are against one edge of the cylinder—which leaves me with only one side to stand on. The side with the attachments for the tracks.

It feels like I'm in some weird ride at a theme park. When the man shuts the door, I half expect him to say, "Keep your hands inside and have fun!"

Instead, he grunts and lowers the pod to a horizontal position. The curving walls and cables of the pod are covered in some sort of protective coating and have enough give to them that they bend slightly as I'm set down on the ground.

I try to keep my body calm now that I'm lying down. Another man feeds each of us a pack of narrow metal tracks that we're meant to install along the tunnels. I tuck the pack between the central cable and the opposite wall of pipes and wires, which is currently directly above me.

I can see why Dr. Grier needed kids for this. As the adults drag us toward the tunnel, I can't imagine how any of them would fit in the pods with all this equipment. The cables, the piping, the tracks, the tools . . . I'm going to hit my head on something if I so much as sneeze.

We're all in a curved line, and I can just see the others ahead of me. Wyatt, being the closest to the hole, has Mr. Stiles heave his pod upright to sink down into the ground first. In a matter of seconds, he goes from horizontal to vertical, and then he's gone.

It happened so fast. I squeeze my hands in their gloves, forcing myself to keep still.

Todd goes after him, and Kenzie, trembling, disappears next.

Trying to ride the coattails of my crewmates' courage, I stay quiet as I reach Mr. Stiles.

My motor starts up, and boy is it obnoxious: loud, repetitive, and churning, like a car that's trying to start. I'm grateful for the ear protection headphones Mr. Fee gave me earlier.

Like the others ahead of me, I'm pulled upright by Mr. Stiles, so that I can descend vertically into the alpha tunnel. The pod wobbles in his grip, and it takes all my self-control not to yell as I'm tipped into a standing position. My feet rest on top of the big fracking drill once again. The drill isn't on, but if I press the wrong button on my control panel, it will be.

Then a cable starts chugging, and I get pulled into the hole below.

The bright floodlights from the cavern cast shadows along the ground, which I watch for as long as I can. Lowering farther and farther, the rocky ground eventually becomes eye level. I can see Mr. Stiles's boots now—they knock bits of rubble loose as he walks around my pod. My breath quickens, hot against my face in its mask. Just as I'm about to shout that I don't want to do this anymore, the cave disappears from view.

CHAPTER SEVEN

The motor is the last part of the pod to sink into the ground. It hooks onto the track that's already installed in this part of the tunnel and starts pushing me down, down, down . . .

The Earth has swallowed me whole.

"Hey, Kenzie?" I call out over our radios. They're specialized ones, called TTE radios—Through-the-Earth communications radios—that allow us to talk even through rock. Miners use them, apparently.

"Yeah?" she answers.

"Nothing. Just wanted to make sure you were still there."

"Where else would I be? There's only one direction to go in here," she says.

I laugh. That is very true.

"I'm here, too," Todd says.

"And we're so glad for that," Kenzie responds.

We continue to chug down the tunnel, and I try desperately not to think about how we're getting closer and closer to actual, real-life magma. Every now and again, I'll move wrong and scrape myself on the metal track speeding by me, connected to the bedrock. All the rock we've moved past so far appears to be rhyolite, if I had to guess. Or granite. It looks like those types of rock from the research I did for my project, at least. I think about the kids who came out of the tunnel before us. If they've been here for a while, maybe they're the ones who set up all this track and drilled the alpha tunnel.

"So, how's everyone doing?" Todd asks as we continue our long descent.

"Fine so far," Wyatt answers.

"Just peachy," Kenzie says.

"Trying not to think about needing the bathroom," I honestly reply.

"Bri!" Everyone starts complaining.

"Come on! They purposefully had us not eat or drink so we could last a few hours!"

"I know! I'm sorry, I know it's not real, but my head thinks it is," I say.

"Great, now *my* head thinks *I* have to go," Todd says.

"Just think about something else," I say.

"I was until you brought it up!"

"Cut the radio chatter," Mr. Stiles's voice interrupts. "Communication should be for work purposes and emergencies only."

"Oh, stuff it," Kenzie says. "I'm not working down here in silence for hours on end. At the very least you could've provided us some music."

"You are saving the world," Mr. Stiles lectures. "You don't need theme music."

"Actually, this is exactly the type of situation that would call for theme music," I can't help but say. Because it totally is. And music would help calm my nerves.

But Mr. Stiles is insistent, so for now at least, we stop talking. A few minutes later, out of jitters and boredom, I turn my camera on.

"So, here we are," I say into it. "Going down a tunnel underground in a supervolcano. Yeah, it's about as terrifying as it sounds. But a girl's got to save the world, doesn't she?"

I film the rock wall moving by, then the cables in the center that I'm clutching with one thick glove. Next, I pan the camera to the metal tracks that my pod is traveling down.

"Today we're supposed to install some of this track stuff down natural crevasses in the bedrock. That will make it possible to get our pods into them so we can drill down to the magma chamber." I zoom in on the tall bag of track pieces I have crammed next to the pipes. "Sorry for the shaky camera work," I apologize. "It's a tight fit."

I know this isn't exactly the scientific recording Dr. Grier entrusted me with, so I decide to save my camera battery and turn it off for a few minutes. I can't risk her changing her mind about allowing me to film.

I loop through the plan and our instructions in my mind over and over. I don't want to mess this up. One, if I use my little hand drill to connect the track to the wall in the wrong spot—say, near a pocket of water—I can get sprayed with scalding steam. Two, if I use the big drill in the wrong spot, I could blow the Yellowstone Supervolcano.

I mean, that second one is way less probable, with all the sensors and equipment I've got and the state of the magma in the upper chamber right now, but still. It's something I'm ultra-aware of, to the point that my skin hasn't stopped tingling for a moment.

We make a gradual turn to go horizontal. The semiflexible bars of my pod bend, forcing me and everything in here with me to bend to match. My fracking drill goes from pointing down to pointing sideways. The bag of tracks falls on top of me, and I have to shove it back up with the piping.

It is *super* uncomfortable.

I travel flat on my back for nearly half an hour. The motor pushes along the tracks under me, screeching, and I try to quash my fears of it failing and getting stuck. I keep my eyes shut, concentrating on breathing in and out and stopping myself from calling over the radio for reassurance again. It's someone else's turn to look scared.

Occasionally, we hit a crack—too small for us to begin working in, but big enough that we need to be careful not to drop anything. Wyatt, who is in front, lets us know over the radio. He'll call something out like, "Three centimeters, stable." Then everyone else will reach the crack before me, because I'm the caboose of our little train.

Wyatt marks the cracks in fluorescent green spray paint. They're easy to see that way. If those kids we saw really did drill all this, they did a great job laying the tracks in a safe and sturdy way over the gaps on the tunnel floor. The pods pass over them easily.

After what feels like an eternity, Wyatt calls with a different message:

"I've got a crevasse big enough for us to drill into," his voice says over our radio. "Bri, are you last? Because this one will be yours. I'll mark it in orange."

My stomach turns.

"Yeah, I'll take that one," I say. As real as this all is, it just got more real. I'd fallen into a rhythm, but with one radio call, my nerves are full-on firing once more.

Wyatt starts our line moving again, until he finds three more places to drill. I continue to travel along, keeping an eye out for the spot Wyatt marked. Finally, the leading edge of my pod goes over the massive crevasse sprayed in reflective orange, and my heart leaps into my throat.

I stop the pod's motor. My body lays over a crack in the Earth that's just big enough that I could slide down it if I wasn't enclosed in my pod. Oh. My. *God*.

"It's okay," I whisper to myself, my voice echoing down the crevasse like a ghost calling back to its foolish body. "Be logical, Bri. You can't fall. You're okay."

But not having a speck of stone underneath my belly as I hover over a gap that potentially leads to molten rock is enough to paralyze me for several moments, regardless of logic.

I swallow about ten times over.

"Come on. You got this. Just install the first track and start your beta tunnel."

It sounds simple. But to do it, I'll have to reach out through the bars of my pod and into the crevasse.

I take several shaky breaths. My mask is tight against my skin. Sweat trickles down my face. Slowly, I angle my head toward the crack in the ground, shining my headlamp into it.

The crevasse goes on and on. There's no telling how deep it is.

Okay, breathe, just breathe. You physically cannot fall, unless you contort yourself and squeeze out of this pod, which you aren't going to do, because you aren't stupid.

"Holy—" Kenzie lets out a string of swear words over the radio that would've gotten me grounded for five years straight.

But at least it lets out some of the tension. I laugh.

"Seriously," I chime in. "I can't budge. I'm too scared."

"It's . . . it's not so bad," Todd says.

"Have you actually started yet?" Kenzie asks.

"I've thought about starting," Todd answers.

"I've got part of a track in," Wyatt says. "You just have to sort of make yourself do it, and then it gets easier. I dropped a screw, which was the scariest part. Didn't even hear it land. Not sure it has yet."

The very thought of dropping something and never hearing it

land makes me shrink up like an inchworm.

"What if we all start together?" Kenzie suggests.

"Okay," I respond shakily. "I'll start if you guys start." Maybe.

"We have to take measurements first," Todd reminds us.

"Right, yeah," I say.

"Okay, I'm going to lower in my instrument pack on the count of three," says Kenzie.

I reach for my pack of sensors on a string. Wyatt, as the lead, supposedly took all these measurements already to confirm that these crevasses are ones we can work in. But double-checking is important.

"One . . . two . . ." Kenzie says. "Three."

I lower my small pack of sensors, hoping they all work right. Their shadows play on the wall, and I wait for them to stop swinging before I press the buttons, like Mr. Stiles taught me. Then I watch for the readouts.

Humidity: 56%.

Temperature: 53 degrees Fahrenheit.

Projected depth: 1.217 miles.

Oh my god.

I want to yank the instruments right out of there, but I stop myself. I still need to check the walls for mineral strains.

It's okay, Bri. We have to drill our beta tunnels down two or three miles, so having the crevasse naturally over a mile deep to begin with is a good thing.

Unless you fall, a voice in the back of my mind says.

"I'm not going to fall!" I say out loud, not to my camera, not over the radio, not to anyone. Just to myself. "I can do this. I have to do this."

But after I finish examining the walls and find no evidence of gypsum or any other minerals that would indicate the dangerous presence of water nearby, it still takes me a while before I can convince myself to pull my small hand drill off my belt and angle it into the crevasse to make the holes for the screws.

I set the tip to the rock, my arms dangling into the nothingness below. My headlamp makes the diamond-tipped edging of the hand drill bit glitter. I go to rub my eyes, but they're behind my goggles, so I can't.

"Got to save the world," I tell myself. "Literally the entire planet is counting on you."

I squeeze the trigger of the little drill. The drill bit slides completely off the mark, skidding along the wall.

"*Shoot!*" I yell, turning it off immediately. For a hot second, I'd thought I'd dropped the drill, but I didn't. It's strapped to my wrists, anyway.

Now I'm just mad at myself. We practiced! I can *do* this. Determined, I grip the hand drill tighter, then set it back on the spot to try again.

This time, I get an eensy bit into the wall before it skids off again.

"Ugh!"

It takes a few more tries before I have enough of a dent to hold the drill bit in place so it can dig in deeper. After that, I have more luck.

Bits of rock fly off in all directions as I drill. I'm super grateful for my enormous face mask and goggles, because they both keep getting pelted. It was startling at first to have flecks of rock pinging off the plastic covering my eyes, but it rapidly just becomes part of the job.

My hands sweat in the large gloves I'm wearing. I double-check the temperature, but it's not reading anything odd or dangerous, so I keep going.

It. Takes. *Forever.*

Every few minutes, I have to stop and clean out the drill bit, which is caked in rock dust. I also have to scrape the dust out of the hole I'm making. I'd thought my face mask was to protect me from dangerous gases, but I think it's mostly to make sure I don't inhale powderized igneous rock.

After about ten minutes, I finally have the first hole done. I drill the second and third holes as fast as I can, and my arms feel like jelly by the time I'm ready to insert the track.

I understand why they couldn't get someone more muscular in here, because I barely have room to breathe, but I still feel like maybe Dr. Grier—or rather, Ms. MacNamary, I guess—made a mistake choosing me for this job. I wonder how the others are doing, but I'm too tired to turn my radio on and check in.

The good news is, once I do bolt the metal track to the crevasse wall, I find that I did an okay job. It's steady. It holds.

I connect the newly installed vertical track to the horizontal track from the tunnel I'm still in, using the special brackets Mr. Stiles gave me. This will allow the motor to push the pod into the crevasse. Then I just have to find the courage to turn on the fracking drill and start drilling my way down to a magma chamber. Simple, right?

I shift my cage pod back up the tunnel until I get the base of my pod lined up with the crevasse. This whole process has taken almost an hour. I must be way behind everyone else.

The cables are holding you up. You can't fall. You can go in, but you can't fall.

When I squeeze my eyes shut, tears pinch out of their corners. I imagine this moment as a video. This would be the point the lead on-screen personality would take the plunge.

I turn on my camera, vowing to delete this section before giving it to Dr. Grier.

"Hey," I whisper. "I'm going to do it. Hero time."

Keeping the camera on me, I angle the bottom of the pod in with my feet, fire up the motor, rotate the giant drill on its hinges, and maneuver in.

The turn into the crevasse is fast and painless—even though my heart feels like it's about to explode.

"Oh my god," I say, once the turn is done and I'm fully vertical. I clutch my camera. It's probably aimed in a super unflattering way at my face, but I don't care right now. "I did it! I'm in a crevasse in the Earth that leads straight down toward one of the most dangerous magma chambers in the entire planet. Just want to state that for the record."

The motor moves me down as far as the track will take me. The fracking drill on the bottom of my pod actually has to do work now, busting up rock to widen the crevasse to allow me to fit through. I turn it on and a slurry of stone gets churned up through the big pipe, heading to the surface. It must be adding to the giant pile we saw when we entered the cavern worksite.

For some reason, that makes me most proud out of everything. I'm no longer just going where others have been, I'm digging my own tunnel.

I line up my small hand drill to make holes for the next section of track. Now that I'm upright, drilling the holes goes *much* quicker.

In the next two hours, I lay nine new pieces of track. I record the process, so Dr. Grier will have something useful on video rather than just my panicked talking. I'm already much farther along than she had expected us to get today, so I think she'll be pleased, regardless. I hope, at least.

"How's everyone doing?" I ask over the radio. I'm not sure when we're thinking about being done, but my body is hitting its exhaustion point.

"*So. Tired*," Kenzie replies.

"It's only midafternoon," Wyatt says. "We should probably do a couple more sections each before we head back."

"Oh god, do we have to?" Kenzie asks. "Can't we just lie down and never get up again?"

"Well, that's an option, I suppose," Todd says. "But I don't think that will actually do much in the way of saving the world."

"You don't know that," Kenzie says. "What if the volcano bubbles up right here and my body stops it? If you make me keep moving, you could be dooming the entire planet."

"While I appreciate the sacrifice you're willing to make, Kenzie, I think we should probably do what Dr. Grier has planned instead," I say, despite totally wanting to be done myself. "She has *just* a few more years of experience with this sort of thing than you."

"She doesn't have squat experience with what we just did," Kenzie complains. "I'd like to see her drill one of these holes."

"Kenzie," Wyatt says. "Come on."

"Fine, fine, fine," she grumbles. "But only because I happen to *like* this planet."

"Three more track pieces each?" I ask.

"Yeah," Wyatt says. "Then we can go back and get some food and rest."

After running my sensors again, I readjust my mask and goggles, put my gloves back on, and start working.

Once I have the three tracks laid, I radio in and confirm that everyone is ready to head back. They are. We're all very much *done*.

I'm in the lead this time, on our way up. My body feels numb. The smooth, cut bedrock zips by me mere inches from my face, but that has already become normal to my mind.

After what feels like ages, I finally emerge. Mr. Stiles and Dr. Grier are there in the cavern, waiting for us. I try to unlatch the cage door, but I'm too tired, so I just fumble with it until Mr. Stiles helps me unhook it.

Out. Food. Chairs. Rest.

My brain repeats those four words as I stumble out of the

pod. Soon after, the next gets pulled up.

"*Yes!* Finally!" Kenzie collapses as she emerges from the ground.

"Welcome back," Dr. Grier greets us.

"I got twelve meters of track into a crevasse," I say, stretching.

"Good start," Dr. Grier replies. That's all she says on that subject, though, and I'm a bit disappointed. "Come on, dinner is waiting."

"Wait, we still have to get Suck-Up and Texas out," Kenzie says, peeling off her face mask and goggles.

"The boys?" Mr. Stiles replies. "I'll get them. You two can go on ahead."

I take off my own goggles and mask. I'm too tired to ask about anything more, and Kenzie apparently is, too. We follow Dr. Grier back to base camp.

Dr. Grier hasn't forgotten about my camera. She takes it from me as we walk.

"Sorry, I was mostly just trying to get a handle on how to do my job," I say. "Probably isn't too much there that's useful."

"It's fine," she says. "You will have plenty more chances to record the process."

I almost stop walking at that. She's right. Somehow, in today's work, I had fallen into the mindset that I just needed to get this done *now*. I hadn't thought about how I was going to do this all again tomorrow. And the next day. And the next. For the whole summer.

Sudden tears spring to my eyes. The muscles in my arms

spasm, and I rush to walk faster, getting in front of everyone so no one sees me like this.

In my rushing, I nearly run into someone.

"Hey, watch it!" a kid says, stumbling backward.

I stare at him. He's definitely not one of the kids from earlier. He's younger by at least a year, much darker skinned, and thicker around the middle than they were.

"Sorry," I say. "It's been a long day."

"Nolan, Ms. MacNamary will find you later," Dr. Grier says.

"Oh, so *this* is Nolan," Kenzie says, eyeballing him. I remember Mr. Stiles and Mr. Fee mentioning someone named Nolan yesterday. "How are you so *clean*? This is super unfair." She reaches out to smear dust on his green sweatshirt.

Nolan takes a huge step back away from Kenzie, ignoring her and easily dodging her attempted swipe.

"I'll go and wait, then," he says. Then he walks a different direction than we're headed. Dr. Grier watches him leave, tapping one finger on her crossed arms.

"Bye!" Kenzie calls after him. "Geez, are all kids here this rude?"

Dr. Grier motions for us to keep walking. "They know they have more important things to do than chitchat."

Just as Nolan rounds the corner, two heads pop up from the hood of his sweatshirt. I gasp. *The person with three heads from the mouth of the cave!*

"Uh, everyone saw those animal things in his sweatshirt, right?" I ask.

"Those are Nolan's ferrets," Dr. Grier says. "They help around here."

"His *what?*" Kenzie asks.

"Aren't ferrets those weird long rodent things with the ugly faces?" I ask, hurrying to keep up with Dr. Grier and relieved that I'm not just seeing things.

"They aren't rodents," Dr. Grier says. "I suppose it's subjective whether or not you find them ugly."

"Why does Nolan get to have pets down here?" Kenzie asks.

"Like I said, Buggy and Baxter help with our work," Dr. Grier says.

"Buggy and Baxter? Which one's which?" Kenzie asks.

"Buggy is the white one with the pink eyes. Baxter is the one with the more normal coloring—the browns and the tans. Careful," she advises. "Baxter bites."

CHAPTER EIGHT

Nolan makes Kid Number Three that we know about who works here and is not from our little group. Apparently none of the adults think it's important to introduce any of us to each other. I mean, at least they're not making us sit together and do one of those silly "get to know you" games, but still—this is kind of the opposite extreme.

Kenzie and I tell Wyatt and Todd about Nolan during dinner, but everyone is too bone tired to do anything practical to reach out to him. It isn't until we sleep for the night and wake up for a new day that any of us can muster enough energy to come up with a good suggestion for meeting the other kids more officially.

"We know at least two of them work in the tunnels," Todd says as we all get ready for the day. "Maybe we can leave a message for them down there."

"With what?" I ask from my side of the changing wall. "*On*

what?" I'm trying to imagine a little paper note tucked behind a track on the alpha tunnel wall, but only see it getting barreled over by a pod and eventually torn off and pushed down a magma pit. There, of course, my imagination has it bursting into flames.

"I've got that spray paint," Wyatt says. "Tough to write in detail, but not impossible."

"We could leave them some sweet graffiti," Kenzie muses.

"Actually, the fluorescent paint is probably a good idea—so they have a bigger chance of seeing it in the dark," Todd says.

"It'd have to be a short message," I say. "But it's a start."

There's a knock at the cabin door, letting us know it is time for breakfast. We all hush up quickly. There's a level of excitement in the air at having a secret of our own. This place is so mysterious—it's our turn to hide something from everyone else.

We get up and eat quickly, then head to the work cavern. Part of me realizes I haven't been outside in nearly forty-eight hours, but another part can hardly believe that just two days ago, I was being dropped off by my parents for what I *thought* was going to be an entire summer of being outdoors. So much has changed.

The four of us reach the cavern and casually switch our radios over to a different frequency than yesterday when the adults aren't looking. We decided that we deserve our own private channel to talk on while we're working to save the world. Having Mr. Stiles or Mr. Fee listen in on our conversations is just weird.

One by one, we get into our pods and begin the trek underground.

"*It's the final countdown!*" Kenzie sings, as her pod gets

lowered into the alpha tunnel after Wyatt's and Todd's. *"Da-nah-nah-nah! Nah-nah-nah nah-nah!"* She's not on the TTE radio yet, so her voice goes muffled as she slides into the ground.

Next, it's my turn. Sinking into the narrow tunnel is only *slightly* less freaky than it was yesterday. At least today I know what to expect.

As I travel down, fully decked out in all my gear, ready for Day Two of this operation, I realize what had been bothering me about Nolan.

He's more heavyset than the rest of us. There's no way Nolan could fit in the drilling pods. Dr. Grier and Ms. MacNamary said they have kids here to help because they need small people to fit into narrow spaces, but Nolan is a kid who's here and definitely wouldn't be able to do that.

I bring up my observation over the TTE radio as we all shuttle down the main passageway.

"Listen, he clearly is here to train his ferrets to fight in the apocalypse in case we fail," Kenzie replies. "He's the Ferret Whisperer. Don't question his purpose."

I laugh. But then I remember what Ms. MacNamary said about what would happen if we didn't want to help. "Maybe he's working with Ms. MacNamary in other parts of the park," I say. "She said she had other work we could do if we didn't want to do the tunnel stuff."

"Let's just figure out what we want to say in our message. At least two of the other kids will get it," Wyatt says.

We debate for a while, and then agree on a simple:

HI! WE'RE NEW HERE. WYATT, TODD, KENZIE,
BRIANNA. WHO ARE YOU?

But by the time I get to Wyatt's message, I see Kenzie has
added to it with her lipstick. Now it reads:

FEARLESS LEADER↘   ↙**NERD**

HI! WE'RE NEW HERE. WYATT, TODD, KENZIE,
BRIANNA. WHO ARE YOU?

↖**ALSO TOTALLY
BEST**   ↖**AKA THE
≈BEST≈**

"Nice, Kenzie," I say.

"What?" Todd asks. "What'd she do?"

"Just made some corrections," Kenzie answers. "You'll see later."

After traveling a ways more, I eventually reach my beta
tunnel and am pleased to see everything still looks good from
yesterday. No water or magma gushing in. All neat and tidy.

I rotate my fracking drill ninety degrees so it faces down my
tunnel, then power up my motor to push the whole pod in. Then
I begin the descent.

I film more of the nitty gritty this time, pausing every few
moments to record my track installation progress and show how
I'm changing my stance and how I grip the drill. I'm also recording what my thermometer, infrared sensors, and barometer say.
Dr. Grier is going to have so much data to work with from this,
she won't know what to do with it all.

The day passes, and by the end, I'm proud to say I installed even more track than I did yesterday. I'm getting the hang of this! Even in the tricky area, where I had to compensate for some impossibly dense granite.

Of course, to get all the way down to the magma chamber will take weeks. I don't know if Dr. Grier wants us to make more than one beta tunnel each, because from my calculations, we'd be lucky to manage two apiece over this entire summer.

Maybe that's what the other kids are working on—other beta tunnels farther down the alpha tunnel. I chat over the radio about that idea as our cables and motors pull us up at the end of the day. But that conversation gets interrupted when Todd reaches the message on the wall.

"Nerd? Really? That's the best you could come up with?" Todd squawks.

"Short, sweet, and most importantly: accurate," Kenzie replies.

"I can't argue with it. I *am* a nerd, and proud!"

"Good for you," Kenzie says.

"I think we're all nerds, to be honest," I chime in.

Then Wyatt reaches the message. "Okay, I was going to be mad that you messed up what I wrote, but I think I can forgive you," he says. I can hear how pleased he is over the radio.

"Thanks, sir," Kenzie replies. "Wouldn't want to upset our Driller in Chief."

I laugh at that. Eventually, we all emerge from the tunnel, looking mildly less disheveled than we did yesterday.

"Whew!" Todd says, wiping his hands on his jumpsuit. "Got twenty-five done today!" he boasts to the waiting Dr. Grier.

"So did I!" Kenzie immediately exclaims.

"Me too," I say.

I watch Todd fight back a reply. I can almost hear his thoughts competing in his brain—both wanting to have done more than us, and also remembering that it's a *good* thing we all got a lot done.

"An improvement," Dr. Grier acknowledges. "Excellent."

I look at Wyatt.

"Twenty-nine," he says, not catching my eye.

I smile for him.

On Day Three, we're all pumped to head back down into the ground, though we can't tell Dr. Grier or the other adults why.

The claustrophobic feeling of being trapped in my pod is almost gone by now—I'm really starting to get used to this. Plus, there's the added distraction of waiting for Wyatt to reach the message and learn who the kids on the opposite shift from us are.

My pod sinks lower and lower into the earth, and I sigh impatiently. My mind wanders to last night, when we sent our first emails home. Those honestly might have been the hardest thing we've done so far. They took ages to write, since we had to make sure our stories lined up in case our families talked to each other. We decided a simple few lines about adjusting to camping life and sitting through some lessons from Dr. Grier was as close as we could get to the truth. Mine ended up reading:

Hey Mom and Dad!

Things are great so far. We have set up at the campsite. I'm sharing with Kenzie, which has been fun. We saw
an elk on the drive in! With a baby!

Dr. Grier has been teaching us a lot, so that we can
help her with her research. We might go to Mammoth Hot
Springs soon!

—That line I threw in so we all had something to talk about
on our next emails.

Anyway, guess that's about it so far. Did you guys
make it home already? Talk to you later.

Love, Bri

As Todd has to email every single day, I've been tagged as
his writing buddy, since I've been to Yellowstone before and can
come up with places we're "visiting" with Dr. Grier. I'm taking
notes on what he writes, so we can all keep our stories straight for
whenever the rest of us choose to email home. Wyatt and I are on
the same page of doing so every few days, but Kenzie is hoping
she can get away with once a week, tops.

I just have to hope my parents will forgive me when they find
out about all the lying I'll do this summer. I feel like I'm in one
of those cartoons with an angel and a demon on each shoulder—
except instead of sitting apart, they're together, high-fiving and
sharing a sundae. I wish there was a way to separate them, but I
guess this is one of those cases where doing something small and
bad is needed in order to do something gigantically good.

In an effort to distract myself, I brainstorm about other
Yellowstone locales that would make sense to do geology research

at as we descend into our tunnels. We're going to need a lot of them to keep the ruse going with our families. But I stop when Wyatt calls out over the radio:

"They answered! They're using blue spray paint. Huh, interesting."

The other kids responded! I jump with excitement and hit my head on the motorized top of my pod. "Ouch!" I whisper, even though no one can hear me.

"I don't care what color it is, what does it say?" Kenzie demands.

"It says, 'Eddie Fuentes and Raquel Soto. Be careful drilling. Steam dangerous.'"

"Eddie and Raquel," I repeat over the radio. It's nice to have names.

"See, this is why we should get to meet with them in person," Todd says. "Who better to train us than the kids already doing the work?"

But later that night, when we ask Dr. Grier if we can meet the other kids, she shrugs it off. I even try to do what Ms. MacNamary said and present the argument as logically as possible. Nothing works, though, so at least for the time being, talking through spray paint in the tunnel is the only way we can think of to communicate. The next day—Day Four—we write back:

THANKS FOR THE TIP. ANY OTHER ADVICE?

Over the course of the next couple weeks, we learn several

helpful hints about drilling, and we learn more and more about each other. Raquel and Eddie have been here six months. They made the alpha tunnel. Now they're drilling farther down the alpha tunnel on opposite hours from us. They're from California. They know Nolan, but he doesn't work with them and they don't know what he does.

The days go along both slowly and quickly, somehow. Twenty to thirty tracks become our average each session we're underground, and Dr. Grier loves to remind us that the volcano could go off any day now, so we really need to hurry as much as we can. I figure out a trick to install the tracks faster by using them as the measuring tool, rather than my tape measure. I also figure out that by entwining my air conditioning pipe around my pulling cable, I can cool the cable down and fight the heat from friction, which keeps my whole pod feeling much more refreshed.

The evenings pass by with games and hang out time. Wyatt and Kenzie discover they share a love for chess and start playing every night. Meanwhile, after our email sessions, Todd and I have started inventing a superhero universe and have been drawing what each of our outfits would look like. The cabin is slowly becoming covered in our ridiculous art. We rarely see Ms. MacNamary, but when we do she usually sneaks us some kind of snack, so we're always on the lookout for her. And sightings of Nolan are nearly as rare—Todd and I have written him into our superhero universe as the Mysterious Ferret Boy.

This isn't at all how I'd envisioned my summer going, but the constant undercurrent of worry that we could blow up in a lava explosion at any second has cemented the friendships among us four faster than any I've ever experienced in my life. Add in the secret messages we've been sending, and I've really come to think of Kenzie, Todd, and Wyatt as my *people*. We share something no one else in the world shares, other than Eddie and Raquel. It's weird, but kind of nice.

Then, one day—Day Sixteen of tunneling—the messages from Eddie and Raquel stop.

As I pass by the spray-painted words from our ongoing conversation, I read the last message we wrote to them:

DOES IT EVER FREAK YOU OUT THAT WE ARE
DRILLING THROUGH A SUPERVOLCANO?

"Maybe it really did freak them out," I say over our radios, as we discuss why they didn't answer.

"They probably just had a busy night," Wyatt replies. "There's only two of them and four of us, after all."

"Yeah, you'd think they'd split us evenly," Todd notes. "Three and three."

"You'd also think they'd let us talk to each other, but I don't think Dr. Grier knows the meaning of the word *socialization*." Kenzie snorts.

I fall silent. Today we are in new jumpsuits. They're entirely reflective, designed to keep heat out. Yesterday, we reached temperatures that were warm enough to turn us into sweaty messes—even my cooling trick couldn't help me. And it's only going to get hotter from here on out, so it was time for a safety gear upgrade.

I reach my beta tunnel and maneuver in. Kenzie and I decided that we were going to try to do thirty-five tracks apiece before dinner—both to speed up the process and to see the look on Todd's face when we tell him.

However, once I'm down my tunnel, I find I'm in a patch of quartz-rich granite, and that is taking absolutely *ages* to drill through. Kenzie is stuck with a ton of quartz in her granite, too. I know, because she won't shut up about it.

"This is the *worst*," Kenzie says. "We're never going to hit thirty at this rate, much less thirty-five."

"You don't have to hit thirty-five," Todd says.

"*You* don't," Kenzie says. I can hear the grin. "But I'm going to. Suck it, quartz!"

"Good grief," Todd grumbles.

I crack a smile and get back to work. From over the radio, I can hear Kenzie holler with glee.

"YES! Quartz *did* suck it! Different minerals now, way easier!"

"Lucky!" I say. I turn back to my own section of wall, my headlamp shining on the mica and making it glitter off the quartz. "Stupid quartz."

But then, Kenzie lets out an entirely different yelp. A giant *whooshing* blasts over the radio—and then silence.

"*Kenzie!*" I scream.

"Kenzie!" Todd yells.

"Kenzie, are you okay?!" Wyatt shouts.

"*Kenzie!* Say something!" My voice rises to hysterics.

There's no reply.

"Oh my god, what do we do?" Todd asks.

"Dr. Grier!" Wyatt calls over the radio on the channel that's meant to reach the surface. "Dr. Grier, we need evacuation! Kenzie might be hurt!"

"Hurry!" I add.

The response is staticky, so I can't tell what the adults are trying to say, but the emergency cable does start chugging, and we begin the ascent out of the tunnels.

"Kenzie, please tell me you're okay! Say something!" I repeat.

"Please!" Todd adds.

There's excruciating silence for several moments. I hug my cable, trembling.

"You know what?" I finally hear crackle over the radio.

It's Kenzie. I collapse against my bag of track pieces in relief.

"What?" I reply, tears springing to my eyes.

"I take back what I said about quartz."

I laugh, gripping my pipe and cables and trying not to totally lose it, as my eyes water more by the second.

"You're okay!" Todd exclaims.

"Are you hurt?" Wyatt asks.

"Not badly," Kenzie says. "I might be burned. I hit a pocket of steam. It was small."

"Oh my god, you're so lucky," I say.

"I know," she says. "But I'm fine. I'm fine, I'm fine, I'm fine . . ." She repeats the phrase, her voice going shaky.

"Kenzie?" Wyatt asks.

"I'm fine!" she insists. "I'm fine. This is dumb, I'm fine, I didn't get hurt, I'm fine." She shuts off her radio, presumably to cry, and I can't blame her.

"We're going to get you looked at, even if you think you're okay," Wyatt says. "Just in case."

She doesn't reply, which tells me she might actually be hurt more than she's letting on.

We travel up faster than usual, thanks to the power of the emergency cables. I check in with Kenzie, as do Wyatt and Todd, every few minutes, but mostly she ignores us.

Once we reach the surface, I hurry out of my pod so they can bring Kenzie out. Mr. Stiles and Mr. Fee are both there with first aid kits on hand.

Kenzie's pod comes up next. Before I can get to her, Mr. Stiles is already opening up her cage door, helping her out. He quickly pulls off her equipment. Where her mask and goggles pressed into her skin, she's outlined in red blisters.

I wince. Thankfully, most of her face looks okay, but she clearly got burned.

"What's going on? What happened?" Dr. Grier rushes over to us.

"We had an accident," I explain.

"Are the tunnels okay?" she asks.

I pause. Two thoughts trip over themselves in my mind. First: *How can that be your first question?* And then: *Oh god, what if they aren't? What if we messed up something bad, and caused some sort of deadly domino effect?*

I glance at Kenzie.

"I don't know," Kenzie answers. "I think so. It was just a small burst."

"Burst?" Dr. Grier snaps her attention to Kenzie.

Kenzie holds her ground, tipping her little chin up. "Yes. I screwed up. I hit a pocket of water, steam rushed out, I probably would have died if it was worse, but then it stopped and we decided to come out." She owns it all, and I would've reached out to hug her, but Dr. Grier looks far scarier than usual.

"Be more careful in the future."

"Shouldn't we get her to a hospital?" I ask.

"It's not third degree," Mr. Stiles says. "She'll be okay with treatment here."

"Kenzie, do you want to go to a hospital?" I ask, ignoring Mr. Stiles. What a dumb answer! Second-degree burns are still awful.

"No." She shakes her head. "If we can treat it here, let's do that. I can get back to work faster that way."

I stare at her.

Behind Kenzie, Todd's pod surfaces into the cave.

"Kenzie, you okay?" he asks, climbing out as fast as he can.

"Of course," she answers. "I eat steam for breakfast."

"Kenzie, I really think you should see a doctor," I say.

"I'm a trained medic," Mr. Stiles says, glaring at me. "Trust me, she is getting professional treatment." He cleans off Kenzie's face.

I shut up. My hands are shaking. I don't like any of this. I exchange glances with Todd, who looks as concerned as I feel.

Wyatt finally emerges from the alpha tunnel. "How is she?" he asks, joining us.

"Not dead," I say. "But her face got a full blast of steam. Everything not covered by her mask and goggles is burned."

"What the heck was she thinking?" Todd crosses his arms. "This is all her fault for showing off."

He's not entirely wrong, but I'm still angry on Kenzie's behalf. "She was just trying to get this job done."

Dr. Grier stands behind us, her eyes steeling over. "We brought you four here so this kind of thing wouldn't happen," she says. "You know the science. You should recognize where it is safe to drill. I don't have time to walk you through Geology 101."

"Kids!" a voice shouts. I spin.

Ms. MacNamary runs down the cave tunnel toward us, and I well up in relief. *Ms. MacNamary's here!* I can hardly believe our luck that she's visiting today when we have a real situation on our hands that needs adult attention—not *Dr. Grier* attention.

"Oh, Kenzie!" she exclaims, showing all the concern Dr. Grier isn't. "Thank goodness. Oh my, my, my."

"We want to take her to a hospital," I say, wiping at my eyes.

"Kenzie, what do you want to do?" Ms. MacNamary asks, kneeling down to face her where she sits.

"I'm okay, really," she insists. Her hands are shaky. "If Mr. Stiles says he's a medic, he's probably good enough for me."

"Yes, he is," Ms. MacNamary reassures her. "And he's seen far worse burns than this one. I trust him, if you do."

"Sure," Kenzie says. Behind her, Mr. Stiles fishes out some cloths from the first aid kit, and I wish I knew a tenth as much as my parents did about healing people. Maybe I *should* learn to be a doctor, like Mom wants. Then I could make sure people are fixing my friends up the right way.

"Laura, you promised me these kids—" Dr. Grier starts.

"Everyone makes mistakes," Ms. MacNamary says. "They're doing the best they can. Look at them!" She gestures at us.

I look up and down the line of us, covered in dust, tear streaks dried on each of our faces.

"We don't have *time*," Dr. Grier tries to say next.

"I know. Trust me, I know," Ms. MacNamary says. "But Samantha, we can't demand the impossible. Accidents are bound to happen. It could have been much, much worse. You know that."

That shuts Dr. Grier up. I watch, fascinated. Sometimes, it's hard to tell which one of them is actually the boss around here.

"Do you three want to stay with me, Kenzie, and Mr. Stiles?" Ms. MacNamary asks, turning to us. "I'm sure Kenzie would appreciate some company."

"They could get more work done today," Dr. Grier suggests, arms crossed.

Mr. Stiles guides Kenzie up and starts to walk her out of the work cavern, back to camp.

"I really think right now everyone needs a break," Ms. MacNamary says. "With some rest, you all will be refreshed and faster than ever tomorrow."

"A break would be good," I say. Wyatt and Todd nod next to me. Together, we walk past Dr. Grier, following Ms. MacNamary.

"Bolivia and New Zealand," Dr. Grier calls after us. I wince, thinking about the quakes in those countries in the past few months—a seismic clock *is* ticking. But a couple hours off can't make a huge difference, can it?

"I know we need to hurry," Ms. MacNamary calls back. "But we can't afford to be reckless, either."

Exactly! I cling to my camera, which Dr. Grier has forgotten to take from me, and head back up through the caves.

CHAPTER NINE

As the afternoon turns to evening, Ms. MacNamary takes us all outside the caves on a walk around the hills. Kenzie's face is covered in an antibiotic cream that is a gross, gooey contrast to her tanned skin and bright red lipstick. But she's in good spirits. I have to hand it to her.

"What's this tree?" she asks.

"Spruce," Ms. MacNamary answers.

"And these?"

"Raspberry bushes," Ms. MacNamary answers next. "Not quite ready for picking yet, but maybe soon." She's been naming every plant we've seen for us as we go. I wonder if she would be open to being a guest star on my documentary.

We follow a narrow trail, which I'm pretty sure was made by deer, and I film as we walk. We all got huge chocolate bars before our outing, and I feel bouncy from the sugar rush. My feet crunch through the leaves, and I film my boots for a few moments, then pan up the trail to the back of Todd's head. He's leading us. Well, "leading." Mostly he's just walking first and turning where Ms. MacNamary tells him.

"Don't get too far ahead now!" Ms. MacNamary calls after him. "We need to stay as a group."

"Or else the grizzlies could get us," I say for the benefit of my future viewers as I pan my camera across the wooded landscape.

Once we've walked a ways and reached a pile of boulders, Ms. MacNamary calls for a rest stop.

"If anyone needs the bathroom, the woods are right over there." She points.

No one takes her up on that. Instead, the four of us sit down, letting the evening breeze cool us off. A few mosquitoes buzz by, and I smack at them.

"Bri, do you mind shutting off your camera for a moment?" Ms. MacNamary asks, setting her bag on the rock next to her.

My curiosity is piqued. "Sure. Just a sec." Overhead, the blue sky is threading with red. The sun is nearing its time to set, and I record a final few moments of the changing sky before powering down my camera, laying it in my lap, and resting my hands on the cool rock we're sitting on.

"Don't tell Dr. Grier," Ms. MacNamary says next. Then she pulls our phones out of her knapsack.

The reaction is immediate. I squeal so loud I think my own eardrums might burst. Kenzie shrieks even louder. Todd and

Wyatt scramble over each other, trying to get to Ms. MacNamary first.

"Seriously." Ms. MacNamary raises her voice above our shouts. "You can't tell Samantha. She won't be happy."

"We won't, we won't!" Kenzie says, grabbing her phone from Ms. MacNamary's hand. We each take ours, powering them on.

"And fair warning—you probably won't get service, so don't get your hopes up too high. I just wanted to at least give you the chance to try." Ms. MacNamary tucks her knapsack back behind her.

I'm only half listening. I watch my phone's start screen spiral until all the logos have passed. Once it's fully on, I try to check my texts, but nothing is loading beyond the ones from before entering Yellowstone.

"I can't get *anything*," Kenzie pouts, her mood doing a one-eighty.

"Wow, service really *does* stink out here," Wyatt says. Todd climbs up behind Ms. MacNamary, trying to get some height on the rocks, holding his phone over his head.

I open up app after app, just hoping to get *anything* to work. No YouTube, no Earth Builder. Nothing. Just how remote are we in this park right now that there's literally zero service?

Ergh! I lower my phone. I can't remember the last time I've gone this long without checking for a YouTube update from Aunt Pauline. I know she's okay, because Mom and Dad have told me so in their emails, but I really miss seeing her videos. I'm going to have to binge watch them all after I go home at the end of the summer.

"Sorry, everyone." Ms. MacNamary's shoulders fall. "Thought we could at least try."

"We appreciate it," Todd says glumly.

"Yeah," Wyatt agrees. "It's nice to at least see my phone again. Know that it hasn't been thrown away."

Ms. MacNamary laughs. "I wouldn't put it past Samantha."

"Why won't she trust us with our phones?" I ask. "She lets us email home. We could tell our parents about all this that way, easily."

"Creeper lady is probably reading our emails to make sure we don't," Kenzie says.

My eyes fly open at that. "Wait, you think so?!" I spin toward Ms. MacNamary.

She adjusts her park ranger hat on her head. "Oh gosh, I highly doubt she's doing anything *that* interesting, but A+ on the paranoia." Ms. MacNamary winks at Kenzie.

My mind races trying to think of a way to test if Dr. Grier has read what I've emailed my parents about. I've felt bad enough that I'm lying to them, but to think someone is checking my lies to make sure they're false enough . . . the very thought makes me want to curl in on myself and pop out of existence.

"What's her problem, anyway?" Kenzie asks. "She's worse than my grandma, and that's saying a lot."

"Samantha is just . . . wary about people," Ms. MacNamary continues. "I am, too, to an extent. But Samantha's a lot harder to win over. Humans tend to be pretty awful, you know? A lot of them claim they want to make the world a better place, but collectively . . . eh." She looks out into the forest, and I can see the exhaustion in her eyes. "The world is falling apart. It's not that there are too many bad people, it's that there are too many *indifferent* people. It's rare to find anyone who sees what really needs to be done and has the courage to do it."

I twist my arms across my chest. I'm still stuck on the Dr. Grier-reading-my-emails suggestion, but this doesn't sound like the time to bring the conversation back to that.

"We're doing it, though," Todd says. "We're helping."

Ms. MacNamary laughs lightly. "You are." Then her eyebrows furrow in concern as Kenzie traces her fingers along her burned face. "Kenzie, what happened to you today was very scary."

Kenzie, actually subdued, nods.

"If you want to stop working in the tunnels, we can find something else for you to do. Or if you really want, we can send you home. This is asking a lot of you, and I didn't mean to pressure you just now with what I said."

"No way!" Kenzie says, shaking her head so hard I'm worried she might pop her blisters. "Look at this place!" She gestures around.

I take in the serene atmosphere. The frogs trilling, the birds settling into the trees for the night. The nearby brook bubbling over its smoothed stones.

"I'm not going to let Yellowstone get blown up. Or the rest of the world, for that matter," Kenzie says. "We're so close to finishing our first tunnels. I'm seeing this through."

Ms. MacNamary considers her. "Okay." She turns to the rest of us. "Anyone else?"

We all shake our heads.

"Oh, you guys." Ms. MacNamary beams. "I'm so proud of you all."

"Yeah, I didn't get almost blasted to death for you guys to give up," Kenzie warns. "So you'd better finish your jobs."

Over the next week, Kenzie and I come up with a way to check if Dr. Grier's been reading our emails. Ms. MacNamary might think we're being paranoid, but I'd rather not take any chances.

Our plan is simple: Kenzie and I sign each of our emails home with an added, seemingly random letter several spaces below our names. If a person was to read *both* of our emails and combine the letters we've been ending them with, they would spell:

HI DR GRIER!

But we're nearing the last set of emails for this plan and haven't gotten *any* sign from Dr. Grier that she's noticed. So either she is pretending really well or isn't reading our emails after all.

I hope it's that she isn't reading them, but I also wonder if she got tipped off that something was up by how much more often Kenzie is writing to her grandmother.

Meanwhile, down in the tunnels, Eddie and Raquel still haven't returned our messages. Ms. MacNamary's been gone even more than usual, and the days are starting to melt from one into another—every night, I go to bed even more exhausted than the last.

However, all our work is finally paying off. We finished our first beta tunnels a whole week earlier than scheduled: on Day Twenty-One instead of Day Twenty-Eight. Which is pretty cool—and also means that today our assignment changes.

We have to insert the explosives.

On my way to our briefing to learn about this ridiculously scary process, I pass someone in the cave. I'm so focused on what we have to do today that I almost don't realize who it is until two ferrets peek out of the person's sweatshirt.

"Nolan!" I say. "Wow, hi, where have you been? We haven't seen you in ages."

Nolan just tries to walk faster, but then one of his ferrets—the white one with the pink eyes—jumps from his hood, scampers down his sweatshirt and jeans, and lopes over to me. I remember what Dr. Grier said about his ferrets sometimes biting and take a step back.

"Buggy! Get back here!" Nolan says, chasing after his pet.

Buggy, meanwhile, hops around my boots, then flops over, yanking one of my laces and doing what can only be described as a side-somersault with it.

"Sorry," Nolan apologizes, picking Buggy up off the cavern floor and putting him back in his hood with Baxter.

"It's okay," I say, bending down to retie my boot. "He's actually pretty cute."

"Yeah, and he knows better," Nolan chides Buggy, who drapes

his head out of the hood over Nolan's shoulder, the picture of pink-eyed innocence.

"So where do you work?" I ask. I'm not going to miss my first real chance to get some answers out of this kid. "We've been here for weeks and we never see you."

"Out, mostly," he says. "I work in a different part of the park a lot of days."

"Really?" I ask, trying not to get *too* excited that I'm finally learning more about Mysterious Ferret Boy. "What do you do?"

"I help Ms. MacNamary with an area a little south of here," he answers. "We—"

"Nolan!" a voice calls. Ms. MacNamary rounds the cave bend.

"Hi, Ms. MacNamary." I wave in an attempt to hide my disappointment. I didn't realize she was here today. Under normal circumstances, I'd be happy to see her, but she's just ruined my super sly interrogation.

"Hello, Bri." She walks over to join us. "It's nice to see you. How have things been?"

"Really good," I reply. "We finished our first tunnels. We're going to put the blasting powder down them today."

"I've heard," she says, smiling. "Nervous?"

"Like you wouldn't believe," I say. She pats me on the shoulder reassuringly.

"You'll be fine," Ms. MacNamary says. Then she turns to Nolan. His ferrets are popping up and down in his hood, as if thrilled to see Ms. MacNamary. I immediately see why, because she gives them each a treat—beef jerky, it looks like. "We should get back to the main camp. Your aunt will want to hear about what we got done."

Aunt?

"Right, yeah," Nolan says. He reaches back to settle his pets down, but they just nose out between his fingers, looking for more snacks.

"Wait—is Dr. Grier your aunt?" I ask, wondering if I heard that right.

"Yeah, I take after my dad," Nolan says, like he's had this conversation a million times before. "He's black, Mom's white. She's my aunt on my mom's side." My face flushes and I shut myself up before I say anything else that makes me sound too much like my awkward dad.

"Good luck today," Ms. MacNamary says to me, steering Nolan along. "You won't need it, but good luck all the same. We'll catch up later!"

I watch them go. I suddenly have a gazillion more questions for Nolan, which is saying something, since I knew nothing about him two minutes ago. *Dr. Grier is his aunt?!* Wow, did he draw the short straw in the aunt department. And what exactly does he do to the south of our caves? And was Ms. MacNamary purposefully keeping him from talking to me? Sure seemed like it.

There's so much I want to know. But I'm going to be late if I don't get moving, so I let out a grunt of frustration and head to our work site.

My boots kick some of the stones underfoot as I descend farther and farther down the caves. The string of lights along the cave walls guide me, and I notice that the fifth lamp from the end is out. I don't like the little patch of darkness that causes. I'm already freaking out enough about today's job, and I would prefer if everything in and around here was working one hundred percent. Not that a single light can mess up too much. But still.

When I reach the work cavern, my nerves fire just as badly as they did on Day One. Today, we go down our tunnels *without* our pods, just attached to the cable, no protective cage around us. Exposed. Dangling. Hopefully not falling to our deaths. All with a pack of explosives strapped to each of us.

Oh, boy.

I meet Wyatt, Todd, and Kenzie at the mouth of the alpha tunnel, where Dr. Grier goes over our final instructions.

"The powder won't blow unless it's detonated by remote control," Dr. Grier says. Dr. Grier's tall shadow, created by the giant floodlights behind the massive cement mixer, stretches across the cavern floor and nearly reaches the far wall. I look more closely than usual at her—I guess I can see some resemblance to Nolan, if I really concentrate. It's in the eyes. "But that's not to say you shouldn't be cautious," she continues. "Your packages are still filled with very volatile substances. And once you've connected the detonator's power supply and radio antennae, there is no undoing it, or it will blow up in your face."

"Trust me, that's not fun," Kenzie says.

"A real bummer," Dr. Grier agrees. "Especially since this will definitely kill you."

Wyatt and I laugh at that. Todd frowns at us, as if we're being disrespectful, but there's a ghost of a smile on Dr. Grier's face. I've known her long enough now to know that she likely meant that as a very dark, very dry joke. A serious threat, but a joke nonetheless.

Mr. Stiles and Mr. Fee come around, handing us each a pack. They're about the weight and size of a bag of flour, with weird padding around them. Before Mr. Fee hands me mine, Dr. Grier steps forward to take it.

"If I may?" she asks.

Dr. Grier sets my explosive pack down in a simulated cutaway of the tunnels we've drilled. I fire up my camera, figuring this might be something she wants recorded.

"Here's what you'll need to do," Dr. Grier explains, demonstrating with the equipment. "After you drill twenty-four holes into the base of your tunnel, you will empty part of your sack of blasting powder into each hole, filling it. Then, you will nestle the remainder of the bag at the center point of your tunnel base, with its antennae on top, connected to the metal of the track, like so." She peels a wire off the top of the sack and brings it to the track, wrapping it through the hole at the edge. "Then, you should cut the corners of the sack, and spread some of the blasting powder out to the edges of your tunnel. Do you have all that?"

We nod. I turn off my camera as Dr. Grier hands me my bag of explosive terror back. I try to keep my hand steady when I take it from her.

"Do not mix up your packs with each other," Dr. Grier warns. "We have assigned you each a pack for your beta tunnel, and if you don't install the one you're given, we may not detonate the proper one when we do our controlled pressure releases."

We all instinctively clutch our packs.

"Okay, Wyatt, you're up first," Mr. Stiles says. He stands at the tunnel entrance, his feet near the edge of it and his hands on the main cable, holding it up to help lower us down.

We line up in our usual order, but this time step into harnesses that attach to the cables, rather than our pods. In between each of us, giant coils of winch rope are attached to the cable for later use. Then, one by one, Mr. Stiles maneuvers us down into the tunnel.

I hold tight to the cable, even though it's unnecessary with my harness. After Kenzie gets lowered with an inappropriate, echoing curse word to punctuate her bravado, I choose to descend silently.

"Good luck, kid," Mr. Stiles says. He hoists the cabling over my head, and I suck in a breath as I'm lowered into the hole on the cave floor.

Darkness soon surrounds me. It's weird going down the alpha tunnel without my pod. My headlamp illuminates the way, shifting with every movement I make. Every time I turn too much, I swing into the hard, rocky wall, so I do my best to stay steady.

I can see Kenzie's light below, past the huge coil of rope attached near her on the cable. She looks up, almost blinding me, then bobs her head back and forth, dancing out a rhythm. I copy her, and soon we're having a tunnel dance party, complete with terrible renditions of pop songs. At one point Kenzie stops to look down and I can hear her yell something, presumably at Todd. I can only imagine how annoyed he must be right now by our singing, but he can just deal.

We stop when Kenzie gets to the horizontal section. She disappears from my view, and I'm left alone in the dark. I try to hum some of the songs we'd been singing, but my humming gets warbly as nerves kick back in.

When I get to the horizontal section myself, my boots hit the curving part of the tunnel, and I have to maneuver slowly to lay on my back. I keep the blasting powder safely on top of my stomach, where I can hold it with the cable so it doesn't scrape on the walls. It's super uncomfortable laying on the metal track, sliding along in jerked motions by the cable. More than once I wish I had a free hand to film something. I could use a distraction.

Eventually, I reach my beta tunnel. Here, I have to attach the coil of winch rope that's hooked to the central cable onto my belt to allow me to drop down. And down. And *down*.

My breath quickens in my mask. The carabiner I'm latching slips a couple of times before I get it clipped. I let out the same swear word Kenzie used earlier without thinking. *Mom and Dad aren't going to be happy with that new habit.* Then I lower myself into my tunnel, a few loose chips of rock falling down it as I slide in.

My feet dangle, and I repeat a few more of Kenzie's favorite expressions, embracing the power they're giving me. Without my pod, I feel completely exposed, heading miles into our planet, toward Yellowstone's magma chamber. I keep checking my sensors. The temperature is rising, but not to dangerous levels.

I'm really glad we only have to do this once.

My headlamp illuminates the sparkling granite I've spent the better part of a month drilling through. It's really pretty, with its pinks and grays and crystals, and it keeps my mind off the fact that I'm absurdly far below the surface of the planet, with nothing holding me up but a cable and some metal clips.

After traveling nearly two miles down at painfully slow speeds, I finally reach the end of my tunnel. For the first real time, I get to see what the impression of my big drill looks like on the rock. There's a chewed up, swirling pattern at my beta tunnel's deepest point. I can't tell if it's attractive or ugly. It's symmetrical, at least. It's not molten, either, so that provides me with some relief.

My feet touch down. The rock below me feels way warmer than rock should. I check the temperature again, but we're in the safe range.

. . . It's just that I'm super close to where the magma chamber is.

"Okay, Bri," I whisper to myself. Sweat pours down my face. "The faster you do this, the faster you can leave."

I take my hand drill off my belt, use my laser-guided ruler, and make a grid of twenty-four evenly spaced spots on the ground of my tunnel, squatting awkwardly to do so. There's no room to bend over.

Drilling this way takes *forever*. I have to shuffle my feet in a minicircle to get at all the drill points. By the time I'm done, my knees are screaming.

Carefully, I open up the blasting powder and pour it into each hole. Then I lay the bag down in the middle between my feet, peel up the antennae wire, and attach it to the track on the wall to boost the range. I connect a couple of wires, completing the circuit to supply power to the little device on top of the pack. This is the part Dr. Grier warned us about—accidentally undoing this will cause everything to blow up by default.

For a brief moment, I worry there's a spark—but then I realize it's just my headlamp gleaming off a less-than-perfect edge to the track. I wait for my pounding heart to calm down, then I cut the four corners open and push out some more blasting powder to the edges of my tunnel.

There. That should do it.

I latch my rope to lock it, radio in to be lifted out, and turn my camera on now that I don't have to keep my hands on the explosives.

The light when I hit record nearly blinds me as I'm hoisted up, but I grin through it, because I'm not missing this historic moment.

"Hi, everyone," I say into my camera. This is going to get more views than all of Aunt Pauline's videos combined. "I may have just saved humanity. Yes, you're welcome."

CHAPTER TEN

With at least four beta tunnels complete—I'm still not sure if Eddie and Raquel finished any more—we now have four chances to stop a supervolcanic eruption of Yellowstone. This deserves a freaking party.

That night, the whole camp is rowdy and lively, filled with games and music. Ms. MacNamary bought several massive tubs of ice cream for us. Our shouts echo through the cave, laughing as we cram ourselves full of Neapolitan and chocolate chip cookie dough.

"Who saved the world?" Kenzie shouts, and points at me and Wyatt.

"We saved the world!" we shout back, grinning our faces off.

"Who saved the world?"

"We saved the world!"

"You're all a bunch of dorks," Todd says.

"Look who's talking." Kenzie flings a spoonful of ice cream at Todd, who just manages to duck in time. "Ooh, MacNamary's setting up bocce ball!" Kenzie exclaims, now pointing over Todd's shoulder to the edge of camp. "Who's in?"

"Sorry, Kenzie, Wyatt and I have a date with destiny," Todd says, straightening his glasses. A new tub of ice cream has just been set out on the table under one of the kitchen tents. "You promised, Wyatt."

"What I promised was that I could totally *own* you in an ice-cream eating contest," Wyatt replies. "If you are ready to be defeated, then by all means." He gestures toward the table.

"You have no idea who you're messing with," Todd says.

"Didn't the two of you already each have several bowls?" I ask.

"Those were just the appetizers," Wyatt says.

"If you guys throw up tonight, you better do it outside of the cabin," Kenzie warns. "Bri, would *you* care to join me in a highly sophisticated game of throwing heavy, multicolored balls at other heavy, multicolored balls?"

"It would be my honor," I agree, tipping an imaginary hat at Kenzie.

She bows in my direction, motioning toward Ms. MacNamary and the bocce ball game. We head over together, leaving the boys to their ridiculous contest. Amid all the partying, there's one thing that I can't help but notice:

Eddie and Raquel aren't here.

Nolan is—but he's in the corner of the kitchen tent, watching a tablet screen of some television show. We tried to get him to come hang out with us earlier, but he flat-out acted like we weren't even there. And he refused to answer any of my questions, especially about being Dr. Grier's nephew.

But where are Eddie and Raquel? Don't they get to celebrate?

I can ask Ms. MacNamary, I suppose. But before we can get to her, Dr. Grier shows up out of nowhere, standing directly between us and the bocce game.

"Hello." The geologist clears her throat, looking down at us. There's an awkward pause. "I uh . . . I just wanted to thank you both for your hard work." It sounds like this is the most difficult sentence she's ever uttered.

"Erm." I try to figure out how to reply. "You're welcome. I mean, it was you who came up with all this, so we should be thanking you."

"Yep!" Kenzie agrees. She points at Dr. Grier. "Who saved the world . . . ?" she leads, a smile spreading across her face.

Dr. Grier just furrows her eyebrows. "We all worked together."

Kenzie drops her arm, obviously disappointed that she didn't play along. Behind Dr. Grier, Ms. MacNamary catches our eyes and gives a sheepish shrug. She clearly knows how awkward this conversation is.

"I could use some help setting up the game," Ms. MacNamary says. "Any takers?"

"Oh, me, definitely me!" Kenzie darts away before I can even open my mouth to respond.

Dr. Grier watches her go, and her shoulders fall slightly. "It's hard to put into words how important this day is," she says, not looking at me, but clearly still talking to me. "I've been working my entire life toward this."

Now I really can't leave, or I'll look like a jerk. I nod, instead. "I'm glad we could help."

"I have to admit, I was not sold on the idea of bringing you in when Laura first mentioned her plan," Dr. Grier says. "But I can see the value now. You're a bright girl, Brianna. If you're willing, I might ask that you help with future projects down the road. You would make an excellent student."

I'd . . . what? I try not to actively gape at her, but it's hard not to. We rarely get any kind of compliments from Dr. Grier. I can't process this many nice things from her in a row.

"The world is full of people who just don't *get it*," she goes on. "But I've watched your aunt's documentaries and your recordings here. You are the type of person I could see becoming a leader for a new generation. Maybe after we are done at Yellowstone, we could have a meeting and I could propose what I'm thinking for our next steps."

Sudden laughter interrupts our conversation. Kenzie and Ms. MacNamary are doubled over, howling about something. I still can't find the words to reply with.

"Go on," Dr. Grier says, throwing her head over her shoulder in their direction. "We can talk later."

I hesitate. Behind Dr. Grier, Kenzie and Ms. MacNamary are chucking bocce balls, punctuating their throws with shouts of,

"Who needs the government?!" and "Yeah, stick it to the man!" It honestly weirds me a little out, especially since Ms. MacNamary technically *works* for the government as a National Park Service employee. I'm definitely not as comfortable befriending adults as Kenzie is. I turn back to Dr. Grier, but she's already walking away.

"Ms. MacNamary?" I ask, interrupting her game with Kenzie.

"Yes?" she answers.

The Dr. Grier thing is something I'll have to sort out later. First, I need to ask my original question. "Why aren't the other kids here?" I stop myself just in time from saying their names, since Ms. MacNamary doesn't know we were talking to them down in the tunnels. "Shouldn't they be celebrating with us?"

She stops, mid-throw. "Oh."

"Oh yeah, good question!" Kenzie agrees, dropping her ball to the mat covering the cave floor and scooting up next to me.

Ms. MacNamary sighs. "I don't know. Dr. Grier said they didn't want to come. I guess they're tired. They are on an opposite schedule than you, so now is their time to sleep."

"That sucks for them, though," Kenzie says. "Do they get their own party at some point? We could host it at 4:00 a.m. or something, so they could come."

Ms. MacNamary smiles at her. "That's not a bad idea. They deserve one, you know? They've been here even longer than you four."

I frown. I don't like how evasive Ms. MacNamary is being. Eddie and Raquel have been missing for a week now. Something's going on with them—something the adults don't want us to know about. But what? And why? Why do grown-ups never tell kids the whole story? We're not even kids, we're teenagers, and we just set explosives miles deep in our planet. I think we have earned some trust here.

Mr. Stiles and Mr. Fee let out huge laughs from across the cavern. I look over at them, both wobbling on their feet, and I realize that they're drunk. My eyebrows shoot up my forehead.

"Those two . . ." Ms. MacNamary chastises. "Excuse me." She nods at us, then heads toward the men. "Bri, take my place in bocce, okay?" she calls over her shoulder.

"Okay!" I reply. But as soon as Ms. MacNamary is out of ear-shot, I explain my feelings about Eddie and Raquel to Kenzie.

"Well, duh," Kenzie says when I'm done. She shuttles a ball between her feet. "Obviously something weird is going on with them. We definitely should figure out where they are."

"Any ideas of what we can do?" I ask, trying to keep my voice quiet.

"Tonight?" Kenzie replies. She stops the ball by setting her boot on top of it. "Tonight we play bocce and eat ice cream. We're literally surrounded by every person who works for Dr. Grier right now. We're not going to be able to sneak away and play detectives."

"Good point," I acknowledge.

"Of course it's a good point," Kenzie says. "I'm full of good points."

I don't want to let go of the Eddie and Raquel thing completely, but I can't think of anything more to do about them right now. I sigh. I wish I could feel better about our accomplishments from the tunnels, but now I just feel worried. "So, who was winning?" I ask, nodding at the bocce set and trying to distract myself.

"Oh, totally me."

I roll my eyes. "Sure you were."

Between wanting to solve the Eddie and Raquel mystery and being totally hyped up from the party, I'm surprised at how quickly I manage to drift off to sleep. I marvel at this as I'm shaken awake at some strange hour of the night. *Maybe I was able to fall asleep so fast because I finally got my tunnel done. . . .*

"Hey! You!" someone's saying.

Or maybe it was the sugar crash?

"Hey!" the voice insists.

It slowly dawns on me that someone's in the cabin with me. Someone with a voice I don't recognize. Someone who is shoving me repeatedly.

I bolt upright.

"Who are—?" I start.

"Shhhhh!" The person covers my mouth.

I struggle backward in my sleeping bag until I hit the wall of the cabin. I focus on the person in front of me, trying to see them clearly in the dark.

It's a teenage girl.

"Listen!" she says. She's wearing a jumpsuit a lot like mine, and her dark hair is pulled back in a ponytail. "I'm Raquel. Eddie and I are here to get you out."

"Wait—Raquel?" I try to ask through her hand. I wonder if I'm dreaming. "Where have you guys been?"

"What?" I hear from the other side of the cabin through the makeshift curtain.

"Shhhh!" someone says.

"Eddie's waking up the boys," Raquel says, as a kid yanks the blankets down in the middle of the cabin.

Todd squeaks, grabbing for his sleeping bag as a blanket hits the floor.

"Oh my god," I say, trying not to roll my eyes. The boy next to Todd moves on to wake Wyatt. He looks closer to our age than Raquel. He might even be a little younger than us. Like Raquel, he has dark hair, but his skin is lighter in tone than hers.

Raquel lowers her hand from my mouth—possibly tired of me talking against her palm. "Be quiet and help me wake up your other friend."

I look at Wyatt, searching for his opinion of the situation. He gives me a small shrug. Then I lean over and shake Kenzie as Raquel covers her mouth. "Kenzie, don't panic, just wake up and be quiet," I say.

She sits up like a rocket going off. It's a good thing Raquel has her hand on her mouth, because her shrieks would've been ear-piercing otherwise.

"Kenzie!" I whisper loudly. "Shh! Just . . . wait a second! It's okay!" I look at Raquel, still baffled. "It is okay, right?"

"What's going on?" Kenzie asks, her voice muffled through Raquel's hand.

"We're here to save you," Raquel says. "This might be our only chance. Stiles and Fee forgot to lock our cabins tonight. Drunk, I'm guessing. I heard them partying, which can't be good. We have to go, now!"

Forgot to lock our cabins? But our cabins are never locked. . . . I watch Eddie and Raquel carefully, and goosebumps prickle down my arms.

"We have to . . . what?" Todd asks. He looks uncertain if he's allowed to talk.

"Do you guys want to stay prisoner or not?" Eddie demands.

"Prisoner?" Todd replies, his eyes widening. "But we're not—"

"Did you think you were here on vacation?" Raquel asks him. "Now come on, we have to get out and warn everyone."

"What are you talking about?" Wyatt asks. "Warn everyone about what?"

"The supervolcano!" Eddie replies.

"Oh!" Todd says. "Is that what you're worried about? It's okay, we just finished our first tunnels. We're safer than ever from that thing."

Something tells me Todd might be missing the point, and that same something is making me tremble uncontrollably in the dark. *Prisoners,* my brain continues to repeat Eddie and Raquel's words. *Warn everyone . . .*

"You think those tunnels are made to keep people safe?" Eddie scoffs. "What kind of messed up story did they feed you?"

My heart pounds in my chest. One by one, all the weird things I've noticed through the past several weeks fall into place. *No . . .*

"You're here to trigger the volcano," Eddie says. "Just like us. We're meant to drill down to the lava and then die in the explosion. If you want to stay and let that happen, go for it, man, but if anyone wants out, now's your chance. We didn't have to come get you, you know."

All four of us stare at the pair of kids. Every good feeling I had from finishing my beta tunnel falls straight down, through my stomach, and crashes onto the cabin floor.

CHAPTER ELEVEN

"That . . . that can't be true," Todd whispers.

"It's true," Raquel says. "I'm sorry you didn't know, but that's what's really going on here."

My breaths are short, shallow, and painful. This has to be a dream. They have to be wrong. *This can't be real.*

Wyatt looks as gray as a ghost. "But we've worked so hard."

"You didn't think there was anything suspicious when they kidnapped you?" Eddie asks him.

"Kidnapped us?" Todd says. "They invited us!"

"Invited?" Raquel asks.

"We were chosen. From a contest," I whisper. I don't trust myself to speak any louder. I honestly might puke. Horrifically shocking news and a stomach full of ice cream don't mix. "We won the chance to work with Dr. Grier for the summer. And when we got here, they told us what our real job was."

Raquel and Eddie just stare.

"You mean the job to set off explosives inside a volcano?" Eddie asks.

"Those are going to release the pressure in a controlled way," Todd tries to explain.

"Dr. Grier—she had research," Kenzie rambles, actually wringing her hands. "It showed that Yellowstone will explode within the decade if we don't do anything about it. Seismic activity is on the rise everywhere!"

"Like all those earthquakes around here," Wyatt jumps in.

I nod rapidly. "Yes!" I agree, desperate for Eddie and Raquel to be wrong. "Those earthquakes prove it, we're in a dangerous situation and have to act before—"

"Earthquakes?" Eddie asks. "What earthquakes?"

"What . . . earthquakes?" I ask, wondering how he could've been here this whole time and never noticed the ground shaking around us every few days.

"You mean the ones we caused whenever we'd have to blow up bedrock to make a new section of the alpha tunnel?" Raquel asks.

Stunned silence crashes over us. Sheer horror rolls through my body.

"You mean . . ." Wyatt's voice is barely audible, and he gapes at Eddie and Raquel.

"Oh my god, we were so *gullible*!" Kenzie gasps.

Now everyone shushes her. I wince at the noise and Kenzie's point.

"Listen," Raquel says, shaking her head and getting back to business. "Whatever you've been told, whatever you believe, it's wrong. You're lucky Stiles and Fee forgot to lock all our cabins tonight, so we can bust out."

"Lock our cabins? Our cabin is never locked," Todd says.

"It's *not?*" Eddie spins toward him.

"How else would we be able to go to the bathroom in the middle of the night?" Todd replies.

"Do you hear him?" Eddie turns to Raquel. "Their cabin's been unlocked this whole time. This whole time! They could've just left! They—"

"They've obviously been lied to," Raquel says.

"O *son estúpidos*," Eddie says.

"O *han sido engañados*."

I wonder if they slipped into Spanish because they assumed we don't speak it. I definitely don't speak it *well*, so if that was their intention, it mostly works. I'm pretty sure Eddie just called us stupid, though.

Eddie crosses his arms and goes silent, turning away from Raquel. I don't think he and Raquel are siblings, since they have different last names and don't look anything alike, but I get the immediate impression that he looks up to her like she might as well be his sister. I've started to think of Kenzie, Wyatt, and Todd as family, in a way, so I can understand.

"So . . . we're leaving now?" I venture to ask. I'm still not sure of any of this, but one thing is certain—I'd prefer to figure this out on the move, and get away, in case Eddie and Raquel are right. My head spins. I can't see how they wouldn't be right. This completely explains why we never see them. This explains the quakes. This explains *so much*.

"Yes!" Raquel looks relieved to see me on board. "Let's go!"

"What about our phones?" Kenzie asks. "We should get those."

"And risk getting caught?" Raquel replies. "No, we need to move, now."

I grimace thinking about my camera, which is in Dr. Grier's possession as it is every night.

"I just can't believe . . . we've worked so *hard*," Wyatt repeats, staring numbly at Eddie.

Then something hits me. "What about Nolan?" I ask, wondering if he has been tricked, same as us. "Should we get him?"

"We don't know where he is right now," Raquel says. "So there's no way to rescue him, even if he'd want us to. The best thing to do is go for help and come back for him."

"Says you," Eddie grumbles.

"Yes, says me," Raquel says. "There's no time to argue. We shouldn't even be talking about all this right now! Are you guys with us, or not?"

I look at each of my companions. To believe that all we've done, all summer, has actually been to trigger the Yellowstone Supervolcano, not stop it . . .

"Yeah, let's go," I say.

"Absolutely," Kenzie says, climbing to her feet, her face one massive thundercloud of glaring eyes and healing scabs.

Fury, confusion, horror . . . the whole mess broils inside of me. I stand up, grabbing my tool belt and headlamp. Priorities have to be getting out of here. We can come back if this is in error. Right?

This would be a heck of a lot easier if the fate of the planet as we know it wasn't on the line.

Todd gets up next, grabbing the stuff he can bring. Wyatt is still on the floor, staring helplessly.

"Come on," Kenzie says, walking over to him and offering a hand. He looks up at her. In the dim light, I can see tears clinging to his eyelashes.

I step forward, but then Wyatt takes Kenzie's hand and stands up.

"I need to get my prosthetic on," he murmurs, shuffling along in the dark, using his other hand to steady himself on the wall.

"Right," Kenzie says. She turns. "Just one more second, guys."

Raquel and Eddie say nothing as they wait for Wyatt to get ready. I want to thank them for that but don't want to do so in front of Wyatt, and then I immediately feel bad for the entire line of thought. But I know we have to move, like, now, so their patience is really touching, especially since I'm guessing they didn't know about Wyatt's foot.

Once Wyatt is set to go, Eddie opens the door to our cabin

and peers out into the dark of the cave.

"Okay," he whispers. "All clear."

We file out, one after the other, a million questions running through my head, but no time to ask any of them.

As silent as possible, we pick our way across the rocks, through camp, and toward the spiral staircase that will lead us up to the mouth of the cave. I feel like we should be grabbing supplies—food, water, *anything*—but also have no idea how to manage that without making too much noise and raising the alarm. And if Raquel and Eddie didn't waste time grabbing stuff, then we probably shouldn't try to do it now.

I watch Kenzie the most as we walk. Her tiny frame is physically shaking from rage. I can't blame her. But I cross my fingers super hard that she keeps it bottled up until we're out of here.

A rock skids from my left shoe out across the cavern floor, and I freeze. The noise clatters in the stillness of the cave. Everyone looks at me, and I wince, shrugging up my shoulders in apology.

Nothing else happens, though. No one comes out to check on the noise. So we keep walking, and I stop watching my friends and start watching my feet.

We reach the spiral staircase. Unfortunately, as soon as we all pile onto it and start the climb, we notice that it creaks under our weight. Loudly.

"Okay, back off, back off!" Raquel instructs, shooing us all off the steps back down. "We're going to have to do this one at a time."

I glance over my shoulder at the camp, where everything is still silent. Fiddling with the sensors on my tool belt, I wish I had something that could be useful, like giant pillows for our feet. But I suppose that still wouldn't solve the weight issue on the stairs.

Raquel sends Eddie up first. He carefully ascends, one step at a time, and I am relieved that Raquel's idea was a good one. The stairs creak far less with only one person.

After Eddie's up, Raquel gestures for Wyatt. Todd had stepped forward, as though to volunteer to go next, but he follows Raquel's direction and stays back until Wyatt's up at the top.

After Todd, Raquel waves me over. I still the swinging tools on my belt, so none of them hit the metal railing, and begin climbing. The first stair creaks immediately.

Bri! I chastise myself. My face flushes, and my ears strain to hear if Dr. Grier or anyone noticed. The camp remains quiet.

I take the next step even more gingerly. It doesn't creak. I try not to exhale with too much physical motion, even though I want to collapse forward in relief. I climb the steps slowly, taking the longest out of everyone. When I reach the top, I step off onto the rocks near the mouth of the cave and shiver. The night breeze whips around up here, and I wish I'd brought my sleeping bag as a blanket. Ugh, supplies!

Kenzie comes up behind me, light-footed like a rabbit. Raquel is last. She doesn't even know us and made sure we got up first. I want to thank her but am also too afraid to talk too much while we're still in the cave.

When Raquel reaches the top, she stares at us. "What are you all standing around for?" she asks, still using a whisper. "Go! Let's get out!"

"We were waiting for you!" Eddie says.

"Don't be stupid," Raquel replies, steering him urgently forward by his shoulders and reinforcing my earlier idea that the two of them see each other as siblings. "Move!"

We all immediately do as she says. The cave entrance isn't far, and we reach it within minutes. When we exit into the dark of the night, I realize we are about to run into untamed wilderness with nothing but starlight and headlamps. When Aunt Pauline and I were filming in Yellowstone, we always made sure to be packed up by nightfall and to tuck our food and equipment safely away from where we camped, to keep bears and mountain lions from visiting.

Maybe it's a good thing we didn't stop to grab food.

We book it down the side of the hill, following the path as best as we can in the dark. To be extra safe, no one turns their headlamps on just yet, and I'm relieved that we're each smart enough to have come to that conclusion on our own. We need to get far away from here before we can risk lighting ourselves up as targets.

And we also need to stay together, in case there *is* any dangerous wildlife around.

The wind bites into my face as we continue down the massive hillside. I accidentally kick a few more rocks, but I think a little bit of noise is okay now. As long as I don't crash a whole bucketload down the cliff or something.

Now that we're out, my mind starts to process the implications of everything. If it's true that we've been doing all this work to trigger the supervolcano, not stop it, then . . .

I can feel my chest tighten.

Have we really been fooled that badly? I can almost see Dr. Grier being a criminal mastermind bent on the death of millions, but I don't want to believe bocce ball–playing, chocolate-gifting Ms. MacNamary could ever knowingly participate in such an evil plot. What could possibly be their motivation? Why have us create ways to reduce the pressure in tiny intervals if they actually wanted to set off the whole volcano?

A thought hits me, like a blast of the cold night air. Once again, I find myself about to throw up.

If Dr. Grier blows all of our beta tunnels at once, instead of one by one, that won't be *anything* like letting a little pressure out of a bottle of soda. That will be like stabbing into the side of the bottle with a knife.

The cave—all of camp—would be flooded with lava. And that will be just the beginning.

"This way," Eddie says when we reach the bottom of the hill. He points right.

There isn't a single part of me that isn't trembling. We *have* been fooled. Our work can *totally* cause a supervolcanic eruption.

"No, this way," Todd says, pointing to the deer trail path that we took a walk on the other day with Ms. MacNamary. "We know where this one goes."

"That means they do, too," Raquel says.

"It's dark!" Todd retorts. "I'm not wandering off in some unknown direction! We could get lost, or fall off a mountain, or slip down a waterfall—"

"We need to find *people*," I say, jumping into the conversation. "Where is that road we drove in on? We can follow that back to the main roads and find someone to help us."

"I'm with Bri on this one," Wyatt says.

"I'm with Eddie!" Kenzie says. I turn to her, trying not to let her words sting. "We have to get away first. Hide. Then we can come up with a plan for finding people."

"Is no one with me?" Todd asks.

"Group vote," Raquel says. "Todd's trail?"

Only Todd raises his hand.

"Find the road Bri's talking about?"

Me and Wyatt.

"Get the hell out of here into the dark?"

Raquel, Eddie, and Kenzie's hands all shoot up.

"Okay. Dark it is. Let's go." Raquel waves for us to follow.

"Wait!" Wyatt says. "This doesn't seem fair—"

But Eddie's already walking, and Kenzie falls into step with him. I don't want to get left behind, so I go after them. Wyatt and Todd follow me, both grumbling, and Raquel takes up the rear.

I keep my eyes peeled as we walk through the woods, crunching through leaves and over fallen logs. I trip more than once in the dark. Somewhere, I can hear an owl calling, but so far, that's the only sound of wildlife.

Still though. The hairs on the back of my neck prickle. There's not even a moon out tonight to help guide us. We could walk straight into a mountain lion and have no warning. I don't like this at all.

"Guys, we need to stay super close together," I advise. "Like, huddled up so we look like a big, scary animal."

"You think so?" Kenzie asks.

"Definitely," I say. I rest my hand on the small drill on my tool belt, thinking how I could use it as a weapon if I had to. "If a bear sees just one of us, we look like an easy meal. But all together, we might weigh about as much as the bear."

"Oh, come on, they can't be *that* big," Eddie says.

"Have you ever seen one?" I ask him.

He doesn't reply.

"Male grizzly bears can be over six hundred pounds," I recite from last year's documentary with Aunt Pauline. "Females can weigh less, but they usually have cubs, which makes them dangerous in their own way."

"A baby bear would be so *cute*!" Kenzie says.

"Not if its mom is eating your face," I retort.

"Let's do as Bri says," Raquel decides from the back of our line. A small surge of pride courses through me. Since I'm pretty sure Raquel's a couple years older than I am, it's a nice feeling to have her agree with me. "Huddle up."

We all squeeze closer together and continue to walk through the woods as a pack, only to break apart when we have to pick our way through some tough branches or narrow rocky passages.

I'm surprised I'm as awake as I am. I can't remember a time in my life when I've ever been up at this hour, doing actual physical stuff like hiking.

"Adrenaline's a powerful thing," I remember my dad saying years ago, as he was telling me about an eighteen-hour shift he had to pull at the hospital when one of his patients was going into repeated cardiac arrest.

But just as I'm thinking about how I'm not tired, I realize how tired I actually am. I need to sit down. I don't want to unless we're safe, though. Which I have no idea how we're going to be out here.

"Should we rest at some point?" I ask Raquel.

Raquel thinks this over. "Let's go a bit farther. When we do stop, we should have someone keep watch. Anyone want to volunteer?"

"I'll do it," Wyatt says.

Raquel nods. "Okay. Wake someone up if you feel like you're falling asleep, though."

"I won't fall asleep," he replies. There's a haunted look in his eyes, and I completely understand what he means.

We go back to walking in silence for another stretch of time. Could've been half an hour, an hour, or two hours. I honestly can't tell. But then Raquel directs us to stop under a large pine tree.

"Let's rest here," she says. "We'll be hidden under the branches."

She's probably right, I notice. The branches bow down,

making a tent-like structure encircling the trunk. I crawl under them, lean against the bark, and will my heart to slow down.

"Raquel?" Todd asks.

"Yeah?" she answers, settling in next to him.

"You and Eddie never thought you were helping, ever? You've been prisoners this entire time? Forced to work?"

She doesn't answer right away. "Yes," is her eventual response.

"Oh my god," Kenzie says. "For six months? You poor people!"

"No," Raquel says firmly. "We were the lucky ones."

We go silent, and I try to figure out what she could mean by that. None of the ideas I have sound good. But then my body, perhaps noticing we're secluded and possibly safe, shuts down and sends me into an uneasy sleep.

CHAPTER TWELVE

"Bri," I hear. "Kenzie. Todd. Someone. Raquel. Eddie."

Wyatt's whispering. I blink my eyes open. It's barely light out. The sun can't be up yet, but it's just bright enough that I can see through the branches in front of us. I sit upright and look at Wyatt, who is frozen.

"Bri!" he whispers, noticing I'm awake. "Bear!"

I freeze, just like him. My tongue is thick in my mouth, and I try to find the words to respond as my eyes dart around. "Where?" I manage.

"*Here*," Wyatt replies, using his eyes to gesture out of the wall of branches.

I turn and look more closely. Sure enough, on the ground under the branches, I spot four massive paws. They lift slowly and begin circling the tree. Next, a snout appears, lowered to the ground and sniffing loudly.

It's gigantic. The nose itself is the size of a softball. And the jowls that come behind it are slick with drool. If it's not a grizzly, it's the biggest black bear I've ever seen. And if it's a black bear, climbing this tree to safety will do us no good.

Shoot.

"What do we do?" Wyatt mouths to me.

My mind races. I reach for my tool belt. "Drills," I whisper to him.

"What about everyone else?" he asks.

I don't know why we're keeping up the charade of whispering. The bear has stopped and is clearly listening to us through the branches. But I whisper back anyway. "Wake them up. Quietly."

I nudge Kenzie next to me, covering her mouth and motioning over my shoulder as she wakes.

She almost squeals, then pulls herself together. I show her how I'm holding my drill, and she gets hers off her belt. Then I turn to Raquel, and Kenzie turns to get Eddie.

Eddie and Raquel don't have drills. They don't have tool belts. They must not have been allowed to keep them in their cabin.

Which means it's up to me, Wyatt, Kenzie, and Todd—who is now awake, thanks to Wyatt—to scare off this bear.

If Aunt Pauline could see me now.

If my *parents* could see me now.

I motion with three fingers. We all raise up our drills. We have one chance to convince this bear that we're not to be messed with.

The bear is getting bolder. Its nose is edging under the branches now, and its snuffling increases in loudness.

I lower one finger and, with my other hand, find my drill's trigger. I hope everyone knows that we're not going to actually stab the bear, since I think that would just make it angry. And that we need to yell when we do this.

Before I can lower my finger to mark "one," the bear shoves his whole head through the pine branches, sending a shower of needles down on us.

"Now!" I scream, firing up my drill and lunging. I let out a roar from deep in my throat—a noise I had no idea I could produce—and throw myself, drill first, straight at the bear.

Kenzie screeches next to me, and Todd and Wyatt follow suit. With four buzzing drills, a gaggle of screaming heads, and a flurry of clenched fists coming at it, the bear takes several quick steps backward. We blast through the branches, continuing our shouting. Raquel and Eddie join in, chucking pinecones at the animal.

It retreats, looking back at us with confusion and annoyance. But it retreats, all the same.

Adrenaline *is* a powerful thing. Dad was right.

Kenzie lets out a warrior's whoop of victory. *"We did it!"* She jumps around in a circle, grabbing Todd and swinging him with her.

Todd, startled and still on the edge of utter panic, actually lets out a laugh. Kenzie hugs him, then moves down the line, hugging everyone in turn. When it's my turn for a Kenzie hug, I feel like my rib cage is being smashed, but I don't care. I leap around with her and kick pinecones and needles up into the air.

"Oh my god, I can't believe we just chased off a *bear*," Eddie says, running his hands through his dark hair in shock.

Raquel laughs, pulling him in for a side-hug. Then she looks at me. "Nice work." She turns to face each of us. "Everyone. We did it. That was really amazing."

I bubble with pride again. Kenzie pulls out her lipstick and applies her first coat of the day, the bright red in contrast to her beaming, toothy grin. I can't believe that she brought it with her—no wait, scratch that. I can't believe it's taken her this long to use it.

"That's one threat out of the way," Wyatt says. "But it's not going to matter much if that supervolcano goes off."

Our moods nose-dive.

"Can we get the whole story now? Please?" Todd asks Eddie and Raquel.

"While we walk," I add, because as much as I want the story, I want to find people to help us with this whole situation. Also, food.

Raquel and Eddie exchange glances, both wiping pine needles off themselves. "Yeah," Raquel says. "Let's start from the beginning."

The sun rises through the trees as we troop through the woods. I hug my arms. It's still chilly, even with the beams of sunlight coming through, and our jumpsuits aren't exactly built for warmth. Raquel and Eddie stay central in our group, so we can all hear their tale.

"It was right after New Year's," Raquel says. "We had just started school up again. Eddie and I are from a city just south of Los Angeles."

"Inglewood," Eddie says.

"They don't know where that is," Raquel replies. "You guys aren't from LA, right?"

We all shake our heads. My skin is already tingling, though. Just after New Year's . . . LA . . .

That's when the earthquake hit.

"Anyway, our families have been friends for years. And we took gymnastics together," Raquel says. "After school, three days a week."

"Raquel was really good," Eddie says. "I was okay."

"You're great, too, Eddie. Don't be so hard on yourself," Raquel says.

Eddie shrugs. Then he jumps up and catches a low-lying branch. He starts to do a pull-up, swinging his legs up as if he's going to somersault backward, but then pauses. "Eh," he says and drops. "It's not fun anymore."

I'm not the only one who's pieced together the timeline. "Wait, were you guys in LA for the earthquake?" Kenzie asks. She tries to jump for the branch Eddie did but can't reach. Her feet land back on the forest floor and she curses.

"Yeah. We were at gymnastics when the quake started." Eddie kicks some pine needles. "We evacuated the building to get next door, which had much better quake protection. But the shaking was really bad. And then . . ." He trails off, his fists balling.

"There was a van outside," Raquel says. "With two men wait-ing. Stiles and Fee, but we didn't know it then. They told us to get in, that they could drive us out of there before the buildings fell around us. Our teacher was trying to get us to go indoors, but we were all kind of freaking out. Stuff was already breaking and falling over. So a bunch of us jumped in the van."

"Benny and Lucy and James and Carlos," Eddie says. "And me and Raquel. We all were in that van for ages."

I listen with increasing apprehension. There were other kids. . . . Where are they now?

"Yeah, we figured out pretty quick that we weren't being taken to safety," Raquel says. "Seeing as we didn't stop for hours, and whenever we did, we weren't allowed out. When they finally did let us out after a couple of days, we were here. In Yellowstone. Of course, they didn't tell us that. They put us in suits and said we were part of a drill team now—and not to ask questions, or they'd kill us."

"I tried to run," Eddie recounts, rubbing his wrists. "That just got me locked up for four days without food."

As horrified as I've been about the idea of triggering the supervolcano, my horror reaches a whole new level as Raquel and Eddie's story unfolds. This is like some nightmarish mirror-world version of what our group went through. Dr. Grier . . . *Ms. MacNamary* . . . they couldn't have seriously done this, could they?

Eddie continues. "Anyway, they put us in those weird pod things and had us drill into the ground. We laid track and drilled every damned day for weeks and weeks, until . . ." He stops and looks at Raquel.

"There was an explosion," Raquel says. "Big pocket of steam got hit. Benny and Lucy didn't make it out."

"You mean they—?" Kenzie gasps.

"Yeah," Raquel says. My stomach lurches. "So then they moved us. Into that cave where you've been working. Locked us up for a couple of months. We just had to sit around, doing nothing, eating whatever they brought us."

"Eventually they came and got us. Stiles and Fee. They taught us how to use the pods again. Made us go over the instructions a million times." Eddie shudders. "Then they sent us into a new hole in the ground."

"And we worked," Raquel says grimly. "We hated it, but we were too scared not to. They'd feed us if we worked. They wouldn't if we didn't."

"We started figuring out where we were over those months," Eddie says. "Overheard conversations. The weather at least told us we were somewhere north and cold. And Fee mentioned Yellowstone once. I thought Dr. Grier was going to murder him right there."

I swallow, scraping a hand against the bark of a tree as I listen intently.

"Then there was another accident," Raquel says softly. "James got burned really bad. Then they took him and Carlos, and we never saw them again."

"That's . . . horrible," Todd says. I nod in agreement, having no idea what to say. Two kids *died*. Two others vanished to who knows where.

"Dr. Grier yelled a lot about us not noticing minerals," Raquel says. "Trust me, we noticed them. But apparently some are dangerous? Some aren't? Which ones are which? Dr. Grier just threw textbooks at us and told us to study."

Kenzie puts a hand to the side of her face, where her scars are fading.

"We did," Eddie says. "A lot. And so far, it worked for me and Raquel. But it was too late for everyone else."

"Then you four arrived."

"As replacements," Todd whispers.

"That's right," Raquel says.

"Willing replacements," I say. "Ones they didn't have to kidnap."

"And we started talking to you underground," Eddie continues. "And you mentioned the supervolcano."

"That was the last piece of the puzzle we needed," Raquel said. "Suddenly, everything clicked. All the hints we'd picked up from listening to the adults. The steam blasts. Everything. Once we learned exactly why they wanted the tunnels and what their awful plan was, we refused to keep working."

"Yeah," Eddie says. "Got locked up all this past week. Lots of debating from Stiles and Fee if they should just kill us."

"I'm so sorry," I say. Guilt weighs on me from all directions, like the bedrock in our tunnels. "We had no idea any of this was happening."

"They lied to us," Kenzie snarls. Something dark has taken up residence in her face. It's almost as scary as the story we just heard. There are shadows in her eyes, even as the sun rises higher and higher.

"We already had geology knowledge," Todd says. "So they didn't have to teach us much about what to look out for."

"We came perfectly packaged, ready to work," Wyatt says. "Like four completely gullible *kids*." A growl rises in his throat.

"Don't blame yourselves," Raquel says. "That's not going to do us any good right now."

"I just can't believe it," I whisper. "I mean, I do believe it. I believe you." I look between Eddie and Raquel. "It makes twisted sense out of what we've been doing all this time. Why it was kept secret. Why we haven't been allowed our phones. Dr. Grier . . . she was always so strict. But Ms. MacNamary—"

"Who?" Eddie asks.

"Ms. MacNamary," I repeat. "The park manager?"

"The lady with the poofy hair?" Kenzie adds. "Bringer of ice cream? Ringing any bells?"

"Dr. Grier was the only woman we ever saw," Raquel says, puzzled.

That makes me pause. A small surge of absurd hope rears up as Kenzie falls silent. Wyatt and I share a look of uncertain optimism—if Ms. MacNamary *wasn't* in on it, maybe she can help.

But that is a big *if*.

"What about that Nolan kid?" Todd asks next.

Eddie turns away, staring into the distance.

"No idea what his deal is," Raquel answers. "Sometimes they'd lock him up with us. Other times, he'd be free to wander the camp with his ferrets. He barely spoke to us."

"He said he worked with Ms. MacNamary south of where we were," I say. "Apparently he's Dr. Grier's nephew."

"Seriously?!" Raquel replies, crossing her arms. "Great. Of course. Of course!"

Eddie kicks more pine needles.

"*Ya ha gastado sus oportunidades*, Eddie," Raquel says. "*Es el sobrino de la doctora* Grier. *Nunca ha hecho nada para ayudarnos. Me alegro que no le hayamos buscado anoche.*"

Eddie's ears go red and he mumbles something I can't hear.

"I just can't believe two kids died," Todd says, shaking his head. "And two others . . . who knows?" His pained face looks like how I felt a few minutes ago. He's working through his denial. "How could they do this?"

"If they're deliberately trying to set off a volcano, I don't think they care," Kenzie replies. The shadows are back in her eyes. "Adults are the worst."

"*Why* would they do this?" Todd asks next.

"Money? Power? Just general evilness? Who knows." Kenzie glowers.

"That's still the one thing we could never figure out," Eddie says.

I wish I knew how to respond to any of this. All I know is that we *have* to get help. And fast. Whether Nolan's in on it or not, or Ms. MacNamary's in on it or not, or if the volcano is ready to blow from the work we did or not . . .

We need help.

I walk faster, desperate to find a road. People. Anything.

"Hey, Bri, slow down!" Kenzie chases after me.

"We can't waste time," I reply. "Do you remember my simulation video? The one I did to win the contest? With the supervolcano? That could actually happen. We have to hurry."

"We *are* hurrying," Kenzie says. "But we don't know if this direction is going to be any better than any other."

"We would have known if we'd followed Bri's suggestion of looking for the road last night," Wyatt pipes up.

"And we also probably would be caught by now," Eddie says. "That's the most obvious way for us to have gone. At least this way, we have a chance."

"A chance of what?" Todd asks. "Getting lost and dying in the woods?"

The whole group is huffing and puffing, because I refuse to slow down. They can argue as we walk. I've chosen southwest as the direction to go in. I figure if we go in a roughly straight line for long enough, we'll have to hit a road or a trail or something. Yellowstone is big, but it's also been around for a long time and has plenty of human influence. And if our cave was where I think it was, southwest should be in the direction of Yellowstone Lake. Which means campgrounds and people. Which means help.

Yeah, that makes sense. My inner reasoning is satisfied enough, and I stumble onward, frustration and hunger driving me. The sun rises higher and higher behind us.

"Wait—seriously, slow down!" Raquel says. "Your friend without the foot can't keep up."

I turn at that, concern flooding me. But Wyatt isn't that far behind.

"I'm keeping up just *fine*," Wyatt says, climbing over a fallen tree trunk.

"Don't hurt yourself," Raquel says, staying back to keep next to him. I can see Wyatt flush with embarrassment from here.

"Leave Wyatt alone," Todd says, narrowing his eyes at Raquel. "He doesn't need your help!"

"Don't yell at Raquel," Eddie snaps.

"I'm *not* yelling." Todd now turns to Eddie. I flail my arms, because now the entire group has slowed down. Ugh, what does everyone not get about *hurrying*?

"She's trying to be nice!" Eddie says.

"She's being patronizing!" Todd retorts.

"She's just worried! If you don't like that she cares so much, then you can go back to the cave. We could've left you, you know, but we *cared*, so we *didn't*."

"That has nothing to do with this!" Todd argues. Everyone's completely stopped walking now. I flail even more, but no one pays attention to me. "If she's going to treat my friend like he's a baby, then *I* get to tell her to *stop*."

"I haven't even heard you say *thank you* yet, so no, you don't get to tell her anything!" Eddie retorts.

"Oh my god, *shut up*!" Kenzie shrieks. That gets everyone's attention.

There's a brief moment of silence. Somewhere, a bird calls in the trees above. A twig snaps as Todd shuffles awkwardly.

Kenzie puts her hands on her hips. "We can't waste *stupid* time arguing *stupid* things."

"Thank you!" I exclaim, throwing my arms in the air.

She ignores my response and instead points at Todd. "You: don't make everything your fight—Wyatt can speak for himself." She points at Eddie next. "You: Raquel can speak for herself, too, so stop arguing for her." She points at Raquel. "You: Wyatt is awesome and doesn't need a babysitter." She points at Wyatt. "You: promise to be honest and tell us if you need us to slow down." She points at me, and I step backward in surprise. "And *you*: we're all freaking out, but my legs are literally half the length of yours, so maybe don't take off like a bat out of Home Depot when we're trying not to get separated in the middle of the wilderness!"

I open and close my mouth. Kenzie's eyes are apologetic when they lock with mine, and I scrunch up my shoulders. She's right, on all counts. "Sorry," I say.

There's a round of awkward apologies. I take some deep breaths, trying to calm down. My stomach has reached the point where it actually *hurts* from not having eaten. It's hard to think rationally when hungry.

"We need to work together if we're going to get out of here and find someone to help stop Dr. Grier," Wyatt says, motioning for us all to gather around a fallen tree with him. "Let's figure out a plan of action."

Thank god for Wyatt and his blessed common sense.

Over the next few minutes, I explain my reasoning for picking the direction I started walking in, and we decide what we should say to people as soon as we encounter anyone. Once we're all on board with our next steps, we start walking again, staying close together so that we can be as safe as possible if we encounter any dangerous wildlife.

We're all starving. We find some wild raspberry bushes, but eating a handful of berries each does next to nothing to help. The only true saving grace is that the tall trees in this part of the forest provide shade so the sun can't drain us further as we walk.

Sometime, midmorning-ish, Kenzie brings up the question that had been bouncing around my head ever since hearing Raquel and Eddie's story.

"How come you guys didn't make the news?" she asks. "A whole van full of kids goes missing, but I never heard anything about it. And I really should've. My grandma plays CNN nonstop. So freaking annoying." She shakes her head.

"You think six kids going missing from Inglewood would make national news?" Raquel laughs.

Kenzie looks my way, discomfort growing on her face. I stay quiet. Missing kids sounds like a thing that should be on every news channel, but the way Raquel said it makes me feel like I might not totally understand.

"I guarantee you they picked us because it wouldn't draw attention. We're not exactly a couple of rich white kids from Picket-Fence-Ville. Plus, I don't think anyone knew we made it out of the quake," Raquel continues. "Our teacher—Miss Roberts—died that day. She's the only one who saw where we went."

Add another punch to my gut. "What?" I ask.

"Yeah," Raquel answers. "The quake killed a lot of people. Our families are okay, though. So we should be thankful for that, at least." That last line sounds robotic and practiced, like this is something she's said to herself before.

I'm still reeling. I knew lots of people died, because Aunt Pauline would text us to celebrate whenever someone was found alive in the rubble . . . and those texts were few and far between. But there's something about hearing about an actual, specific person who died that's way harder than hearing that a bunch of nameless people did.

"You're sure your families made it out?" Kenzie asks.

"Kenzie!" Todd exclaims.

"What, who told them? Grier? She's lied about everything!" Kenzie retorts. I wince.

"Seriously, Kenzie," Wyatt says. "Not cool."

"No, it's fine, it's a legitimate question," Raquel says.

"We wouldn't do any work until we knew what happened to our families," Eddie explains, speaking up for the first time in several minutes. "We got Grier to let us go online and read the lists of the missing and dead people. Our families were marked as safe. Miss Roberts . . . was not. But that was the last time we got anywhere near a computer or phone or anything, because Lucy tried to send a message to her mom."

"Grier stopped us before Lucy could finish," Raquel says. "It was the angriest I ever saw her."

"Explains why she was so strict with us about tech stuff," Wyatt pieces together. I nod.

"Yeah, we got in big trouble for that," Eddie says.

"Okay, so what you're saying is that no one knows what happened to you guys that day," Kenzie says. "And that your families think you're dead."

"Yeah, probably." Raquel's eyes are tired.

"*Kenzie*." Todd covers his face with his hands. "Think. Before. You. Talk."

I groan. Some squirrels dash past us to one side, climbing up a tree.

"Hey, this is going to turn out good, though." Kenzie elbows Eddie, who looks just about as morose as Raquel. "Because they're going to find out you're *not* dead. And you'll get to celebrate and see them again, as soon as we get the hell out of this doomsday park."

A smile slowly grows across Eddie's face. "Yeah." He climbs over a large tree root, a touch more spring in his step.

"We'll make it happen," I promise. Raquel looks at me like she wants to believe me but can't risk it.

We go silent again, no one bringing up the supervolcanic elephant in the room. The morning ticks by. I cycle between guilt trips. What Raquel and Eddie have been through . . . the crushing knowledge that we have set up another geological event worse than the LA quake . . . even the small guilt from walking ahead of the group earlier and getting called out by Kenzie. It's all spinning around in my brain, weighing down my heart. It doesn't help that I'm so thirsty I could scream. Midday, when I see a stream a ways up through the thicket, I temporarily forget my promise to not run ahead and dart forward.

And then I stop in my tracks. Because climbing out of the stream is a moose.

"Whoa!" Kenzie says. "It's Bambi on steroids!"

The giant animal lifts its massive antlers up so it can get a better look at us.

"Oh my god, nobody move," Raquel says. No need to tell me that—my feet might as well be rooted to the ground.

The moose steps forward, water dripping off of its brown fur, soaking the forest floor. I've seen moose before, but never, *ever* this close. In our documentary last year, we compared a moose to the size of a large horse, but in this moment I realize that comparison was *way* off base. This thing is more like a tank.

"Why don't we chase it off with our drills, like the bear?" Todd suggests quietly.

"They're very powerful animals," I whisper. "It's better to let it do what it wants."

"Hopefully what it will want will be to leave us alone," Eddie adds.

"It's just an herbivore," Todd replies. His voice wavers, and I wonder if he's trying to convince himself not to be scared. "Its teeth aren't even sharp."

The moose regards the conversation with interest, as if it understands what Todd is saying.

"Ah yes, the gentle herbivores," Kenzie says. "Horns, antlers, massive body weight tonnage . . . none of that poses any danger to anyone ever. That's why prey evolved those things. To be cute, harmless, and fluffy toward their predators."

"Okay, I get it, you can shut up now," Todd mumbles.

We wait several grueling minutes. It's like the worst staring contest in the history of the world. Eventually, though, the moose moves on. Its giant body slides into the forest with scarcely a sound, like it was a ghost all along.

"Oh thank god," I say, my body relaxing.

"That thing was *huge*," Eddie says. "I didn't know they got that big!"

"Let's just be thankful it decided we weren't a bother to it," Wyatt says.

"Agreed," Raquel says. We start to pick our way over to the stream. I'm *so* tempted to drink from it, but remember what my aunt said about how streams and lakes can host Giardia. I don't want to catch that gross disease and spend the supervolcanic end of times with diarrhea. I warn everyone else about it, and we decide not to risk it, though Kenzie's reasoning is that she doesn't want to drink moose water—also a legitimate concern.

As we continue our trek, Wyatt, Todd, Kenzie, and I tell Raquel and Eddie our stories from the summer. It's hard to explain our role in everything, now knowing what they've been through. I still can't get over how vastly different our experience has been. We just get to the part where Kenzie got her face blasted with steam and Ms. MacNamary brought us chocolate when we finally reach a trail. An honest-to-god *trail*.

"Guys!" I exclaim, stopping.

"What?" Kenzie asks. "Another moose? Oh, a trail! Look at that, we aren't doomed."

What's left of my hope gets a resurgence. Maybe we can really do this. Really find help—really stop Dr. Grier's plan.

"Way to go, Bri," Wyatt says, patting me on the shoulder.

"Which way do you think we should go?" Raquel asks me.

"Yeah, you got us here," Kenzie says. "Now what?"

"Um." I squirm. All eyes are on me. "Let's go . . . left."

Left is mildly downhill. Downhill probably means a better chance of reaching some sign of civilization. Trail heads are usually at the bottom of hills, not the tops. It's my best guess.

"Left it is!" Kenzie exclaims.

We walk down the trail for about an hour. I do my best to keep up an air of confidence about my navigational decision. The four of us finish telling our summer's story, and Kenzie is back to groaning about how gullible we were. She's my friend, but I am getting seriously tired of her rollercoaster of moods. How am I supposed to stay calm and collected when someone is fluctuating between laughter and swearing as frequently as Kenzie is?

"We really should've known what was going on," she says, tossing a fistful of pine needles.

"How?" Todd asks her.

"I don't know, by not being idiots?"

"We were tricked," Wyatt says. "That's all there is to it. There's no use being upset. Sometimes bad things happen, and you just need to move on to whatever the next steps are."

Kenzie turns to face Wyatt, balling up her fists. "Oh my god, you sound like my grandma." Then she raises her voice up into a scratchy, old-person impression. *"Stop wasting time, Kenzie! Get a handle on your emotions! You're never going to accomplish anything if you can't calm down! Do you want to end up like your parents?"*

Wyatt just stares at her.

"What happened to your parents?" Raquel asks.

"What *didn't* happen to my parents?" Kenzie mumbles. "Everything that'll never happen to me, if my grandma has anything to say about it."

The wooded landscape around us gives way to open fields. The breeze picks up here, rustling through the grasses. I'm suddenly very aware of how out in the open we are. That could be good if there are other people around to see us and rescue us, but also bad if Dr. Grier is looking for us. But I guess it can't be helped.

"Are they alive?" Wyatt asks her.

Kenzie looks at him. "What?"

"Are your parents alive?" he repeats.

"Unless they faked their overdoses as a cover to run away and join a secret spy organization, no." Kenzie turns away from Wyatt, kicking a rock down the grassy hill.

My eyes widen. I knew Kenzie lived with her grandma, but I never felt right asking her why. My annoyance with her fizzles away in an instant. I want to give her a hug, but she kind of looks like she's going to physically tear apart the next person who touches her, so I stay back.

"I'm sorry," Wyatt says. "I know what that feels like. Kind of, at least."

Todd is clearly going through the same struggle I am. I catch his eye, and we share a helpless look.

"Yeah," Kenzie replies. "Your mom."

"Cancer."

"Sucks."

"Yeah."

I think about my parents and wrap my arms around myself. I never really thought about how lucky I am to have them both. And Aunt Pauline. I don't have any siblings, but I have a family who loves me, and who are all alive. Even my grandparents.

That could all change if we don't find a way to stop this supervolcano. Oregon will be buried.

A large rocky outcrop is just ahead of us. Looks like volcanic tuff to me—old volcanic ash, compacted together. I shudder, trying not to let my imagination get carried away. Just as we move to walk around it, I hear a noise from the other side.

We stop. Without even saying it, I know we're all anxious it's another bear or moose. But then something else comes out from behind the outcrop.

"Kids!" Ms. MacNamary sobs, running toward us. "Oh my god, you're okay!"

CHAPTER THIRTEEN

I instinctively pull back, lining up in tight formation with Wyatt, Todd, and Kenzie, as Raquel and Eddie stare in bewilderment.

"Ms. MacNamary!" Kenzie exclaims.

"Whose side are you on?" I ask, reaching for my drill.

Ms. MacNamary comes to a halt. "I'm so sorry," her voice cracks, breaking down. "So, so sorry. You have no idea." Ms. MacNamary's eyes have gigantic bags under them. "I've been tracking you down all day. I had to get to you first."

"Tracking us?" Wyatt asks. "How?"

"Your tool belts," Ms. MacNamary gestures. "They have GPS chips in them."

We all immediately undo our belts, flinging them away from ourselves.

"No!" Ms. MacNamary says, reaching out to stop us and

wincing as the belts hit the ground. "Don't do that! You'll break something, and then we'll be doomed for sure!"

"What are you talking about?" Raquel asks. "Who are you?"

"I'm Laura, Laura MacNamary." She sits down on the edge of the outcrop, rubbing her hands over her face. "And this is all my fault."

"You didn't know," Todd says, a look of realization dawning on his face. "Oh my god." His expression evolves into something like confused pity.

I have no idea what to think. I look around, desperate for signs of other hikers across the sunny meadow. I'd feel a lot better if we could reach other people.

"Samantha told me you two were here by choice." Ms. MacNamary turns to Raquel and Eddie. "At least, at first. I thought you'd only gotten locked up later. I didn't know, I swear."

"You *what?*" Eddie asks.

"I'm sorry!" she gasps. "I thought what we were doing was right! I thought we were saving the world! I thought you two were helping, but wanted to stop, and I knew we were running short on time, so I agreed with Samantha's decision to keep you here against your will. That was so wrong of me, but I was desperate!"

Eddie does not look at all convinced. I can't read Raquel's expression, but she does take a step closer to Eddie. Disgust at Ms. MacNamary floods through me. She misled us about Raquel and Eddie. She kept them locked up. She's a *kidnapper* and now she wants us to trust her? To believe she's sorry?

"Wait," Kenzie says carefully. Never one to hide her emotions,

I can see the same war raging across her face that's playing out inside of me right now. "Do you know what Dr. Grier is really planning?"

"I do now." Ms. MacNamary hangs her head. "It all came out after your escape. She's trying to set off Yellowstone's supervolcano. She's not trying to stop it. She hates people and wants to kill as many as she can. And she's about to succeed." Ms. MacNamary's eyes fill with tears. "I'm so sorry. I didn't realize. I thought . . . for *years* I thought . . ."

"Why should we believe you?" Wyatt asks.

"Yeah," I agree. "You're the one who invited us to join her."

"I didn't know!" Ms. MacNamary repeats herself, wiping at her eyes. I've never seen an adult look as disheveled as she does in this moment. It's unsettling. "Please listen—we have to hurry. I'm no geologist, but I got ahold of the schematics. I think there's a way to stop her." Ms. MacNamary pulls out a tablet. "I'm not sure, but if you all agree with what I'm seeing, we may still have a chance to save my park—and save the world!"

Trembling from hunger and confusion, I can't find any sympathy at all for her tears. Thoughts crash around in my brain. Ms. MacNamary sure sounds like she's being honest now, but if she's not . . .

But if she *is*. . .

I take a step forward, hardly daring to even suggest that I trust Ms. MacNamary's word, but needing to see what the schematics show. If there's a chance we can stop the eruption, it's worth at least a look.

Kenzie, looking even more torn than I feel, lets out a guttural scream. Then, after furiously kicking some grass, sending clumps of it flying, she trudges up to the tablet to read. She and I crowd over it, soon joined by Wyatt and Todd. Eddie and Raquel stay back for a moment, but curiosity gets the better of them and they eventually join us, too. Though they stay as far away as possible while still being able to check out the tablet.

On the screen is a cutaway map of a huge section of Yellowstone's caldera. On one side is the cave we were working in. The alpha tunnel can be seen going down for a long ways underground, then turning horizontal to join up with the beta tunnels we spent July creating. Below those, down, down, down, is the magma chamber.

Ms. MacNamary swipes the screen. This time, our tunnels are shown to explode at the bottom. Pressure is released.

She swipes again. Bubbles build through the magma, causing the rock that was almost cool enough to be solid to melt down and foam, rising up through the beta tunnels.

She swipes a third time. The alpha tunnel floods with magma. It spews out of the mouth of the tunnel, into the cavern. This newly created eruption causes even more pressure release from the removal of mass. More bubbles form deeper in the magma chamber.

She swipes a fourth time. The bubbles down deep continue. The rhyolitic magma heats up so much that the basaltic magma below it begins to rise in temperature.

She swipes a fifth time. The basaltic magma starts to bubble.

From what I remember from my Earth Builder project, basalt is easier to melt. I feel my heart rate kick up.

She swipes a sixth time. The basaltic magma heats up so much that it sends hydrothermal fluids up through the rhyolitic magma, making for more bubbles and frothing than the chamber can handle. At this point, this looks like it could've been taken right out of my project.

She swipes a seventh time. Everything has melted in the chamber. It's all froth and bubbles now. The explosion of the supervolcano is imminent.

She doesn't need to show us another slide. We know what comes next. An explosion that will decimate the Northwest. An eruption of not just lava, but of poisonous gases and glass-filled dust that will cover the continent. Unbelievable amounts of smoke and aerosols will enter the atmosphere, causing the world to drop in temperature so drastically that we'll be sent into winter for ten or more straight years.

"So what's your idea?" Wyatt asks, breaking our horrified silence. "I thought disarming the explosives down our tunnels would result in them blowing up in our faces?"

"Yeah, Dr. Grier did sort of stress that point when we were laying the blasting powder," Kenzie says.

"And she was right," Ms. MacNamary says. "We can't tamper with the explosives. They're designed to blow if the circuit gets broken. I thought it was a failsafe in the event of a big quake—a way to ensure a tunnel would open to release the pressure during high-risk times for the supervolcano, even if we weren't pressing the button ourselves. But now I see why those bombs were *really* designed as they were." She shakes her head sadly.

"So what do we do?" I ask.

Ms. MacNamary swipes all the way back to the beginning and points at the alpha tunnel. "We use our *actual* failsafe. We fill the alpha tunnel with the cement we've been making out of the churned rock from all your drilling."

I remember the vat in the cavern and the cement mixer next to it. Is that what it's been for?

"We had it there in case something went disastrously wrong and we needed to close up the tunnels and keep the pressure contained underground. This *should* also work if the disaster is actually Samantha pulling the trigger." Her face darkens as she says the name of her former partner.

"Won't closing off the tunnel just make the lava explode out of somewhere else instead?" Wyatt asks.

"There are only four tunnels with explosives in them right now," Ms. MacNamary says. "That's actually not too many. We were aiming for more originally, but thanks to you two," she nods at Raquel and Eddie, "we're still down some. And the tunnels we have are small enough that even if it did trigger some pressure drop, if there's no exit, it should just harmlessly filter up through the Earth and then calm down. Might see some more geysers for a few days, and the hot springs may get interesting, but the rest of the fallout won't happen."

I wish I had Earth Builder right now. I'm trying to run through this like a simulation in my head, but it's hard without the game in front of me.

"We should call for help," Todd says. "We can't risk this not working."

At that, I regard Todd carefully. It sounds like he's already set to trust and help Ms. MacNamary.

"If Samantha sees any signs of police or government, she's going to pull the trigger," Ms. MacNamary says, looking pained. "Right now, she thinks I'm looking for you all to bring you back to her. If she gets the slightest hint that we've alerted any authorities, that I've betrayed her, or that you six have found a way to get the word out, that's it. Game over. We have to take care of this as secretly and as quickly as we can. The world literally depends on it."

My heart skips a beat. The thought that all it would take to set off the supervolcano is Dr. Grier getting spooked—oh my god.

"But how do we get back in there without being seen?" Todd asks next.

"That I don't know," Ms. MacNamary admits. "But everyone's out looking for you kids right now, so the caves will mostly be empty. Maybe our escape artist masterminds can help?" She looks hopefully at Raquel and Eddie.

Eddie and Raquel have been silent this entire time, and I've been anxiously waiting for them to weigh in.

"I don't like this," Eddie says, arms crossed. "You conveniently say we can't call for help. You track us down before anyone else does. And even though you say you didn't know what Grier was planning, you kept us locked up. *For months*. Forcing us to work for you. That makes me really not feel like trusting you and definitely not feel like helping you. What about you, Raquel?"

Raquel squares her jaw and looks out over the meadow. She's quiet for several moments and we all are, too. Ms. MacNamary fiddles with her hat in her hands. "I don't want to trust you, either," Raquel finally begins, turning her gaze back on the woman. "Benny and Lucy died because of you. I don't care if you weren't the one to kidnap us—you let people keep us as slaves. That's just as bad. Worse, even." Raquel's voice trembles. "You're going to have to face that evil inside yourself somehow."

Ms. MacNamary stops her fiddling and stands frozen in place.

"But I don't know if you want your park to blow up. Maybe that means more to you than our lives." Raquel pauses, then turns to the rest of us. "You know this woman better than we do. Can we trust her on this?"

My eyebrows shoot up. I look at my team. Wyatt and Todd don't look certain, but clearly don't want to say no. Meanwhile, Kenzie's eyes flick between Raquel and Ms. MacNamary, lingering on each for long stretches of time.

"Her idea is the only one we've got for keeping that supervolcano from erupting," Wyatt points out, sounding as exhausted as I feel.

"That's true," I say. I turn back to Raquel. "She's done terrible stuff for sure, but I don't know what other option we have here. Maybe think of it as less helping Ms. MacNamary and more helping to stop Dr. Grier."

She and Eddie exchange glances.

"I know I didn't make the best choices before," Ms. MacNamary starts to apologize again. "I—"

"Shut up," Kenzie says. Her hands are on her hips. "You did awful things. But weirdly, you were the only adult at camp who ever cared about any of *our* group. I don't know why you screwed up so bad with Raquel and Eddie, maybe because you thought you were saving the planet, maybe because you're racist trash or something. But now that you know you *weren't* saving the planet, you're here, at least trying to fix that. Sometimes people make crap choices. But I'm not my grandma. I'm willing to give second chances. Especially when the survival of our whole freaking continent depends on it."

Ms. MacNamary squeezes her hat even tighter in her hands. I'm still not sure Raquel or Eddie are convinced, but neither of them say anything more.

"Whatever we do, we should get away from those tracking things," Wyatt says.

I give him an appreciative nod. That, at least, we can all agree on straightaway.

Kenzie picks her belt up. "Where are those creepy chips, anyway?" she asks.

"They should be sewn into the inside of the belts," Ms. MacNamary says, finding her voice. She lowers her tablet and takes Kenzie's tool belt from her, then pulls out a pocket knife and cuts into it. "Here."

From the middle of the leather of Kenzie's tool belt, Ms. MacNamary pops out a small chip, no bigger than a grain of rice.

It falls to the ground and Kenzie stomps on it repeatedly, even though I'm pretty sure it's small enough to just slide between the cracks of her boot. In fact, I double check the ground when she's done to make sure it hasn't lodged itself in the sole of her shoe. That would entirely defeat the purpose.

I hand Ms. MacNamary my belt next, and she removes the chip. Then she does the same for the rest of the group. As I clip the belt back on, I realize, in a way, I just made up my mind about Ms. MacNamary. I've trusted her to remove the tracking device.

If she's lying, then I've already let her endanger us.

I suck in a breath. This is one of those times where I have to make a choice and stick with it. Like Aunt Pauline would say when we were filming with only one camera and had to make the call about which angle we were going for: *"Own it, Bri!"*

I nod to myself. Okay, owning it. Trusting Ms. MacNamary.

About the volcano stuff, at least.

"Let's get you all some water," Ms. MacNamary says. "There's a field station nearby for park rangers. It's not in use full time, but it should have a sink. Maybe even some stale snacks! But probably not, because bears."

"Because bears should be on a T-shirt," Kenzie says.

There's some nervous laughter at that. I'm not sure any of us are in the mood to truly find anything funny, but I appreciate Kenzie for trying to lighten the atmosphere.

Ms. MacNamary starts walking. Kenzie, Todd, and Wyatt follow. I stay back a moment, because Raquel and Eddie don't budge.

"I don't trust her," Eddie says.

"I get that," I say. "You don't know her."

"Do you?" he retorts. "Do you really know her?"

I wince. "No. I guess I don't. At all, really. But if she's taking us to a ranger station, they'll probably have a phone there. You can call your families."

Eddie falls silent at that.

Some dandelion fluff floats past us on the breeze. Raquel uncrosses her arms. "We wanted to find help," she says slowly. "And if you guys are right about this MacNamary lady, maybe we have. You have no idea how hard I'm trying right now to be objective about this. There's so much at stake."

"Oh, I know," I say, letting out a mirthless laugh at all that we're dealing with. "We're literally trying to save the world. I guess that's why I don't want to risk passing up her plan—it's the only real idea we have to stop Dr. Grier. I can't think of anything else. Not if Dr. Grier's going to pull the trigger if she hears of anyone from the military or something coming into the park."

Raquel stares into the distance. "So you think we should go with her."

"*¿Y vas a confiar en su juicio?*" Eddie asks Raquel.

"*Nos dirijió bien en el bosque.*"

"*Los árboles y las personas son cosas distintas,*" Eddie says.

I know my Spanish isn't great, but it must be even worse than I thought, because it sounded like Eddie just said something about trees not being people, and I have no idea where that would have come from. Regardless, the rest of the group is way ahead of us now, and every second we waste is another second Dr. Grier could decide to blast us all off the face of the planet. I fiddle nervously with a blade of grass, wanting to run ahead and catch up, but also not wanting to leave Raquel and Eddie behind.

"This does sound like our best bet," Raquel says to Eddie, in English once again.

"It's our only bet," I add. I hate to sound pushy, but it is what it is.

Raquel nods at me while Eddie makes a frustrated noise from the back of his throat. But he joins Raquel as we all hurry to follow the rest of the group.

Ms. MacNamary leads us down the path to another side trail where the stream splits off. We walk for an hour, back into a wooded area, until we reach the station she was talking about. It's devoid of people, as Ms. MacNamary had guessed it would be, and unfortunately devoid of phones or radios. This earns me a harsh glare from Eddie but, surprisingly, no real reaction from Raquel. Maybe that's because we *do* find a sink. All of us gorge ourselves drinking from it. We also find a jeep. This second find even raises Eddie's spirits.

"If things turn bad, we can use this to get away," he quietly says to both me and Raquel. "There's a lot more of us than there are of her." He nods at Ms. MacNamary.

He's right, but I don't think any of us are old enough to know how to drive, even Raquel.

"Who leaves a jeep in the middle of the woods?" Todd asks Ms. MacNamary.

"It's for emergencies," Ms. MacNamary says. "A handful of our stations have them. We're very lucky, so let's not look a gift horse in the mouth."

Eddie climbs over the top of it to drop into the driver's seat and throws some leaves out the window. "Hmm. One thing. No keys."

"Let's hotwire it!" Kenzie says.

"You can do that?" Todd asks her.

"Nah, probably not," she says. "I watched a YouTube video of it once, though."

"We're not hotwiring the jeep," Ms. MacNamary says. "The keys are likely hidden somewhere around here, anyway. That's protocol."

The seven of us hunt around the station, looking for any hidey-holes where car keys might be kept. It's a quick search. After a few minutes, Todd finds them under a log that has a downward-facing arrow carved into it. "Okay, worst hiding spot *ever*," he says.

"Useful if you've forgotten where the keys are, though!" Ms. MacNamary says. She sounds much more like her usual cheery self now that we aren't all actively accusing her of kidnapping, murder, and worldwide terror plots. I hope she doesn't think we've all forgiven her, though.

We climb into the vehicle. Wyatt takes the front seat. Kenzie, Todd, Eddie, Raquel, and I all squeeze into the back. Kenzie is practically on my lap. Then we hit the road.

Riding in a jeep is really loud, I quickly discover. I can only hear half of what Ms. MacNamary's saying as we drive. Something about wanting to park a good distance away so they don't get suspicious, and how there's a side entrance we can use to sneak in, but not being sure about how many guards might be there.

As we travel back to the very place we'd been fleeing, I think about how if Ms. MacNamary really was tricked, then she's just set up the destruction of the park she lives for. I also realize that she is trusting us to *save* her park. Six kids. We're her only hope.

The enormity of what we're going to attempt to do seeps into my bones. I mean, earlier this summer, we were told we were working to stop the supervolcano, but this time around—it's so much more real. Back then, I guess I always sort of assumed they would find someone else to replace me if I left. And while I knew the odds were high for the volcano to blow, they weren't literally a button push away.

Everything has changed. But Ms. MacNamary still trusts us and still needs us. I swallow, trying to muster courage. I'm pretty sure I'm about to do the real-life equivalent of switching from "challenge" mode in Earth Builder to "Olympic-tier."

We arrive as far as Ms. MacNamary's willing to take us, and she stops the jeep. We all climb out—for those of us in the back, it's more like we *fall* out—and regroup around the front of the jeep.

"Okay, we need a distraction," Todd says. "If there are guards, we have to split them apart if we have any hope of getting past them."

"And when we do encounter one, what do you suggest we do?" I ask him.

"Umm." Todd clearly hadn't gotten that far. Though, his idea for a distraction probably is worth some consideration.

"How long will it take to fill up the tunnel with cement?" Raquel asks.

"I'm not sure," Ms. MacNamary says. "We'll need as much time as we can get."

"Distracting the guards might not be the best idea, then," she says. "Who knows how long we'd have to keep it up?"

"Then what do we do?" Kenzie asks. "Kill them?"

"Holy crap, Kenzie, no!" Todd says, aghast.

"We'll have to capture them," Raquel says. "Take them with us."

"How?" I ask.

Ms. MacNamary frowns. "We're going to have to physically overtake them."

"Us?" Todd asks, looking around at our team with serious doubt.

"What if there are, like, a whole ton of them?" I ask. I'm with Todd on this one. It's not bad enough that we're all kids—we're all kids who were deliberately picked because we're *scrawny*.

"There shouldn't be," Ms. MacNamary says. "Most are out looking for you. We had fourteen men working for us total. So that's sixteen people, including me and Dr. Grier. I saw at least ten of them leave this morning."

"So four or less," Raquel says. "That still sounds like a lot."

"Let's go up there and find out," Wyatt says.

Without any better ideas, we edge through the woods in the direction of the caves. Thankfully, we don't encounter anyone along the way. They must've fanned out much farther than where we are by now.

"Okay," Ms. MacNamary whispers. "See that big rock over to the left?"

We all nod. Just to the side of the main entrance, about half a person's height lower, there's a huge boulder.

"Behind that is another entrance," she says. "If they're low on guards, they won't have many there. Maybe one or two at the most."

"That sounds like my kind of entrance," Kenzie says. Her face is flushed with adrenaline, making it almost as pink as the healing skin on its edges.

Ms. MacNamary picks up a large stick. "We need something to intimidate them with."

I pull out my drill, which I've become rather attached to since the bear incident. "How about this?"

She smiles at me. "Yep, I wouldn't want to come near you with that thing."

"Do they have guns?" Raquel asks.

"No," Ms. MacNamary answers. "At least, I don't think so. They never did to my knowledge."

"I don't think so" isn't the answer I'm looking to hear from that kind of question.

"Let's hold half of us back in reserve," Raquel suggests. "That way, if the first half gets attacked, we'll still have some of us available to come up with another plan."

Ms. MacNamary regards her. "You're a smart girl."

"I'll go first," I say, ready to just get this over with. "Who's with me?"

"I am!" Kenzie jumps forward.

"Me too," says Wyatt.

"And I'll go," Ms. MacNamary says. "That'll be a strong showing. Four of us against hopefully just one guard."

I've never fought anyone before. I'm not sure I can. Though, not for nothing, we did fend off a bear this morning.

"Okay," I say. "Let's do this."

We near the boulder. So far, I don't think we've been spotted. But that's about to change, I'm sure. Whoever is on the other side of the boulder will see us. We just have to make sure they don't have time to radio for backup.

"On three?" Ms. MacNamary says.

"On three," Wyatt confirms.

"One," Kenzie says. "Two . . . "

"Three!" Ms. MacNamary shouts.

We leap forward, past the boulder and into the hidden second entrance. There, as predicted, is one guard: a man I recognize from camp but whose name I never learned. He backs up in alarm, clearly not expecting us. Which is perfect.

Ms. MacNamary dives at him, while Wyatt and I each go for an arm. He tries to kick out, but Kenzie throws herself onto his legs. Wyatt shoves a work glove in his mouth so he can't yell. I'm thrown up against the wall, but when I hold my drill out in the direction of his face he stops.

Ms. MacNamary leans her stick length-wise into his throat, and his eyes bug out. "Now, Kenzie," she says.

Kenzie gets to work with her tool belt's tape measure, wrapping it around the man's legs and tying him up. He lays on the dirt, completely pinned. I lean against a rock, trying to catch my breath.

It all went so fast, I can barely believe we did it.

"Are you alone?" Ms. MacNamary asks.

The man glares at her. He must realize that she's no longer on the side that he is.

"Yes or no!" she demands, motioning to me to raise my drill higher.

He nods.

"You're alone?" she repeats.

He nods again.

"How many more are left at camp?" she asks.

He can't answer, with his mouth full of gross old work glove.

Ms. MacNamary holds up four fingers. He shakes his head. She lowers it to three. He shakes his head. Two.

A nod.

There are two others around here, somewhere, though not down this particular section of cave. I wonder where they are and how we're going to take them down.

After Kenzie gets him suitably tied up, I lean out the mouth of the side entrance.

"Come on, guys!" I call. "We've got this one taken care of. We can get in!"

Todd, Eddie, and Raquel come out of hiding and scoot up the hillside toward the cave, ducking behind the boulder with us.

We begin to head deeper into the caves and the dark, when I look behind me to see Raquel and Eddie still at the entrance.

I jog back. "What's wrong?" I ask, wondering if they've changed their minds. Food and water are ahead, and I personally don't want to waste any time getting to them.

They just look at me.

"We fought so hard to get out of here," Eddie explains.

My shoulders drop. Of course. "I'm sorry," I say. "It won't be long before we're out again, now."

I don't know if either of them believe me. I don't know if I believe me.

Raquel crosses her arms. "It doesn't matter. We don't have a choice. Benny, Lucy, James, Carlos . . . they deserve to have meant something. If we die without stopping Dr. Grier, then all this will be for nothing. This is our only plan. We have to try."

"Right," Eddie agrees. That gets him moving. Even though it was Raquel's motivational speech, it still takes her another moment to follow us.

CHAPTER FOURTEEN

We come up the tunnel in the dark, and I see light ahead. Our campsite. The guard we've captured is currently dragged along by Ms. MacNamary and Kenzie, who looks ready to rip him to shreds if he tries anything funny. He clearly notices that, because he stays very still and behaves himself.

Kenzie and Ms. MacNamary heave him off to one side once we're in the camp area. The other two guards could be anywhere.

"We need scouts," Ms. MacNamary says.

Eddie and Raquel both volunteer. Before anyone can object, they dash off into the cave, looking around our camp. I wonder if they offered to go search because they still don't trust Ms. MacNamary and are checking around for signs of betrayal. After several minutes, they return.

"They're by the main cave entrance," Raquel says. I blink. I hadn't even noticed her climb up the stairs to check. "How do we want to handle them?"

"Blasting powder," I say.

Kenzie grins a feral grin. "Okay, scary, but yes!"

"No," I say quickly. "I don't want to use it. I want to intimidate them with it."

Ms. MacNamary beams. "Excellent plan, Bri!"

Todd and Wyatt exchange wary glances, but I don't know what to tell them. Desperate times, desperate measures.

We enter the camp and Ms. MacNamary takes us to a shed where the blasting powder is stored. I pick up a bag of it, grim resignation coming over me. This stuff is dangerous. If I make a mistake, or get too close to a flame, it could kill me. But after all we've already been through, I'm surprisingly calm about that fact.

Todd and Wyatt have secured the first guard in one cabin. Raquel says they practically used all the rope in the camp, and Todd pouts at that.

"Hey, I'm not going to apologize for being cautious," Todd says. "You want him to get free and warn Dr. Grier?"

"It was my idea to double tie everything," Wyatt says. "You can laugh at me if you want."

But Raquel doesn't. Todd and Wyatt stay behind with Ms. MacNamary so they can sort out exactly how we're going to get the cement into the tunnel, while the rest of us head through camp in the other direction toward the cave entrance. The element of surprise is a major part of our plan, so when we reach the spiral staircase, we ascend it one at a time again, carefully and quietly.

I get to the top and notice it's starting to get dark outside. It's hard to tell where the cave ends and the outdoors begins. But two men move by the entrance, and my eyes adjust.

Once we've all reached the top, I give Kenzie a nod.

"Hey, dipwads!" she shouts.

They spin.

Kenzie ignites her blowtorch, and I raise my bag of blasting powder up into the air.

"If you make any moves, we blow all of us up, right here, right now."

One of them freezes, and the other frowns, not buying it. "You wouldn't do that," he says. "You'd kill yourselves."

Raquel, who had been hiding in the shadows behind us, comes up with her own blowtorch. "If she won't do it, I will."

I'm surprised by the effect that has on the second guard. At Raquel's declaration, he completely complies. My heart reaches out to her, seeing the lines on her face in the light of the blowtorch fire.

"Now get walking," Raquel says.

They do as we ask.

We head back into camp, tying the other guards up with the first. That should be all of them. Eddie takes great pleasure in locking the door to their cabin. Then Ms. MacNamary settles her shoulders, ushering us all over for a meeting.

"Okay, now comes the work," she says.

Todd and Wyatt show us a diagram they drew. "The cement mixer in the cavern can be attached to slurry hoses," Todd says. "We need to fill up the vertical section of the alpha tunnel with cement—from way down where it begins to curve, all the way up to the very top where the exit hole is."

"But we have to be thorough and pack the cement in tightly," Wyatt says. "Which means we're going to have to go down there with it. One person, with the hose of sludge mix, to start filling it neatly, getting the edges and everything. And whoever is first will need to take something with them to block the turn in the alpha tunnel, so the cement doesn't accidentally ooze all the way down into the beta tunnels. If anything drops into those, we could risk setting off the explosives."

"We'll probably need to take turns so no one tires out," Todd says.

"And what? We just have to hope Dr. Grier doesn't come back and find us or get bored and blow everything up in the meantime?" Kenzie sniffs.

"Yes," Wyatt says. "So we really should hurry."

I nod, more than ready to get this plan going. We head to the inner caves, down to where our worksite is. The walk is fast, which is good because it's also painful. With every step, I'm reminded of the pride I'd felt in our work all summer. The rocky walls of the cave taunt me now. The light from the strung-up lamps dances along them, laughing cruelly.

Your fault, they seem to say. *You did this. If the volcano erupts, it's on you.*

When we finally reach the cavern, I'm shaking worse than the false earthquakes we'd felt throughout July. I shine my headlamp around our worksite, trying to channel the single-minded focus I can get when editing videos for Aunt Pauline. We have a job to do.

My light shines to the far edge of the cavern, where the cement mixer lies. The good news is, we're going to have plenty of cement to work with. We've churned up so much rubble over the summer that the mixer must be filled to the brim. And more can easily be made from the vat of water and piles of rocks in the cavern near it.

We locate a piece of scrap metal about the diameter of our pods to use as a plug for the bottom of the vertical portion of the alpha tunnel.

Kenzie volunteers to go first, as she'll need to take the metal plate in addition to the hose and safety cable. As the smallest of us all, it'll be easiest for her. After we load her up with everything she needs, she steps into her harness like we did on the day we installed the blasting powder.

Then she gets lowered into the tunnel. The rest of us plan out an order of who will keep watch. Luckily, Ms. MacNamary seems to think we have some time before Dr. Grier and the men return, even though it is already dark.

"As soon as you are done with the cement, I'm radioing for help," Ms. MacNamary promises. "And if Samantha finds us before help arrives . . . well, I'll try to direct her anger onto me, so you all can get away." She grimaces, and I shudder. I don't know how any of us will escape if that situation happens.

After nearly an hour, Kenzie radios up, asking for a trade. Todd presses the button that gets the cable moving up and out of the tunnel. When Kenzie eventually emerges, I see that her gloves are caked in drying cement and her face is covered in gray dust where her goggles and mask don't cover. I hope that doesn't hurt her healing skin.

Eddie goes next. The rest of us make and eat some oatmeal, which is unfortunately the only large-group-serving foodstuff we can find at the camp. After Kenzie comments that her oatmeal looks a lot like the cement she was pouring, I have an even harder time forcing it down.

Ms. MacNamary doesn't eat. She just paces, looking for all the world like she's on the verge of a heart attack. She must feel so useless right now—she can't fit down the tunnel to help us, she can't call anyone or risk the volcano blowing, and she's got the guilt on her shoulders for being responsible for this entire situation and having to face Raquel and Eddie after what she's done to them. I'd feel bad for her, but honestly, for a lot of that she deserves to feel rotten.

After Eddie comes out and dives into his own bowl of oatmeal, Todd goes down. Wyatt offers to go after him. I look at Raquel at that point. Neither of us have signed up to go in yet.

She seems to like bringing up the back of the group, so I probably should go after Wyatt. It's something I've observed about her time and time again.

"Hey, Raquel?"

She looks at me from her camp chair. "Yeah?"

"I'm guessing you want to go last, right?"

"If you don't mind," she says.

"I don't."

"It's not because I want you guys to do all the work," she says quickly.

"Oh, no! I didn't think that at all," I clarify. "I just noticed you always bring up the back of the group pretty much everywhere we go. I guess I've just been wondering . . . why?"

She leans back in her camp chair, folding her knees to her chest. "Benny and Lucy took last shift the day they died. James was in the back of our group when he got injured." Raquel's voice goes quiet. The churning of the cement mixer behind us is the only sound for several moments. "I was in front. They looked to me to lead, so I did. But that also meant it was my responsibility to watch for dangers. It's my fault. Now . . . well, if I go after everyone else, then anything that's missed falls to me. And whatever curse there is on being last . . . that falls to me, too."

I reach one tentative hand out and set it on her shoulder. She flinches, so I take it off. "It's Dr. Grier's fault. And Ms. MacNamary's." I know that won't be enough but need to say it anyway. "Not yours."

"It's their fault we're here," Raquel says. "But they weren't in the tunnels those days. They weren't the person everyone looked up to and trusted." Helpless, I watch her get up and walk over to Eddie, who has passed out asleep in his camp chair. She picks up his empty bowl of oatmeal and takes it over to the pile of dishes.

I stretch one arm over my shoulders, trying to get my muscles to come back to life before it's my turn to head down. I have no idea how to get Raquel to see that this isn't her fault. None of this is her fault. That'd be like saying Kenzie got blasted by steam because I didn't take third spot on our crew.

I pause, watching Kenzie. She didn't die, though. Maybe that's the difference.

I wait for Wyatt to come out of the tunnel and let my mind wander to the likeliness of any of this working. The high temperature underground allows for the cement to cure faster, but in Earth Builder it takes a week at normal temperatures for cement to harden fully. If the volcano blows sooner than that, will it hold, even without being fully cured?

Maybe the weight of the sludge will speed up the process. With that kind of pressure . . .

I do some mental math, figuring out the volume of the tunnel and then trying to figure out the weight of the cement filling it. Heat can speed things up, but so can pressure. That's basic geochemistry—something I read a lot about while trying to perfect my simulation.

But then my calculations get interrupted. The radio squawks, and it's Wyatt, announcing he's ready to be extracted. I straighten in my chair—it'll be my turn next.

A couple of minutes later, Wyatt is pulled from the tunnel, and he sets down the giant slurry hose. The handles on the end of it glint, reflecting the floodlights in the cavern.

"Phew!" he exclaims, peeling off his gloves. "Done."

"Done?" I ask. "Wait, like I-don't-have-to-go-down-there done? Like, *done* done?"

"Yes," he says. "*Done* done."

I get up from my chair and walk over to the tunnel's entrance on the floor of the cavern, shining my headlamp into it. Sure enough, a few yards down, there's a nice layer of cement. We can easily finish the tunnel now from the cavern's surface. "Whoa."

Kenzie squeals. "Heck yeah, Wyatt!" She darts over, hugging him. Dust poofs off of him, and I can see a very flustered expression on his face under flecks of drying cement.

"It's done?" Todd asks, waking up from a nap.

We stopped it. The supervolcano can't blow up now. Probably.

The tension that's been threaded through me floats away. The worst of it is stopped. If we can get the detonation trigger back from Dr. Grier, there won't even be minor issues, like geysers and such. It'll be like none of this ever happened. We did it.

Eddie wakes up next, and he and Raquel share an exhausted hug of relief. Wyatt collapses in a chair, free from Kenzie, and rubs his hands over his face.

Kenzie's the only one of us actively cheering. "Bri!" She spies me and full-on tackles me. I fall back on a chair, the fabric sinking under our weight.

"Oof!"

"We're done!"

I laugh, but probably not as much as Kenzie wants me to. "I know! I can't believe it," I say, trying to muster some enthusiasm. I wish I could feel happier about this monumental thing we just did, but I felt like this once before and had it horribly snatched away from me. Maybe I'm just tired, but something still isn't sitting right with me.

"Where's Ms. MacNamary?" Todd asks.

Kenzie looks around, climbing off of me. "No idea. She was here a minute ago. Yo, Ms. MacNamary!" she shouts. "Come party with us! We're done!"

Ms. MacNamary appears from the edge of the cavern entrance. She must've been on guard duty. "All done?" she asks.

"*Hella* done!" Kenzie declares, beaming.

"Fantastic," she says.

And that's when a dozen men with guns step out from behind her, with Dr. Grier and Nolan in the lineup.

"See?" Ms. MacNamary says to Dr. Grier. "I told you positive motivation always works better than negative."

CHAPTER FIFTEEN

No. The cavern might as well be collapsing around me. I shake my head, refusing to believe it. *No, not again. We saved the world. We saved it! I swear this time! WE SAVED IT!*

"Ms. MacNamary?" Todd asks. "What—what's going on?"

I get to my feet, vomit threatening to build up and explode out, like the sludge cement we spent all evening pouring.

"No," Kenzie whispers. Her face drains of color. To our other side, Raquel and Eddie edge backward.

"Round them up," Ms. MacNamary says. Then men with guns, including Mr. Stiles and Mr. Fee, move toward us. I take a swing at the one who reaches me first, but he easily scoops me up, carrying me across the cavern.

"Let me go!" I scream. Fury rides off me in waves. "How could you?" I spin toward Ms. MacNamary, pounding my fists into the back of the man holding me. I kick at his stomach, but he doesn't seem to care.

"You were supposed to be on our side!" Todd yells.

Kenzie, swearing up an inarticulate storm, gets shoved into one of the pods by the wall and locked into it. I realize that's where I'm heading, too, and fight even harder.

"*Why are you doing this?*" Wyatt screams.

"We had to get you to finish the job," Ms. MacNamary explains. Her entire demeanor has changed. "We can't fit down those tunnels, and we needed the cement laid."

"I should never have trusted you," Raquel says, getting locked into a pod herself and glaring at Ms. MacNamary. She might as well glare at me, too. It's my fault she and Eddie went along with any of this. The guilt rips through me like a white-hot bolt of lightning.

My fingernails scrape into the man carrying me—more like *dragging* me by now—and I'm thrown into a pod, as well. The cage bars slam in front of me, locking me in.

"You filthy *snotfaced*—!" Kenzie launches into a string of swears. The betrayal pours out of her in painful bursts, like a string of manic geysers, and my heart crumbles into pieces in my chest. We're all locked up now, helpless as the men lower their guns and go back to stand with Dr. Grier, Ms. MacNamary, and Nolan.

"Nolan!" Eddie reaches out. "Why are you doing this? Why are you *with* them?"

Nolan sets his shoulders, shoving his hands in his sweatshirt pocket. His hood weighs down behind him, presumably because his ferrets are in it. "Because as backward as it first sounds—and trust me, I know where you're coming from—this is the only way to save Earth," he says.

"They're not saving it, they're trying to *trigger* the supervolcano!" I say.

"I know," Nolan says. "That's the whole point."

I stare, my mouth falling open. He's *on their side.* Raquel was right not to try to save him!

Dr. Grier steps forward. "Listen," she says. "You may yet understand and agree to join us. Our work isn't done. Yellowstone is just the first site."

"Why'd you have us stop it up, then?" Kenzie turns to Ms. MacNamary, shaking her cage bars. "If you want to make it blow, why'd you have us block it with cement?"

Ms. MacNamary regards Kenzie, her eyes cool and calculating. There is nothing about her that even *remotely* reminds me of the warm and caring park manager we've gotten to know all summer, or even the broken woman we've been working with all day today. No, she's someone else entirely. And this is the first time we're seeing her for who she really is. "We had to save our equipment. The real site of eruption will be over a mile south of here. That's what Nolan's been helping me with. He's worked on the surface, directly above your beta tunnels, laying charges to make a different opening for the eruption. The vent we've always intended on using."

Nolan straightens at that, looking serious and important.

"Blocking the alpha tunnel was part of the summer plan all along," Ms. MacNamary says. "You all just ran away before we could get you to do it. We had to convince you to come back, you see?"

Pain and rage pound inside my chest. "I just . . . I don't understand."

"Then let me tell you a story," Ms. MacNamary says, her voice biting. "About a young girl, like you, who cared a lot about saving the world." She walks back and forth between us. "Her family was wiped out in the floodwaters of a hurricane—the first storm to be directly linked to climate change. She grew up and went to law school. She landed a job in the government. She was an environmental lawyer—fighting to get the whole world on board with lowering carbon emissions, going green, saving wild spaces, everything. And do you know what her government did?"

Nolan crosses his arms.

"They fired her. She was 'too much trouble.' And then they went ahead and made it *easier* for people to get away with destroying our planet. But that's when I met Samantha. She saw things my way. And that's when we figured out how to make a real difference."

"A real difference," I repeat, shaking my head. "Are you *hearing* yourself?"

"My mom wasn't happy about the government ignoring the environment, either, but she never decided the best thing to do was to kill off billions of innocent people," Wyatt says.

"Then she wasn't thinking big enough!" Ms. MacNamary snaps.

Wyatt's eyes harden, and I can see tears glisten in them even though he's several pods down from me.

"The point is," Dr. Grier cuts in. "We've been fighting this fight for decades, and nothing is changing for the better. We are officially in the sixth mass extinction. Earth has always bounced back after mass extinctions, if it gets the chance to heal. We are going to speed things along to give it that chance."

"Samantha found the way," Ms. MacNamary says. "Not only will we kill most of humanity, we will trigger global cooling in the process. That's what's so brilliant about using volcanoes!"

"Yellowstone is our starting point," Dr. Grier explains. "Easily, a decade of global cooling, just from the aerosols that will enter our atmosphere from this one alone. But we'll need others to keep the process going, especially if we want to permanently reduce the human population of the planet. We've begun work on two other supervolcanoes. That's where you all come in."

"Us?" Eddie asks.

My stomach churns with the knowledge that Yellowstone is just the *first* supervolcano they're planning on blowing.

"You are the experts," Dr. Grier says, looking at each of us in turn. "You can help us at our other sites, just like James and Carlos are doing."

Eddie gasps. "They're alive?!"

Raquel lets out an inarticulate noise somewhere between relief and terror.

"Yes, of course," Dr. Grier says. "Why would we waste their experience? They're valuable members of our team."

"*Valuable members*—what?!" Eddie asks. "After how you treated us, that's what you think of us as?"

"She doesn't mean *we're* valuable," Raquel says. "She means our work is valuable. Big difference."

"Their sites are underway, but not nearly as far along," Dr. Grier continues, as if not hearing them at all. "We'd hoped the LA quake would be enough of a distraction for the world's geologists, but they're starting to sniff around."

"Wait—did you *cause* the LA quake?" I ask, my brain tripping over itself with the influx of all this horrific information.

Now Raquel and Eddie both cry out.

"It was a relatively simple seismic event to control," Dr. Grier says. "But as I said, it's not providing as much of a distraction as we'd hoped, so we need to move on all of our sites more rapidly than planned. I've really appreciated your recording of your methods, by the way, Bri. Those will be of great use."

I gag, thinking about my videos serving as a training resource for more destruction.

"You caused the LA quake, killed our friends, stole us from our families—" Eddie can't get the words out fast enough. He grips the bars of his pod, shaking them. "You're monsters!"

"We're human; we tend to be monsters by instinct," Ms. MacNamary says.

"We're trying not to be, though," Dr. Grier explains. "If you'll help us, you'll see."

"Why would we help you cause a mass extinction?" Todd asks, paling more by the moment.

"Because we're already in one!" Ms. MacNamary snaps. "Weren't you listening? We are just moving it faster and setting the world back to the way it should be."

"You want to save the environment by destroying it?" I ask. "That makes no sense!"

"Bri, I would think you would understand better than anyone." Dr. Grier looks at me in surprise. "Your documentary with your aunt last summer was about regrowth—the fires in Yellowstone that allow for new trees to grow into new forests. That's a crucial part of our ecosystem."

"The natural ones, maybe," I say, gripping my bars like Eddie gripped his. "What you're doing is the opposite of that."

"As Samantha said, we're already in a period of unnatural disaster," Ms. MacNamary explains. "We have to take responsibility for that and come up with a solution. The time for small efforts has long passed. Drastic action is the only choice we have."

"So your solution is to set off not just one but multiple supervolcanoes, kill billions of people, and throw the planet into an endless winter," Wyatt says.

"If all goes well, yes," Dr. Grier says.

"People will survive," Eddie says, his voice filled with determination. "They always do. I've never seen an apocalypse movie where they don't."

"Of course they will," Ms. MacNamary says. "At least, the right people will."

Dr. Grier nods. "Yes. And that *could* include the six of you. We'd like to invite you to join us, like Nolan has."

I squeeze the bars of my pod so tight my knuckles hurt. Once upon a time, Dr. Grier had said she wanted me as her student in the future. Was this what she was talking about?!

"Are you freaking *serious*?" Kenzie retorts. A tear falls down her dusty face and she hocks a massive wad of spit in Ms. MacNamary's direction. "How far out of reality are you *living* right now? You think there's any chance any of us would want to help you kill everyone?!"

"I told you she'd swing one way or the other," Ms. MacNamary says to Dr. Grier. "With her loathing of authority, there was the chance she'd take our side."

"Like hell I would!" Kenzie screams.

"She's not someone who is going to change her mind once it's made up, though," Ms. MacNamary continues. "We should probably just kill her before she causes any real trouble."

"You kill her, and you lose any chance of anyone else joining you," I say quickly. I'm seething and shaking. Ms. MacNamary fooled us all. She's worse than Dr. Grier. She's . . . she's . . .

Dr. Grier and Ms. MacNamary both turn, regarding me. I let my hatred flow out of my eyes and stare them down.

"Bri, I've always admired your creativity and logic," Dr. Grier says. "I told you—I would be very interested in working with you more. I hope you give our offer to join us serious thought while we're gone. Don't let your peers sway your decision."

"Gone?" I ask, even as I feel like I might hurl at the idea that these murderers think I would ever join their side.

"We have to set this in motion," Dr. Grier says. "You will be safe in here during the initial eruption, don't worry. Plugging up this tunnel ensured that. Though, I really would caution against trying to escape. We can't predict exactly where things will be safe beyond this cave."

"Then where will *you* all be?" Raquel asks.

Ms. MacNamary narrows her eyes at her. I get the feeling that Raquel is someone Ms. MacNamary wouldn't mind losing along with Kenzie. "We'll return here to take shelter and gather our things once the last pieces are in place. Nolan," she says, turning. "We'll need you with us."

He nods. I glare at him. Even though he was never really a part of our group, he still feels like a traitor for siding with the adults. Buggy pops out of his hood and sniffs around.

"We'll leave Fee and Stiles as guards, so don't try anything," Ms. MacNamary says. "They can escort you for bathroom breaks, and they'll see that you get food and water. Until we know you're with us, we can't risk you wandering around on your own. Hopefully you'll see some reason before we pack this whole place up. Then you can escape with us. I'd hate to leave any of you to wait for the supervolcano itself. After all, even after we set off the initial eruption, the full supervolcano could still be days or weeks away, which would mean a pretty slow death for you, probably from starvation."

Then Nolan, Dr. Grier, and Ms. MacNamary are gone.

Hours tick by. We all go through various stages of crying, yelling, or staring numbly at the wall. Our guards, true to Ms. MacNamary's word, do allow us out for bathroom breaks, but so far I haven't been able to figure out a way to escape during any of those. Not when there's a gun pointed at me.

I wait for the return of Dr. Grier and Ms. MacNamary, cursing myself out for trusting Ms. MacNamary in the first place. Especially after knowing what she allowed to happen to Raquel and Eddie. What was I thinking? How could I let myself be tricked so easily? *Twice?*

But I know how, and I know why. Locked in this pod, remembering all the videos I took in here, all the time I spent daydreaming about view counts . . .

It's because I wanted to save the day. But it's also because, deep down, I wanted other people to *see* me save the day. I wanted to impress Aunt Pauline. I wanted to prove to my parents that I was destined for *way* more spectacular things than simply going to med school.

"Nobody gets famous by being a doctor," I'd always tell my mom.

"You're famous to the people you save," she'd reply.

But now I'm saving no one.

I slowly chew on a bite of granola bar that Fee gave me a few minutes ago while I look up and down the line of pods at my friends. I think about everything they've worked toward and suffered through, and wonder why I never thought about any of *them* becoming famous. *How did I ever believe I had what it took to be a hero when I couldn't even think about anyone but myself?*

But before I can answer my own question, we're plunged into darkness.

CHAPTER SIXTEEN

"What the heck?" I hear Kenzie ask.

"Fee, go check on that," Stiles says.

Fee flips on his headlamp. Then it shatters as someone clubs him in the head.

"What the—?" Stiles begins, but then he's hit, too. "Son of a—!"

Neither of them are struck hard enough to be knocked out, but the blows are enough to make them both stumble about and cry in pain.

"Come on!" I hear a voice say from several pods down. Someone's door swings open. For a brief moment, I think it might be Ms. MacNamary, as some sort of triple agent. But then the next door opens, and the mystery voice is closer, and I realize it's not a woman's voice—it's a boy's.

It's Nolan!

"Get him!" Stiles yells, finding Nolan in the light of his head-lamp.

Fee dives after him, but Raquel and Eddie are both loose now and each jump on one of them. I can only make parts of the fighting out. But then another door swings open, and I realize Nolan must've gotten free from the men to bust the next person out.

Unfortunately for Mr. Stiles and Mr. Fee, the next person is Kenzie.

"*I'm going to rip your faces off!*" she hollers, grabbing a rock off the cavern floor and leaping into the fray.

Everyone's shouting in the dark now: Todd trying to tell them to be careful, Wyatt trying to direct them how to fend off the men, and me trying to cheer them on.

I hear a whimper, and I realize that Raquel's been hit—bad. Nolan unlocks the last three pods, including my own, and I leap out. "Raquel!" I call, looking for any sign of her.

There, on the floor, not far from me. I can just make out her outline in the flashing, twisting light from Mr. Stiles's head-lamp. I run toward her. She clutches at her stomach, rolling to one side.

"Stay still," I say. She winces and nods. I turn, trying to figure out where in the fight I'd be most useful. But then—

Bang!

Someone's shot a gun. Everyone stops.

Stiles turns to face Wyatt, who stands with a gun aimed at the mess of people on the cavern floor. I don't know whose gun he got—Stiles's or Fee's—but Fee is buried under Nolan, Todd, and Eddie, and Stiles doesn't look like he's ready to reach for anything, so I'm guessing it's Stiles's. Kenzie is on his back, wrapping her arms around his neck in a chokehold.

"Okay," Wyatt says. He aims the gun at Stiles. "You, get in a pod."

Stiles, who is struggling to breathe, glares. Spittle drips from his mouth.

"I'm not messing around here," Wyatt says, stepping forward. "I live in Texas. My dad's taken me to gun ranges. I know what I'm doing. Pod. Now."

Fee tries to lunge forward, but Nolan, who was sitting on top of his back, holds on tighter. Todd helps Nolan push Fee back down, and the man's face slams into the rocky cave floor. Fee grunts, rolling to one side and clutching at his nose.

Eddie, who had been on him, too, grabs for Fee's gun. Shaking, Eddie stands up, aiming it at Fee despite looking really uncomfortable.

"My mom would kill me if she could see me right now," he mutters. "Don't make me use this."

Fee and Stiles both back up toward the pods. Kenzie releases her chokehold on Stiles and drops to the ground.

"That's it," Wyatt says, far more calm about this than Eddie. "Into the pods."

They each climb into one, grumbling. Fee still clutches his nose, which is gushing blood, much like the cut on his forehead under his bashed headlamp.

I take the chance to help Raquel to her feet. "I'm all right," she reassures me. "Just got the wind knocked out of me."

Nolan locks Mr. Stiles and Mr. Fee into the pods that used to contain Kenzie and Eddie. It is a tight fit for them, even without the equipment stored in there. They're crammed, smushed against the bars, both bent over. Todd takes Stiles's headlamp and brings it over to us. Nolan moves to join our little circle.

"Not so fast," Kenzie says, stomping up to Nolan's face and glaring. The lights are still out, but I can see Todd wince thanks to the headlamp he's holding. "What's your deal? What are you doing? Why are you here?"

Nolan whistles, and the lights pops back on. His two ferrets come bounding out from around the cavern's edge and climb right up his legs into the hood of his sweatshirt.

"Did your ferrets just turn the lights on?" Wyatt asks in awe. I blink in the sudden brightness.

"Yeah," Nolan answers, giving them each a small treat of some sort from his jean pockets. Eddie looks impressed.

"While cool, very cool—*don't care right now*," Kenzie says. "What are you *doing*?"

"Seriously," I agree. "We've had way too many side switches. You'd better have a real explanation here, and one we can trust."

"I'm playing the only card I had going for me," Nolan replies. Baxter pokes his head out of the sweatshirt hood, looking for more treats. "You have no idea how long I've had to pretend to agree with my aunt's plans. I'm throwing it out now, because we have to get to the eruption site and stop them from syncing the receivers."

214

"The receivers?" I ask. "For what?"

"For the bombs." He turns to me. "Your tunnels aren't the only things set to explode. Ms. MacNamary had me working at the site where they want the first eruption to happen. Not drilling, like you. Just weaving a net of explosives from the surface down toward where your tunnels are. That's what's going to create the real exit spot for the magma. We have to catch up and stop them, and I can't do it alone."

Wyatt sets the gun down and readjusts the layers of socks that his prosthetic fits over. "Last time we helped someone do something that was supposedly for good, we just made things worse," he says, pulling his prosthetic back into position. "How's this supposed to be any different?"

"Exactly," I say, even though my mind is already running with the tidbit of information we finally got about what Nolan has been doing this whole time.

"Look," Nolan says. "I get it. I have no idea how to make you trust me. Maybe because I sprung you out? What more do you want from me?"

"Come on, guys," Eddie says, stepping to stand closer to Nolan. "I believe him."

We all exchange glances. Raquel gives Eddie an exasperated look, but he doesn't notice.

"Please," Nolan begs. "I *suck* at people things. I have no idea how else to convince you. But we really can't waste time."

"Nolan," I say slowly. I think I have a way to test him. "What would you say if I said we should go call for help? Get some adults here to handle this instead of kids?"

"Help sounds like a really good idea," Nolan agrees. "They must have phones back at the camp. Let's check on our way out."

My stomach knots unfurl. Someone who actually is in favor of calling for outside help. Finally!

"I think we can trust him, guys," I say. "Even Ms. MacNamary couldn't come up with a scheme that has *this* many double crosses."

Raquel regards me. In turn, Eddie watches her, holding his breath. "Okay," she eventually says.

I give her the giantest look of thanks I can muster. She really doesn't have to trust my instincts after I failed her with Ms. MacNamary. Meanwhile, Eddie gives Raquel a solid, relieved nod. Raquel smiles at him, and I realize with a small degree of embarrassment that maybe Raquel isn't just trusting *my* opinion about Nolan.

"I'm with Bri on this, too," Kenzie says. "But I've got my eye on you, buddy."

"Todd? Wyatt?" I turn to the other boys.

Todd looks hesitant but nods. Wyatt does the same. Then Wyatt picks the gun near him back up and he and Eddie drop both guns into the extra cement sludge, where they sink slowly into the gunk. We head back to camp, leaving Stiles and Fee locked up. Wyatt kicks some rock dust at them on his way out, and they shout some nasty remarks back at him.

"So how did you train those ferrets to do the lights thing?" Kenzie asks, falling into step with Nolan as we walk.

"Baxter and Buggy have won several awards," Nolan says, straightening up like a proud father. Eddie jogs up to walk with Nolan and Kenzie. "Ferrets are very smart, you know. I have them trained to follow certain commands. It's why my aunt wanted me here. She needed Buggy and Baxter to maneuver through animal burrows and cracks underground to lay a bunch of explosives."

"Can ferrets do something that complicated?" I ask.

"Baxter and Buggy won the National Ferret Agility Awards two years ago—it's like a huge obstacle course challenge, where ferrets have to thread string the whole way," Nolan replies. "Once upon a time, ferrets were used to run wiring in airplanes and buildings."

"That's so cool!" Eddie says. "Why'd people stop using them for that stuff?"

"Because ferrets sleep eighteen hours a day," Nolan answers. "They'd pass out on the job and not get it done. Buggy and Baxter do that from time to time, too, but not as much as some people's. I've got them well trained. My parents never really liked it, though. They barely ever came to any of my competitions."

I try to imagine my own parents sitting and watching their kid whistle and clap for two small furry creatures as they weave through pipes on stage somewhere.

"Anyway, Aunt Sam always did. She was the only one who seemed to care about my hobby. In hindsight, I know why. When she kidnapped me and brought me out here, she had me use Buggy and Baxter for her creepy plan," Nolan continues. "You know those tunnels you built?"

"The beta tunnels?" Wyatt asks.

"Yeah," Nolan replies. "Well, if you add up the full distance the alpha tunnel runs, those beta tunnels are actually located over a mile south of this cave. And straight up from them, way above the alpha tunnel, there's a smaller series of cracks through the Earth that are way too tiny for drills, but just big enough for ferrets. That's where Buggy and Baxter worked. I sat above ground, and they ran down animal burrows, finding cracks off of them to thread explosives through. When your beta tunnels burst, Aunt Sam will also blow up the web they made."

"It'll be like an explosion sandwich," Kenzie says, her eyes widening. "The alpha tunnel is the peanut butter, our beta tunnels are the bread on the bottom, and the network your ferrets ran is the bread on the top!"

"Uh, sure," Nolan says. "If that makes sense to you."

"The pressure drop from above will not only cause a nice big exit path for the magma, it'll also collapse what remains of the roof of the bedrock," Wyatt realizes. "That'll really get the eruption started."

"And after that eruption goes, the supervolcano is basically inevitable." I think back to Ms. MacNamary's slides. Once there's an exit for even a small amount of lava, it's only a matter of time before the supervolcano blows. It's a constant feedback loop of pressure drops: as mass is ejected through an initial eruption, space is cleared underground for more froth and bubbles to form. And that encourages more erupting. It'll build until the underground chamber has a catastrophically huge amount of magma—and then . . . boom.

"How did they get you to do all this?" Todd asks. "Were you lied to at first, too?"

"Not even close," Nolan says. "They made me wear a vest filled with explosives for the first couple of months. Even Buggy and Baxter had some rigged into their harnesses, to make sure I'd do exactly what they asked."

My hand covers my mouth. I nearly trip over a rock as we walk. "Your own *aunt*—?"

"But then I started to play a game," Nolan continues. "I pretended that they were winning me over. That I was interested in being one of the survivors in their new world. Aunt Sam began to trust me, slowly. Ms. MacNamary took longer, though, so she often insisted I stay locked up—which is when I'd be thrown back in with you guys." Nolan gestures at Eddie and Raquel. "But I kept up the act, and eventually Ms. MacNamary bought it. She even gave me a tablet as a present for keeping my mouth shut when you four showed up." Now he nods at me, Wyatt, Kenzie, and Todd. "What you have to understand is that they really believe what they're doing is the right thing. And they think others will believe it, too. The other adults here agree with them. Why not a kid like me? Or you guys? It's why you're not dead yet."

"Oh my gosh," I say, a thought hitting me.

"Yeah, Grier and MacNamary have absolutely no idea how

wrong they are," Kenzie says.

"No, not that—well, yes, but that's not what I meant." I stare at Nolan as we reach the camp. "Your tablet."

"What about it?" Nolan asks. Baxter climbs out of his hood and scoots down his sweatshirt to move into the front pocket. Buggy follows suit.

"We could search all we want for our phones, but they don't work, and I'm willing to bet it's *not* because we don't get signal. They must've blocked them somehow," I say as the group gathers around me. "But Nolan could watch shows on that tablet. It's got internet access. We can use it to call for help."

"I don't know," Nolan says. "I was just watching previously downloaded stuff. I couldn't stream anything. They've got it locked so only a few apps work—none that actually allowed me to communicate with anyone. Not even my parents." His eyes drift for a moment.

"Puh," Kenzie snorts. "Child locks? My grandma put those on everything we own. I can get past them, no problem."

Our faces light up.

"Where do you think it is?" Raquel asks.

"Probably with my camera in Dr. Grier's cabin," I say. "I'm sure she wanted to keep a close eye on any electronics."

No one wastes another second. We all pound our feet across the camp. Dr. Grier's cabin is locked when we reach it, but that doesn't stop anyone.

Raquel drags a chair over, and Todd climbs up it to take on the door hinges with his drill. He decimates the wood, making hole after hole after hole. Kenzie goes after the lower hinge. Sawdust flies, and finally, enough damage is done that we can bash the hinges out. Then Nolan and I grab the door and yank it back, pulling it to the ground.

There's my camera, lying out in the open on her desk. Right next to Nolan's tablet!

"Yes!" I dart into the cabin and grab the tablet. "Do your thing," I tell Kenzie, handing it to her.

She doesn't take the tablet from me, though. "Guys . . ." Kenzie slowly spins, staring at the walls. "Look."

I glance around to see what she's talking about, and my mouth drops open.

Dr. Grier's cabin is lined with headlines from articles.

CONGRESS VOTES TO DEFUND ALL CLIMATE RESEARCH

THIRD ARCTIC OIL SPILL IN AS MANY YEARS

BLACK RHINOS OFFICIALLY EXTINCT IN THE WILD

AIR POLLUTION LINKED TO SPIKE IN LUNG CANCER DEATHS

OZONE HOLE BACK WITH A VENGEANCE

ISLANDS DISAPPEAR WORLDWIDE AS OCEANS CONTINUE TO RISE

SOUTH AMERICAN RAINFORESTS DROP TO TWO PERCENT OF ORIGINAL ACREAGE

EIGHTY-FIVE PERCENT OF SPECIES WILL BE LOST BY 2045

A NEW HURRICANE STATUS DECLARED: THREE
STORMS ELEVATED TO CATEGORY SIX
THE TURNING POINT FOR CLIMATE CHANGE
HAS LONG SINCE PAST: THIS IS THE END

"Well, I can see her motives," I say.

Eddie lets out a low whistle, and we all huddle a little closer together. The air in the cabin is still, and my hair prickles on my arms.

"Hey, um," Raquel says, breaking the tense atmosphere. "Just throwing this out there, but if Dr. Grier left all her stuff in here, don't we think she might be back for it at some point?"

"And not just for her stuff—for us, too, remember?" Wyatt adds.

That is a very good point. They did say they were coming back to get their supplies. We can't stay here.

Kenzie snatches the tablet from me and throws it in a backpack from under Dr. Grier's desk.

"Let's take the tablet and catch a signal somewhere else!" Todd says.

"Yup, yup, yup," Kenzie agrees. I take the bag from her, and everyone runs out the door. I hesitate, looking down at my camera. It's not the fun toy it once was. Now it's just a reminder of how I let my ego blind me. But yet . . .

I still can't part with it. I put my camera and charger into the bag with the tablet, heft it onto my back, and hit the ground running, chasing everyone else.

The herd of us clamber up the spiral staircase—not at all

worried about noise now—and straight out the cave entrance.

The sun hits me. It's morning. Which means we were locked up all night. No wonder my body feels like jelly. I put a hand up to cover my eyes.

"This way," Wyatt says, motioning us down the hill.

"Wait!" Eddie yells. "Look!" He points, and I walk backward so fast that my back slams into the cliff wall. I wince as the electronics get jabbed into my spine.

Down the hill from the cave, in the open field, Dr. Grier, Ms. MacNamary, and their miniature army are getting out of their cars.

"No," Kenzie whispers. "No way, they can't be back from setting up already!"

"There wasn't much left to do," Nolan says, his voice grim.

My fingernails dig into the rock behind me, scraping along its edge. One of the men looks up at us and points.

They see us. No one moves.

"We can still stop them from pressing the button," Eddie says, hoarse. Puffy clouds float behind him, making it look for all the world like we're just out enjoying a peaceful summer morning.

"How?" Todd asks.

Eddie doesn't have an answer.

"We run," I say, desperation flooding me. Dr. Grier and company have already started walking up the main path, trying to shout something at us, but still too far for us to hear them well. "We run, we try to signal for help, and we hope they don't set it off before we can stop them."

"You all better get back inside!" Ms. MacNamary yells from

the path below—her voice finally audible. "It's about to get really unsafe out here."

"*You* all better give up now!" Kenzie retorts. "We're going to tell everyone what you did!"

One of the men steps forward and takes aim with his gun.

"Stop it!" Dr. Grier says, forcing his hand down. "Calm down. Just everyone, calm down."

"Nolan," Ms. MacNamary calls. "What happened? Why would you betray us like this?"

"There are other ways to save the world!" Nolan yells back. "How can you think that triggering the volcanic version of an endless winter is our only option?"

"You're too young to understand!" Ms. MacNamary says. They continue their climb, and I look behind me at the sloping cliffside, wondering if we could manage to run down it without falling. "We can't wait around for the countries of the world to magically band together and save our planet."

"Nolan, please," Dr. Grier begs. "Whether or not you appreciate it now, you've been a major part of this solution. You should get to survive it."

"We're not going to join you!" Kenzie stomps her foot. "You'll have to kill us, and then you won't have anyone left to help you next time!"

"You think you're the only kids we've got?" Ms. MacNamary asks. The whole gang of adults draws closer, and I just want us to stop yelling and *get out of here*. "You're hardly irreplaceable. If you don't agree with us, we aren't going to waste any more time trying to convince you." She turns to the man with the gun. "Shoot them. Better than them messing up our plans."

Kenzie's mouth drops open, and her eyes flood. She looks like she's already been shot.

"Not Nolan!" Dr. Grier insists.

"Guys, move!" I shout, pushing Kenzie and leaping off the side of the entranceway. For a brief moment, we're airborne. Then we hit the ground and tumble down the hill.

Raquel shoves Eddie, and Wyatt, Nolan, and Todd dive after them. Soon, we're all rolling down the cliffside. Raquel and Eddie are the only ones who manage to do so with any kind of grace. The rocky surface slams into me over and over, and I pull my arms and legs in, throwing my hands over my head to protect it.

"Run!" I instruct when we reach the bottom where the meadow is. I scramble to my feet in the grass, trying to ignore the fresh bruises all over my body.

"Now, do it now!" I hear Ms. MacNamary screaming. *"Do it now!"*

"Wait!" Dr. Grier shouts. "We need to get our equipment packed out!"

We race across the meadow, their voices getting farther away.

"We don't have time for that, they're about to ruin everything!" Ms. MacNamary yells. "Give me that!"

There's one moment of complete stillness as my brain processes that they must be fighting over the detonator. Then a massive rumble starts up below our feet. The ground shakes, waves rolling through it. I clutch at a tree as we reach the meadow's edge. After catching my footing, I bolt into the woods, jumping over roots and dodging branches, trying desperately not to fall over as the ground moves under us. Raquel pushes Wyatt along, refusing to let him fall behind, and I can hear them arguing.

They've set off the explosives. It's too late, I realize.

Oh god.

It's too late.

In a blur, we exit the patch of trees, reaching the second drop-off point. Everyone pauses here, catching our breath, no one daring to get near the edge of the hill for fear of it collapsing from the moving earth. It's like an amusement park ride that doesn't know how to stop. I hear cracks behind me—trees toppling, crashing through each other. Animals race past us. A whole family of elk bound across the meadow in the valley below.

"No!" Kenzie shrieks. She falls to the ground, grabbing fistfuls of grass and chucking them. We all drop to the dirt with her, flattening, trying to hold on and hoping the quake stops soon.

For a brief moment, the ground calms. Then, an enormous, bone-shaking *boom* sounds in the distance. It's like a gunshot, but a million times louder. My eardrums *scream*.

I stumble to my feet, throw my hands over my ears, and look southwest over the park. I don't want to see it. *I don't want to—* but there's no way to ignore what just happened.

From a deathly dark ruptured hole in the ground, a massive cloud of ash explodes upward into the blue sky. And raining down from it are the unmistakable drops of glowing bright orange molten rock.

CHAPTER SEVENTEEN

"No," Wyatt whispers.

I can't tear my eyes away from it. Lava falls as heavy splotches and tiny flecks. Dark, billowing gray clouds expand upward as the roar of the explosion continues. A tidal wave of ash, dust, and gas—pyroclastic surge, my mind reminds me—bursts out in all directions.

Including straight at us.

"Run!" Todd yells.

Even though we're uphill from the surge, I do as he says. We flee back into the trees, each using one as a shield and cowering.

The noise is tremendous. I wonder if that family of elk in the valley made it out in time. The eruption is over a mile away, but at the speed that cloud of hot ash is moving . . .

There must be death. A great deal of death. And not just the elk. This is peak tourist season. People have just died. A lot of them.

I clutch my chest, having no idea if we'll be next.

Ash falls from the sky, filtering through the pine trees overhead until it lands on our skin. Warm flakes. The tree I'm hiding behind starts smoldering.

"There's going to be a fire!" I stand up quickly, shouting at the group. "We have to move!"

"Where?" Wyatt asks.

"The caves!" Eddie suggests.

"They'll kill us if we go back there," Nolan says, keeping his hands in his front pocket to stop his ferrets from escaping and fleeing into the deadly surroundings.

"We have to get someplace rocky," I say. "Where the fire can't reach us."

"Let's move up," Raquel says. "High ground first, then we need to find a way down to low ground or we may end up trapped."

"None of that will matter if the full supervolcano erupts!" Kenzie says. "What then? Huh? What then?"

"We have some time before that point," I say, thinking about my simulations. "Let's worry about *this* eruption first!"

Besides, if it does go faster than it did in my simulations, there's nowhere in Yellowstone that will be safe. Nowhere in the Northwest that will be safe.

So it's better to not think about.

We start moving. The ash cloud rains more and more as we struggle over branches, walking through the forest. Everything is hot and gray. Squirrels run by, kicking up clouds of dust. Birds continue to scatter in all directions—which is a little intimidating when they're doing it all at once, but also a relief that none of them are dropping dead. The air is still okay to breathe.

Behind us, even though it's over a mile away, I imagine I can feel the heat of the lava pouring out over the park landscape. Or maybe that's a forest fire starting.

Either way, my heart breaks. Yellowstone is dying.

Then—I hear it. Trucks.

"Stop, guys, stop!" I say. Raquel holds out her hand, and we all pause. We're at the edge of the wooded area where we first met Dr. Grier all those weeks ago. In the distance, I can just make out some of Grier and MacNamary's men, dusting off pickup trucks and backing them through the meadow to the cave hill.

"They must be preparing to move the equipment out," Wyatt says.

I nod, watching one truck with a giant coiled up hose.

"How do we get away now?" Eddie asks.

"We don't, until they're gone," Raquel says. "Stay low. Don't let them see you."

We hunker down behind a shield of large shrubs and young pine trees. I try not to think about all the death and destruction that's taking place, but I can't help it. We played a part in this. It's on us. Yellowstone is dying. It's going to take us all with it soon enough. And I had a direct part in making that happen.

It's like some awful, real-life version of Earth Builder.

"*Sólo quería regresar a casa,*" Eddie says to Raquel from

behind the bushes hiding us.

"*Lo sé. Yo también*," Raquel replies, putting a hand on his back.

I think I know what they said. *Home.* But there's no more home for any of us. Not after this. The smell of smoke only grows. It's the beginning of the end.

Around me, I can hear all of us crying. Some loudly, some hiccupping out tears, others barely letting more than a whimper escape. We're all petrified. Unable to move. Unable to process. Just . . . horrified. Horrified and lost.

In desperation, I pull out my camera from the backpack and turn it on.

"Hey, everyone," I say into it. "Bri here. I want to say I'm sorry." My eyes water, stinging through the hot air. "I messed up. I thought we were helping to stop the supervolcano under Yellowstone, but it turns out we were helping to start it up."

"What are you doing?" Raquel asks me.

"Bri's a documentarian," Kenzie says, wiping her face on her sleeve. "For her aunt's YouTube channel."

It's like their voices are miles away right now. I retreat farther into myself, repeating my apology over and over into the camera.

"I'm sorry," I say, choking. "I'm no hero at all. I don't know why I ever thought I could be. Look where that got us. I'm *sorry.*" The camera shakes in my hands. "I'm *so* sorry, this is my fault, it's my fault, I'm sorry . . ."

Something bumps my shoulder. I startle, looking down. Kenzie scoots into frame, shoving herself into me.

230

"*We* screwed up," she agrees, steely eyed. A cloud of smoke billows past her. "But we're trying to find a way to fix it."

I gape at her. A hiccup escapes. "We are?"

"Yeah," she smiles rebelliously at me. "Do you want your documentary to have a happy ending, or a tragic one?"

"Um . . . happy?" I say. The sky darkens overhead, and the last bit of sunlight gets blocked. Our shadows disappear on the forest floor. "But—"

"The supervolcano hasn't erupted yet," Kenzie says. Half of her ponytail has fallen out of its hair tie, but she doesn't seem to care or notice. "Just because murder pals MacNamary and Grier said we can't stop it once the process starts doesn't mean we have to listen to them. Listening to adults is overrated anyway, am I right?"

I watch, amazed. Kenzie rises to the occasion, with all eyes *and* a camera on her. She really *is* a natural. Aunt Pauline would love her.

"We just have to think—what can stop a supervolcano? Wyatt?" She turns, pointing at Wyatt, who looks startled.

"Me?"

"Yeah? Ideas? You were from Hawaii before you moved to Texas. Your mom worked for the national park there. What did you guys do about volcanoes that got out of hand?"

"Well, people would build barriers," he says, playing with a twig from the bushes next to us. "Ways to direct the lava flow or contain it. No one ever could stop an eruption, though."

"Where would you direct the lava?" Todd asks, half paying

attention and half watching the men in the meadow move their trucks around.

"To the ocean, usually."

"Water," I realize, wiping at my eyes. "We need water."

"Water?" Nolan asks.

I hand my camera to Kenzie, who takes it greedily. "Water to freeze the lava," I explain, sliding a bunch of leaves aside on the ground to get at the dirt. "To turn it solid and plug up its exit. Contain the pressure, just like Ms. MacNamary was saying about the cement in the cave."

"But that cement thing was a trick," Eddie says.

"Yes, it was. They made another exit for the magma." I nod to Nolan and begin to trace out a replica of our tunnel system in the dirt. A long, swooping line for the alpha tunnel. A magma chamber deep down. Beta tunnels linking the alpha tunnel to the chamber. "Your site is where the eruption's really happening." I make a crosshatched network above our beta tunnels to show where Nolan worked.

Buggy's rear end gets shoved out of his sweatshirt pocket as Baxter tries to hide from the increasing amounts of smoke. Nolan nods in return to me, then coughs.

"So we need to plug up the real exit to stop the pressure release," I say, trying not to cough myself. I draw in the eruption and the magma coming up through the beta tunnels, then bursting up to the surface through Nolan's crosshatched area. "There've been plenty of quakes in this region before—quakes that shake things up a bit, causing increases in geyser activity and stuff. But then they settle as the pressure goes back to a stable point. We need to stabilize things underground. Stop the ejection of lava, keep it crammed in there."

Todd looks thoughtful. "Volcanoes *do* need just the right circumstances to blow up. As long as there's not another easy way out for the magma, it should stay underground, settling over time."

"Like a bottle of soda going flat in the fridge," Kenzie says.

"Exactly," Todd says, blushing as Kenzie zooms in on him.

"But how do we plug up an actively spewing volcano?" Eddie asks. "Walk up to it and dump buckets of water on top?"

"The water will explode," Todd says. Raquel winces. "We superheat water like that, and it's just going to blow up in our faces."

"Tell me about it," Kenzie says. She spins the camera at herself and arches an eyebrow, showing off the remains of her scars. I *knew* she would make a great filming partner.

"Well, then we're back to square one." Eddie frowns.

"No, we're not," Wyatt says. "If we have enough water— continuous water—we can stop it. That's what we do with the ocean."

"Where are we going to get that much water?" Nolan asks.

My mind is already on top of that. "Yellowstone Lake," I say, my thoughts returning to last summer's documentary. "It's huge. We just need to pump the water from it—"

"What, straight down the lava vent?" Kenzie asks. "That won't work."

"No, not at first." I shake my head, then point at the place on my diagram where the magma rises to the surface in the newly exploded exit tunnel. "First, we need to get at it from below ground. Narrow the exit tunnel to slow the amount of magma that can come out of it. Maybe after that, we can control it from above."

"You don't mean . . ." Raquel looks at me.

"I do," I say, the plan forming in my mind. "We need to drill another tunnel. One that goes underground and connects to the tunnel of rising magma. Then we need to run some kind of hose down the new tunnel." I trace it out, then look between all my friends. "And . . . yeah. Whoosh."

Everyone stares at me. I know it sounds ludicrous. But what else can we do?

"You're serious," Nolan says, blinking.

"How are we supposed to do that?" Kenzie actually lowers the camera in shock. "It takes weeks to drill, even if we had the right equipment!"

"No idea," I say, wiping sweat off my face as the heat rises. "But I can't think of any other way to stop this thing. Can any of you?"

Raquel and Eddie exchange glances.

"Actually . . . " Eddie starts slowly. Next to him, Raquel wraps her arms around her knees, burying her head. "We might not need to drill much. When we started here, we were drilling in a different location until the accident."

Raquel nods into her knees. "They moved us then. But we were pretty far along."

"Where is this other location?" I ask them, trying not to get too excited.

"I didn't know it at the time," Eddie says. "They didn't tell us much. But I think it's near your lake. We could hear people during the day. We were in a cabin someplace—I'm not sure exactly where. But once someone stopped by and asked for directions, and Stiles told them to follow the signs to Yellowstone Lake, and that they weren't far."

Excited, I add their old tunnel to my drawing. It swoops in from the opposite direction of the alpha tunnel, but I make it turn horizontally far earlier. "Perfect. We can work from there, extending it to reach the magma tunnel!" I exclaim, stretching the horizontal line I'm drawing until it hits the exit path of the magma.

A crack in the woods behind us makes us all jump—a tree has caught on fire and fallen over.

"Okay, running now, planning later," Todd says.

"What about the men?" Wyatt asks, pointing at the trucks being loaded in the distance.

I bite at my lip, chancing a glance at the meadow over the bushes—it would be great to steal one of the trucks with all that equipment they're loading if we really are going to try to tackle my plan. But I don't know how to drive, and the men loading the trucks are armed and dangerous.

"Anyone have any ideas for how we could take one of their trucks and the equipment with us?" I ask. "We're going to need a drill. And a pump. And hoses."

Another tree catches on fire behind us.

"I like your thinking," Raquel says, "but if we stay here any longer, we won't be alive to try your idea at all."

I nod. Avoiding dying is a good priority. Kenzie shoves my camera back at me, and I flip the power off and put it in the backpack. Then we all move along the forest edge, brushing ash off ourselves as we go. I really hate leaving behind everything we could use to do this job, but when fire is closing in and men with guns are guarding the stuff you need, I have to agree with Raquel—it's just not possible.

At least we have Nolan's tablet, and if we find somewhere with signal, we can call someone to help us with our plan. It's not much, but just having this sliver of hope is enough to fuel my own internal fire.

Raquel directs us through some rocks by the trail Todd wanted us to take the night we first escaped. I hope the deer that made it have used it already today to flee to safety.

We hurry down it, coughing as smoke billows past every now and again. In the distance, there is a never-ending rumbling roar: the eruption. I've never heard anything like it. It's like an explosion, except it doesn't quit. It's *constant*. Yellowstone opened its mouth to yell and clearly has no intention of stopping.

Every now and again, I can see rocks fly above the tree line. It's hard to spot any orange lava—most of it has solidified into gray chunks by the time it's high enough in the air for us to see it. But it's a good reminder that it's not just noise coming out of the eruption site. It's ejecting tons of pent-up molten material from below our feet. And the longer it goes, the closer that magma chamber below will be to triggering the basaltic layer down deep.

Then, no amount of water, not even from a hundred-thirty-six-square-mile lake, will be able to stop it.

Our feet pound down the path, and then there's a new roar overhead—much higher pitched. I look up. Helicopters zoom by, lights searching the ground, creating streaks through the sky as they reflect off all the dust and ash.

"*Hey!*" Kenzie shouts up at them between coughs. "*Down here!*"

But the copters don't seem to see us through the smoke and trees, no matter how much we jump and wave.

They must be evacuating the park—that would make sense. I wonder if we'll find anyone at all when we get down the hills toward the public areas of Yellowstone. Anyone alive, at least.

More trees crash behind us. The forest fire is truly coming into full swing now. We break into a run, each of us coughing in the oppressive smoke. Finally, we reach the edge of the forest at the far side of the hilltop.

From here, we can once again view the eruption in its entirety.

Seeing it for a second time is almost worse than seeing it for the first. We all pause to catch our breath, safely on the far side of some rocks and out of range of the fire. I unzip the backpack and pull out my camera. When else I'll ever get a chance for footage like this, I have no idea.

"It's kind of amazing," Kenzie says. "In a sucktastic, dooms-day way."

"Tourists would always want to go see the lava back at home," Wyatt says. "We took a class trip to it once. My mom let us get special access to see the lava up close. Some stupid kids tried to roast marshmallows on it behind her back and got mouthfuls of glass shards."

"They *what*?" Eddie asks.

"Turns out the air right above lava? Kind of filled with pop-ping bits of volcanic glass," Wyatt says.

"Ow," Todd comments.

"Yeah," Wyatt agrees.

I pan across the landscape and actually have to zoom out to take in the full scope of the eruption. I swallow, my throat dry and stinging. But it's all I can do to try to steady myself as I stare at the spectacle in front of us.

This . . . this *thing* is a colossal beast of ash and smoke. It has none of the beauty of any volcano I've ever watched or read about online. There's no orange or red to be seen. No fountain of liquid lava. No—this is dark, bulky, and ugly as hell.

Rock flies *everywhere*, bursting out like it's being shot by a thousand angry canons. Ash billows up hundreds of yards into the sky. Gray flying flecks of cooling lava tumble through the smoke. And all this comes straight out of the ground, from a dark pit of horrors that wasn't there just hours earlier. The edge of the pit looks deceptively calm, but the chunks of lava just keep coming, chugging out of the crack in the earth, marching onward, piling up . . . and spreading death.

"How are we supposed to *stop* that?" Todd asks.

I stare at the hideous thing, worry setting in that my ego got the better of me again. That I was too ambitious with my plan.

"Do you really think cooling the exit tunnel underground will stop all the magma?" Raquel asks me.

I lower my camera. "No," I honestly say, thinking through my simulations. "There will probably be a part of the magma tunnel, on the farthest edge from where we're flooding it, where it will stay hot and continue to allow magma to rush out and do . . . that." I wave my hand in the general direction of the eruption. "But it will be less, at least." *I hope.*

"And then we pour water on top of whatever's left, right?" Raquel asks.

"It's not like a fire that you can just dump a bucket on and call it a day," Todd says. "It's still going to cause the water to burst and turn to steam."

"Remember," Wyatt says, "we're planning on using a *lot* of water. Ideally enough to overcome that."

"We'll pump it from the lake," Eddie says, determined. "Like we're going to do with the underground part."

Nolan nods, and Eddie straightens up even more.

"Oh, we could make a pool!" Kenzie says.

Todd wipes his glasses clean on his jumpsuit. "A *what*?" he asks her.

Kenzie practically bounces. "Like an aboveground pool to

contain all the water. We have to make some kind of barrier in a big circle, and then just go to town flooding it. Spray it down from the top and totally swamp it on all sides." She makes a whooshing noise and accompanying hand gestures.

"I like that," Raquel says.

I nod. "Yeah. That could do it."

"But how do we know the dimensions to make any of this stuff?" Todd asks. "And the actual amount of water we'll need? And where will we get the equipment to do any of it?"

All very good questions. I look to Nolan, who is transfixed by the eruption in the distance.

Then I realize what we can do. "I can't answer that third question, but for the first two, we just need the internet."

"We're not Googling 'how to stop a supervolcano,'" Eddie says.

"No." I shake my head. "We'll download the Earth Builder app onto Nolan's tablet. And then we'll run some simulations."

CHAPTER EIGHTEEN

We race through the park. My feet are covered in ash, my jump-suit is covered in ash—everything is covered in ash now. We've all torn strips of material off our sleeves to tie around our heads and cover our mouths.

Our goal: find someplace with internet. As fast as we can. We are on a proper trail now, speeding down the hills. Last time we found a trail, we found a ranger station. If we follow this, we may be lucky a second time around.

Though last time, that was all part of MacNamary's plan.

We just need to get somewhere with Wi-Fi, or data coverage, or computers, or *something.* Of course we had to be in the middle of nowhere for a cataclysmic disaster. The movies always have them in New York City—there's *tons* of WiFi there!

We reach the end of one trail and find it connects to an even larger one. That trail leads directly toward the beastly eruption, but if that's the most likely direction to signs of civilization—even abandoned civilization, at this point—then that's our best bet.

"Come on," I say, gesturing. The seven of us turn and continue on our way, desperately searching the skies for more helicopters as we go.

I realize this must be all over the news by now. My parents are probably worried sick, and they don't even know the half of it. All they know is that I'm in Yellowstone—I think the last place I told them we were visiting was Sheepeater Cliff, which luckily is pretty far away from the eruption site, so maybe they are hopeful that I'm okay. Aunt Pauline said that was the hardest part of working the LA cleanup: all the families clustered around, praying each day that the cleanup crews would uncover their loved ones, miraculously safe and sound.

I shudder. Then I glance at Raquel and Eddie. With the timing of their kidnapping, their families must think Raquel and Eddie were lost to the quake. There are just so many reasons why we need to find a way to get in touch with the rest of the world.

"Whoa, look!" Kenzie says.

We turn. Off to the side, across some distance, I see what appears to be a field of large boulders, slowly moving away from us.

But they aren't boulders. They're bison—covered in ash.

I come to a complete stop. "Oh," I say softly. I don't know why, but at the sight of them, I start to cry.

"Hey, hey," Raquel says, putting a hand on my shoulder. In the distance, the bison continue to lumber away. One shakes itself, and a cloud poofs out around it. "It's okay. Look, they're alive."

"I know," I say, wiping at my face. There are gray streaks on my hands from the ash. "I don't know why I'm crying, I'm sorry." Gosh, if anyone deserves to break down and cry, it's Raquel, and here I am—doing it twice in one day.

"Don't apologize," Raquel says.

The bison continue onward, moving away from the eruption and on to unknown territory. Yellowstone isn't safe anymore.

"I'm sorry," I whisper again—to the bison, and to a lot more.

"Come on." Raquel tugs on my shoulder. I let her direct my tired feet back to the group.

Just as we are nearly caught up with everyone else, the ground starts to shake again. This has happened a lot today, and each time I'm convinced it's the last and we're going to die.

This time, I might be right.

"Look out!" Eddie yells.

The rumble grows louder, and the ground splits in front of us. Jets of steaming water come rushing out, hissing like a chorus of furious cats with scalding claws. I grab for Raquel, and we cling to each other as we attempt to flee.

But we're not fast enough.

The geyser spray falls down on us. My skin prickles into instant blisters, and the ash below me goes so slick that I slip and fall onto my face. Raquel topples next to me. The pain *sears*. Scrambling desperately, we get back on our feet and join Wyatt and Eddie in racing away from the burning jets.

Shards of glass sting my cheek from where it hit the ground.

My palms feel like they're on fire, though I know it also must just be the microscopic glass embedded in them, too.

"Holy *moly*!" Kenzie screams, once we're all far enough away. The crack in the ground continues to sputter. Then it splits wider, and another burst of water sprays upward.

We all clutch one another, catching our breath, out of range of the worst of it. I can see the back of my hands turn red in spots and streaks from where the geyser got me.

"Guess we should watch where we're going," Nolan says.

I think we all want to laugh at that, but we're still trembling too hard to do so. The sizzling fountain continues to blast in front of us. Water jumps several feet in the air, jerkily, with no predictable pattern.

Todd sighs. "We need to keep going. I did my project on geysers. I'll walk up in front and try to pick safe paths."

Eddie looks at him sharply.

"Todd," I say, my eyebrows pinching. "That's a dangerous place to be."

"Someone has to be in front," he counters. I can't really argue with that. Raquel looks like she's going to try, but stops, instead going back to take the rear of the lineup.

"If you're going first, I'll go with you." Eddie leaves Nolan's side and walks up to join Todd.

"You should stay behind me," Todd says. "I know what to look for."

"Dr. Grier had us memorize warning signs for this stuff after . . . well, after all the accidents," Eddie says. "If you miss something, I can pull us back."

"I won't miss anything," Todd retorts.

"Then I won't need to pull us back," Eddie replies.

I watch, holding my breath. But Todd doesn't argue any further. Maybe he's tired. Or maybe he's finally growing up a little. Whatever the case, he and Eddie walk ahead of us all, a few awkward paces apart from one another.

Kenzie drops back near Raquel, and I stay near Nolan and Wyatt. Nolan's ferrets are still hidden in the pocket of his sweatshirt—perhaps they understand the nightmare we're in. I try not to be jealous of them. I wish I could hide and have someone carry me out of this.

We continue through the grassy meadows, which are all covered in ash, like an awful gray-brown snow. A couple of times, off in the distance, we see new geysers erupt. But Todd and Eddie do manage to keep us away from any areas where that's happening. Instead, we continue toward the worst danger visible: the giant, billowing eruption.

I move my tongue around in my mouth. Makeshift mask or no, my saliva feels like paste. I'm rapidly dehydrating, and my eyes that had been damp with stinging tears now feel like their lids are made of sandpaper.

But then, through the pain, I see some lights. I squint at the pinpricks in the distance, hardly daring to believe it.

"Cars!" Eddie points. "Oh my god, *cars*!"

"We're saved!" Todd nearly collapses in relief.

Hope roars back into existence. Sure enough, far, far up

ahead, we're approaching a road. A real road, with real cars. A giant lineup of them, exiting the park in a slow crawl. They look like ants from here, but we all cheer anyway.

I never knew the sight of a traffic jam could make me this happy.

"Aw, yes! Let's go!" Kenzie says.

"Wait," Wyatt says. "Look, there!" He points.

It gets even better. Down not far from us, there's a building. It looks like a much bigger style of the ranger station we visited in the woods. This one probably has modern stuff, like phones and bathrooms!

"We can call for help there!" Eddie says. "And then we can go catch a ride with all those cars and get the heck out of here."

"Yes, and yes," I say. Everyone else agrees, too. Eddie leads the way, and we all pick up the pace, tiny ash clouds kicking up around our feet as we walk. Todd jogs up close to Eddie, still keeping his eyes peeled for danger.

There's an intense wind as we near the structure. Ash blows sideways into us now. We reach the building and Todd flings the door open.

"Hello!" he calls out, as we all pile in.

No one's inside. Maybe the park rangers have evacuated already.

"Look for phones, computers, anything," Raquel directs, pulling down the strip of cloth she'd been using to cover her mouth from the smoke.

"There's a sink over here," Wyatt says. Water is almost as thrilling a prospect as communication right now. I head his way, until something catches my eye.

"And a router!" I shout, climbing up on a chair to get at the device held up in the corner of the room. I look all over it, trying to find a label with its password. Not finding any, I can only hope it's public Wi-Fi. I pull the backpack off, still standing on the chair, and power up Nolan's tablet.

"Great," Raquel says. "Let's hurry and get some internet going."

"Kenzie!" I call, handing her the tablet. "Do your thing."

Kenzie darts over, wiping her dusty hands on a chair cushion, and takes the tablet. "Child-locks, meet your match," she says. I have no doubt that they have.

"Hey, uh, guys, over here!" Nolan says. He's behind the information desk. I climb off the chair and run over. There's a desktop computer!

"And here's a phone," he says, pointing to his right on a wooden console.

"I'm calling home," Eddie declares, rushing over.

"Me, too," Todd says.

"Not before me and Raquel." Eddie shoulders Todd back as he tries to line up next to him and Nolan. "Our families think we're dead."

"*All* our families probably think we're dead right now." Kenzie snorts, not even looking up from the tablet. "But yeah, if anyone gets dibs on calling first, it's you and Raquel."

"Wait." Raquel puts a hand over the phone just before Eddie can pick it up.

"What?" he asks, startled.

Raquel's shoulders slump. "I . . . I don't think I can call my mom and tell her I survived the earthquake, and then break her heart all over again by telling her where I am now. And if you call your parents, then they'll call mine."

Eddie's eyes narrow, moving her hand aside and picking up the phone anyway. "So wait, you *don't* want *either* of us to call home?"

Raquel inhales slowly. " . . . No."

I watch the conversation carefully, not daring to say anything. We're all silent, as Eddie and Raquel stare each other down. I can almost see Eddie's bloodshot eyes get redder by the moment. Eventually, slowly—like it's physically paining him—he sets the phone down.

"Nolan?" Raquel turns to face the other kid who's been missing from his home for months. "What about you?"

Nolan shakes his head. The three of them step closer together, and a lump of emotion in my throat thickens.

They're not here because they were fooled or tricked. They're here because Grier and MacNamary thought the world wouldn't notice if they disappeared. That few people would care to search for them, for one reason or another. That they would be easy to steal away, either because of where they're from, who they're related to, or what disaster concealed their kidnapping.

And now they're choosing not to get in touch with the people who would care the most about where they are, all because they don't want to hurt their loved ones worse than they've already been hurt.

I . . .

"I'm sorry," I say to them. It's not enough. But I literally played bocce ball and ate ice cream while they were held against their will, fearing for their lives. Nothing will ever be enough.

"Okay, so what's the plan?" Eddie asks, refocusing us. "Who *do* we call first? And what do we tell them?"

Todd starts to speak up, but is quickly interrupted.

"In!" Kenzie says, hefting up the tablet. "Who wants the internet?"

I abandon the desktop computer and race back to Kenzie, nearly tripping over a wooden chair in the process. "Yes! Okay, let's download Earth Builder on here. We can use the big computer to send for help if the phone doesn't work."

"Already downloading the app," Kenzie says.

Todd picks up the phone. "I'll call 911."

"We need people to bring drills," I tell Todd. Nolan has taken my place at the big computer, and logs in as a guest. Meanwhile, I log in to my Earth Builder account on the tablet. "What did Dr. Grier say those drills were—fracking drills? That's what we need. We also need hoses—lots of hoses. And pumps. Sturdy ones. People have to pump water down from the lake and can't stop. It has to be high-powered and continuous. Yellowstone Lake has three and a half trillion gallons of water," I recite from

249

our documentary last summer. "If we need to mimic the ocean, like Wyatt said, we're going to need a lot of that lake. Maybe most of that lake."

"What about the supplies to build the pool?" Eddie asks.

"Yeah, there's all that, too," I say. "They'll have to stop the eruption above ground once they've slowed it. So we need even more pumps and hoses and anything that can transport water. And we need huge barriers to make a circle around the eruption site, so we can trap the water in like Kenzie's swimming pool idea."

Todd nods. "Anything else?"

"We need lots of people who are willing to risk their lives," Raquel says. "Because this might not work."

"That's why we'll run a simulation," I say, holding up the tablet. "We can make sure it'll work, no matter what."

"As long as we do it soon, you mean," Wyatt corrects me.

Todd takes the hint and punches 911 into the phone. I can see sweat forming on his forehead, beading up through the layer of ash that's covering each of us.

Earth Builder finally lets me in, and I access my supervolcano simulation, dialing it back to the initial burst phase. Then I go to the EB store and trade a bunch of my credits in for modern-day EB items, like cement blockades and hoses. I should sit down, but I can't help but pace back and forth in the ranger cabin.

"It's not going through," Todd says. I glance over and see his crestfallen face by the phone.

"Lines are probably flooded," Wyatt says as Kenzie groans. "I bet everyone's calling them right now."

Todd hangs up, runs his hands through his hair in frustration, and marches over to one of the chairs where he collapses, putting his head between his knees.

"Why don't we call the park emergency line?" Eddie asks, pointing at a number on a laminated sheet next to the phone. "Maybe that's internal."

On the tablet, I start building the blockade walls around the eruption site. I'm half listening to everyone's worried conversation, but also half focused in on Earth-Building faster than ever.

"Good idea," Nolan says. Eddie scoots aside as Nolan reaches over for the phone and tries the line Eddie suggested. He puts it on speakerphone, and there is an immediate answer.

"Yellowstone emergency line. Please state your location, number of people, and any injuries for a rapid evacuation," a voice says. Todd looks up from his chair.

"Um, there's seven of us," Nolan says. "But we're actually calling about something else. We have a plan for stopping the supervolcano and need to tell someone right away."

The tablet blinks at me. Low battery warning. *No!* I quickly finish the blockade and start to dig a J-shaped tunnel from the surface down to connect with the magma's exit passageway underground.

"Are any of you hurt? Can you walk to meet a copter? What's

251

your location? This phone is reported to be from the ranger station at—"

"No, we don't need evacuation," Nolan insists. "We need to talk to someone who can get the right people to help with our plan."

This tunnel is taking *forever*. I pause the simulation then head to my settings. It's a punch to the gut, but I change my difficulty level from highest to lowest. Then I head back in to bash through the bedrock at faster speeds.

"I'm sorry, but that's impossible," the voice on the phone says. "The priority is—"

"The priority is stopping the park from exploding and destroying half the planet!" Kenzie interrupts. "We have a plan to do that, so are you going to help us or not?"

The voice pauses for a moment. "How old are you all?"

10% battery life . . . 9% . . .

"That's not what's important," Eddie says. "Are you even listening to us?"

"I am," the Yellowstone emergency line representative replies. "But there is a mandatory evacuation. Not just for Yellowstone, but for entire *states*. Wyoming, Montana, Idaho, Utah, Nevada, Colorado, Nebraska, the Dakotas—"

"No, *you* listen!" Nolan says. "We need you to send—"

Then the phone fizzles, followed by silence. My shoulders slump.

2% battery life.

"Um," Kenzie says. "Hello?"

Everyone looks at each other through bleary eyes. So much for that option. The phone must've died, just like Nolan's tablet is about to.

"Great," Todd says, crossing his arms. "Now what?"

But then the voice comes back. "Hi again, sorry, that was my manager checking in. You wouldn't happen to be the seven kids she's missing, would you?"

CHAPTER NINETEEN

Nolan slams the phone down so fast I'm sure it broke something.

I want to scream. I look to Kenzie, hoping she'll do it for me, but instead I see tears in her eyes. She's tired. We're all tired. Why can't we just catch one break?

The tablet dies in my hands, and I set it down on a chair. I don't even have the emotion left in me to throw it at anything.

"They're going to come for us now," Raquel says.

"What do we do?" Eddie asks. The ranger station no longer feels like a safe, hopeful haven. Now, with its ash-covered windows, it just feels like we're sitting right inside of one big trap.

Weary and frustrated, I set my shoulders. Aunt Pauline and I would run into snags filming all the time. But she always insisted that the job had to get done, no matter how far our enthusiasm for it fell.

"Is the computer up?" I ask Eddie. He nods numbly. I move back behind the desk, and Nolan slides over to give me room. "If she's monitoring the phones somehow, we can try to get our message out online."

I open up the web browser. Its homepage is set to a news site. The leading headline is:

YELLOWSTONE ERUPTING:
DOOMSDAY FOR NORTH AMERICA

For a second, I wonder how that would look on Grier's cabin wall. But I click past it quickly, so I can Google the email addresses for some of the local emergency service people, like the firefighters we interviewed last year for the documentary.

"I don't think this computer has a camera or a microphone," Wyatt says.

"Email could still work," Todd says, getting up from his chair and joining us at the computer.

"But who's going to believe us?" Raquel asks. "If you got a random email from someone during a disaster saying that they had a way to stop it, would you really drop everything and go help them?"

I slide the backpack off my back. "Probably not. At least, not without proof that they know what they're talking about. But luckily, I have a whole SD card full of that kind of proof." I take my camera out of the bag and hold it up.

"Hell. *Yes*. Bri!" Kenzie yanks out her hair tie and starts making a new ponytail, gripping the tie in her teeth as she grins at me.

"I hate to be the pessimist here," Wyatt says. "But if we take the time to upload all of your videos, we're giving Grier and MacNamary more of a chance to come get us."

"I'm fine with that," Kenzie says, finishing tying back her hair. "Let them try to catch me. I'll beat the crap out of them. Did it once already, right?"

"I'm willing to stay to upload our message," I interrupt before anyone can say anything more. I straighten with resolve. "No one else needs to. You guys can get going. Get out of here."

"Don't be ridiculous. You aren't staying alone," Raquel says, glaring at me. "And besides, we're all missing something big: Grier and MacNamary have equipment perfect for the first half of our plan. And now, they're coming here."

I blink.

"We couldn't get it when you wanted to earlier, Bri. But now . . ." Raquel trails off, shrugging at the group. "What do you think?"

"Are you suggesting we somehow steal it from them?" Todd asks.

"I'm saying that we have very few options and chances to make this plan work, and we need to take advantage of all the ones we can," Raquel replies. "It'd be a lot faster to get their stuff and use it to drill down and do whatever Bri's figured out. Then the only thing we'd be waiting on are the supplies to make the pool above ground."

"So, we take care of the first half of the plan ourselves?" Todd asks next, more quietly.

I look around at everyone. We never said out loud whether

or not we were going to stay to help with this plan we'd come up with. I know each of us hoped that those cars exiting the park would be our ticket out of here. That other people would learn of our plan and take over for us so we could finally escape.

I lock eyes with Raquel. If she's willing to stay, I'll follow her lead.

On the other side of the desk, Kenzie balls up her fists. "I'm all in. Let's take out Grier and MacNamary, steal their stuff, and drill that tunnel."

"We never finished the simulation," Wyatt says. "How confident are you that it was going to work?"

I sigh, tucking some stray strands of hair behind my ear. "I can't think of anything else that could have as good of a chance of working. How's that for confidence?"

Wyatt nods, his face lined with determination. "I'll take it."

"What exactly do you need us to do for the first half of your plan?" Raquel asks me.

Oh, boy. Doing this ourselves . . .

Clearing my throat, I begin. "We need a drilling pod and one of the slurry pipes and pumps. Then we need to get it all to that first site that you never finished. One of us needs to extend your abandoned alpha tunnel, getting as close as possible to the magma tunnel. But whoever does that has to know when to stop so they don't break *into* that magma tunnel, or they're going to die. Then we need to drag one of the super long hoses all the way to the end of our tunnel and get out of there. The hose needs to be hooked up to the pump, which needs to be hooked up to the lake."

Raquel drums her fingers on the edge of the counter, puzzled. "If we don't actually drill into the magma tunnel, how does the water get into it?"

Todd's eyebrows shoot up his forehead. "Oh. That's dangerous, Bri."

"It's the only way," I say. Todd gets it, and yeah. It's scary. But what else can we do?

"What are you two talking about?" Raquel demands.

I hesitate. Out of all of us, Raquel and Eddie are the last people I want to explain this part of the plan to. "It's . . ."

"The water," Wyatt realizes from next to Todd. "Todd's right, Bri. Holy cow, that is *so* dangerous."

"What is?" Nolan asks, glancing between us all.

There's no dancing around it now. I shut my eyes. "We send in the water. When it hits the end of our tunnel, just feet away from the rising magma, it'll superheat from all the thermal energy. It'll expand and explode a connection from our tunnel into the magma's tunnel."

Raquel doesn't reply. I still can't look at her or Eddie. It's the same principle that killed their friends. I don't know how to soften that blow.

"It's a good solution," Wyatt reassures me.

"Dangerous, but as long as we're out of there in time, it should work," Todd agrees.

I pinch my nails into my arms through my jumpsuit. "Yeah."

"Listen, if this is what it takes, this is what it takes," Nolan says.

Eddie shakes himself, as if pulling himself out of a nightmare.

"Right," he says. Then his eyebrows furrow. "But even if we steal the equipment from Grier and MacNamary, what about all the stuff we need to seal up the top of the volcano?"

"That's what calling for help will do for us," Todd says. "Or rather, emailing for help."

"Yes," I say, typing up a list of supplies into an email with every emergency services address I could find. "We'll have to count on others to step up and help."

Pain fills Raquel's eyes. "I hope you're all aware that if we stay—if we're the ones doing the plan, with *maybe* some help from people who get our email—there's a really good chance we aren't going to make it out of this alive. You all know that, right?"

Everyone pauses.

"Honestly?" Nolan says, breaking the silence. Buggy is out of his pocket, nosing around in his arms. "I've known that for a while."

"Yeah," Wyatt agrees. "I guess I've been half expecting to die this whole time already. At least if we do, we'll maybe be saving everyone else, right?"

Todd looks down at the floor. Eddie watches him, then looks out the ash-covered window, nodding slowly to himself.

"I mean, so what?" Kenzie shrugs. "Life is short. We make the most of it. Right?"

Everyone turns to me now, as if waiting for my opinion. I'm still not used to being in one of the leadership positions. I'm not entirely sure how that happened. But I do know there's only one thing we can do right now.

I fire up my camera. "We don't have much time," I start, aiming it at myself first. "And if this doesn't work, this might be the last you see of us. I'm Bri Dobson." I pan the room.

"Kenzie Reed." Kenzie waves.

"Eddie Fuentes."

Everyone picks up on what I'm doing.

"Todd Henning."

"Wyatt Cayanan."

"Nolan Branford."

"Raquel Soto."

I nod at Raquel, then turn the camera back at me. "You've got our names, but I hope you don't need them. We're in Yellowstone. We're the reason it's on fire. We helped Dr. Samantha Grier and Park Manager Laura MacNamary set off the eruption. This is just the first stage—the longer this eruption goes on, the more pressure release happens below ground. The supervolcano will explode if we don't stop this first phase."

"We didn't mean to do it!" Kenzie adds. "Just for the record. They tricked us!"

"And kidnapped us!" Eddie adds.

"We tried to call for help," I say. My eyes go to Nolan, but he stays quiet, so I continue. "But officials are concentrating on evacuating everyone. Which is smart. But we need some people to come help us. We've figured out how to stop the eruption, and we have a list of supplies we could really use. Can you pull that up for us?" I ask Wyatt.

Wyatt nods and clicks the email I've been working on. I zoom in on the screen, reading off each item, one by one. Wyatt adds a few more items as I do so.

"High-pressure hoses. Water pumps. Bulldozers. Concrete barriers. Fire trucks." I nod at Wyatt for thinking to add that, and read through all the remaining items as quickly as I can. "Basically, anything that can move a lot of water really fast," I sum up. "We're going to use Yellowstone Lake. We have to take a hose through a tunnel down under the eruption site to flood the rising magma, but it won't solidify completely unless we create a pool and flood over where the magma is exiting, too. Maybe some planes or something would be good to drop water? I don't know. But we need help. We can't do this alone."

"Dr. Grier and Ms. MacNamary are also planning on triggering eruptions at other locations," Todd adds, straightening his glasses as he leans in behind me. "Anywhere where there's a supervolcano. Might be Bolivia and New Zealand, since they've had big earthquakes lately, and we already know they caused the LA quake. If they escape here, it's on all of you to catch them and stop them. If you don't, and they manage to set off a chain of supervolcanoes . . . well, that's pretty much the end of the world."

"We can't guarantee we'll make it out to stop them ourselves," Raquel adds. "Please." Everyone falls silent for a moment.

It's unspoken, but we all suddenly know what we have to say next. I can feel my throat tightening.

"Dad," Wyatt bravely starts. "I love you. If I don't make it, I'll be with Mom. It'll be okay."

I leave the camera on him for a moment, and then move it to

261

Todd as he speaks up next.

"I love you, Mom and Dad. Thank you for everything. I've . . . I've been really lucky to have you as my parents. And Bill—take care of Jamie, okay? You'll have to be the big brother now." Todd hangs his head, done with his message.

"Hey, Grandma," Kenzie says, as I pan the camera to her. She crosses her arms, not looking directly into the frame. "You're not so bad. Sorry I always let you down with stuff. Too much like my parents, I know. But hey, at least I kept your old geezer life interesting, right?" She pauses, then scrunches her shoulders. "Fine, okay, I love you." She turns away before she can cry.

"*Mamá, Papá, Lily, Mia* . . ." Eddie says, his voice hesitant. "*Ojalá pudiera haber estado allí con ustedes estos últimos meses. Sé que probablemente piensan que me haya muerto en el terremoto. Pero prefiero que sepan la verdad. Les amo tanto, y voy a hacer todo lo que pueda para asegurarme de que nadie más sea herido.*" He clears his throat. "And for the families of Benny Rodriguez, Lucy Banner, James Hill, and Carlos Diaz . . . I'm sorry. They were brave. All of them. James and Carlos may be out there yet somewhere, maybe at another supervolcano site. We don't really know. Please look for them."

"Dad," Nolan says, after Eddie finishes. "Mom. I love you. Aunt Sam has had me for all these months, and I've tried my best to do what I could to stay safe. Now I'm going to try to do my best to do what's right. Like you taught me. Stephie, I love you, too. I hope you remember me when you get older. You're in charge of

Buggy and Baxter if they make it out and I don't, okay?"

I turn the camera to Raquel, who's sitting still. She says nothing. I realize she might want to go last, so I start to move the camera back to me, and then she says, "¡Mamá! Te quiero. Lo siento."

I pause on Raquel for another moment, but after that outburst, she seems to be done. So I spin the camera back at myself. "Mom, Dad," I say, trying to keep my voice from cracking. "Keep saving people. I'm proud to be your daughter. I love you both. And Aunt Pauline—I'm sorry for the bad editing job. I'm just going to dump all my footage from our time in the tunnels, so that people believe us and hopefully then trust that we know how to fix this. If we survive, then I'd love it if you'd help me turn this into a proper documentary."

I stop recording.

There's a lot of sniffling as I plug in my camera and start uploading all the videos onto the Google Drive I share with my aunt.

"We have to hurry," Nolan reminds us, glancing outside.

"We still need to figure out how we're going to get all the equipment we need from Grier and MacNamary," Wyatt says.

"We can't overpower them," Raquel says. "Not all at once."

"So what do we do?" Kenzie asks.

I'm exhausted from coming up with solutions and instead stare at the upload progress on the screen.

"Positive motivation," Todd says.

That gets my attention, and I glance up. Todd's jaw is set, and his glasses are nearly sliding off his nose, but he has a look in his eyes I wouldn't want to mess with.

"Positive motivation?" Eddie asks.

"Like MacNamary did to us," he says. "She made us think we were heroes. Then she made us think it was our only option to fill that tunnel back in the cave. Now we need to make her think that drilling *this* tunnel is *her* best option to be the hero she thinks she is."

"My god, Todd, you've actually had a good idea." Kenzie gasps dramatically, throwing one hand over her mouth and the other onto his shoulder.

"It does happen, you know," he replies.

The upload says it is going to be another forty minutes before it's done. I groan. I guess I'll send the email to the emergency services now and tell them to get in touch with my aunt if they don't believe me.

"Okay, so how do we convince MacNamary that this is all her idea?" Wyatt asks next, as I wrap up my email and click send.

"We have to give her a reason to want to blow open another exit for the magma," Todd says. "She won't know we won't *really* drill into the magma chamber with our tunnel, or that we'll then flood the tunnel with water."

"How about we tell her part of the truth? That's always fun," Kenzie says.

"What do you mean?" Eddie asks.

"We tell her we've asked for help," Kenzie continues. "That

we've come up with a plan to stop the eruption. So unless she has another eruption site up her sleeve to set off, that's going to be the end of her pressure-release plan and the supervolcano will never blow."

"I like that," I say.

38 minutes, the Google upload says.

"It's always good to have truth mixed into your lies." Kenzie pulls out her tube of lipstick, which she somehow still has on her. "Keeps people on their toes."

"Grier won't believe us," Raquel says. "She knows we hate her. Why would we offer up information like that for no reason?"

"Gloating?" Todd suggests.

"No." I shake my head. "Raquel's right. There's no reason for us to tell them that we've called for help."

"We have to play into what they believe," Nolan speaks up. "That's how I fooled them for so long. I acted the part they wanted from me."

Everyone turns. Nolan goes quiet, and his cheeks darken with embarrassment. I can tell he's still not sure how he fits into our group. But he is the expert on tricking the adults, so I give him an encouraging nod.

"So what do they think of us now?" Kenzie asks.

"They wanted us to join them, right?" Todd says. "Could we pretend to do that?"

"I don't think so," Eddie says. "Last time we saw them we screamed at them and they tried to shoot us. I can't see them believing we have suddenly changed our minds after that."

"They think we're a bunch of stupid, selfish kids," Nolan says. "They probably hate us like they do most of humanity."

"Then stupid, selfish kids is exactly what we'll be," I say, brightening. "We can stage an argument. Fight with each other. Put the idea in their head that way. Great thinking, Nolan."

He straightens where he stands.

"I love it," Kenzie says. Everyone rapidly agrees.

"Okay, let's outline what exactly we're going to say," Raquel says. "We need to—"

But the time to plan passes, because we hear the roar of a large vehicle drawing near.

"Oh, no." Eddie pales.

I look at the video upload progress on the computer screen. It still says thirty-six minutes.

"Shoot," I whisper.

"We'll run a distraction." Nolan's eyes land on the loading bar. "Draw their attention off."

"They'll catch you," Wyatt says.

"Maybe," Nolan says. "But that'll at least add to the believability when we trick them into taking us to the drill site, right?"

"I'll come with you," Eddie says. "We can stage the argument when they catch us."

Raquel looks between Eddie and the computer, torn. "I don't like us separating."

"Guys, if we're sending anyone as a distraction, it's going to be me," Kenzie says. "Especially if it's leading up to a dramatic fight scene between any of us."

266

I smirk. I can't argue with that.

"Then I'd better go, too," Todd says, dusting some ash off himself and looking at Eddie and Nolan. "You two haven't had as much practice with Kenzie as I have."

The vehicle's engine stops outside.

"Good luck," is all I can say, helpless. There's no time to debate this.

Wyatt and Raquel sit down next to me, watching the file progress bar tick slowly. Kenzie, Todd, Eddie, and Nolan exit the ranger station. I have no idea what their plan is, but all I can imagine is Kenzie shouting, "*You'll never take me alive!*" and running wild.

Then I hear voices outside.

"Which way?" Dr. Grier asks.

"*No!* Get back here!" Ms. MacNamary shouts.

"*Run!*" Kenzie yells.

The car engine revs back up. Inside, the three of us don't dare to move.

"Where are the rest of them?" MacNamary demands.

"Check the cabin," Grier orders someone.

"Bri, we have to go," Raquel says.

The upload time is back to saying forty minutes. That's even longer than before! "We can't let them find out what we're doing," I say, my hands shaking over the keyboard.

"Then we can't give them a reason to come in here," Wyatt says. "We have to go out there, so they've seen all of us."

Ugh, they're right. They're so right. Oh god, this isn't going at all like we'd hoped. I type a quick email to my aunt, in a last-ditch effort.

Check Google Drive. Upload everywhere. Only chance to save everyone!!!!!!!

Love, Bri

"Let's go," I say, hitting send. I just have to hope the upload completes itself.

Wyatt nods. I back away from the computer, leaving my camera hooked to it. I take one last look at the best present anyone has ever gotten me and then jog around to the front of the desk, joining Raquel and Wyatt by the door.

"We have to make this convincing," Raquel says. "Like we don't want to be captured."

My adrenaline is back up to ten thousand. When the door to the ranger station opens, I scream at the top of my lungs and hurl myself at the man who tries to enter.

Wyatt is right on my heels. Together, we shove the guy. He doesn't fall, though, until Raquel kicks him from over our heads—she's gripping onto the rafters, swinging in midair. Dropping, she lands next to us and we all run outside.

"Wait up!" I shout, trying to call after the other half of our group. I can see them in the distance through the woods. Whatever their plan had been seems to have fallen apart, and horrified, I see why.

There's a forest fire raging in all the surrounding trees.

"No, don't wait!" Raquel yells. "Run! Go! *Go now!*"

Behind me, Wyatt gets tackled. Raquel immediately stops,

turning back to go get him.

I look out through the trees, just catching Kenzie's eye.

For a brief moment, I think she's going to run back toward us. But then two flaming trees fall, blocking her path. Kenzie turns to follow the three boys. They disappear into the woods—vanishing in the hazy air.

Then I get slammed to the ground.

CHAPTER TWENTY

"After them!" Dr. Grier directs, while Ms. MacNamary swings a truck door open.

"Get those three in here!" Ms. MacNamary yells.

Wyatt, Raquel, and I are heaved into the narrow backseat of one of the pickup trucks. The front seat gets pushed upright, trapping us in. On the windshield, ash collects.

"We have to get the others," Ms. MacNamary says, hopping into the passenger seat as Dr. Grier takes the driver's seat. "They could ruin everything."

Dr. Grier turns on the windshield wipers, sending ash sailing. We're thrown backward as she floors it in the approximate direction that our friends fled.

Raquel, Wyatt, and I all struggle to lean forward and exchange glances. It's up to us. We have the perfect opportunity—both

MacNamary and Grier are here. I don't have Kenzie's flare for the dramatic or Nolan's practice at lying, but we can't waste this chance.

Making sure I've still got Wyatt and Raquel's attention, I give them a small and deliberate nod. "They know!" I say, loud and clear enough for the women in the front seat to hear me.

"Shut up, Bri!" Wyatt says, after only a moment's pause. He returns my nod.

"They don't know anything, just calm down!" Raquel adds, glancing between the two of us.

"No, no, they know," I continue my charade, "and now they're taking us to—"

"Shut up!" both Raquel and Wyatt say now.

"Don't tell me to shut up, you shut up!" I reply.

"What's going on back there?" MacNamary asks.

Dr. Grier swerves again to miss a fallen tree.

"They're taking us to the other drill site, you can't tell me they don't know!" I say even louder.

"You're just giving them ideas!" Raquel yells. It sounds a little over the top, but it's not so bad that I worry Grier and MacNamary won't buy it. "Stop it!"

"What are you all fighting about?" Dr. Grier growls. I resist the urge to smile in triumph. They're taking the bait!

"Great," Wyatt says. "Just great. Now they *want* to know."

"They already know!" I say. "Look at which way they're taking us!"

"Pull over," MacNamary orders. Dr. Grier slams on the

brakes, and MacNamary spins in the front seat to face us. "You're going to tell us *now*."

Grier radios the other cars to tell them to continue pursuing in the direction Kenzie, Todd, Eddie, and Nolan ran. Several trucks full of equipment sail by us on the road toward Yellowstone Lake.

"We don't have to tell you anything," I say. "There's three of us and only two of you."

"Bri, there may only be two of us in here, but you know how many others I have at my disposal," MacNamary says. "I can do whatever I want. So you'd better tell us, or I'll radio my men and change their orders from capture to kill for your friends who got away."

"Except Nolan," Grier cuts in.

MacNamary gives a small eye roll. "Except Nolan."

"No," Raquel whispers.

I wonder if it would be believable now to go into details. It has to be, right? If they were really threatening my friends, I would tell them.

"We thought you figured out what we did," I mumble.

"Bri!" Raquel exclaims.

"Shut up!" I snap. "I'm not letting our friends die!"

"And what *did* you do?" Grier asks carefully.

"We got help," I say. "We called for help to stop the eruption. So that the pressure will stop releasing and the supervolcano won't be able to blow."

"So you did tell people about us," MacNamary replies, her face paling.

"You can't stop a volcano." Grier snorts. She starts up the engine again. "This is a waste of time."

"We can at least settle it down," Wyatt says, holding his chin up. "We've got tankers coming in with water and barricades. We're going to make a pool around it and flood it from the top."

"That won't fully stop it," Grier says, though she doesn't pull away and start driving just yet.

"But it will slow it, won't it?" MacNamary seems less sure. "That would buy people time to figure out how to stop it or reduce its impact. And perhaps even catch up with us before we can get to Bolivia."

"That's why you thought we were taking you to that other drill site," Grier says, turning back to look at us. "You thought we were going to make you drill a second escape route for the magma, so the supervolcano would still erupt in time. Smart."

I hang my head.

"You really shouldn't have said anything," MacNamary gloats. "We didn't know. But boy, have you given us a great idea."

"Way to go, Bri," Raquel says. I want to smile at the compliment hidden in her sarcasm, but hold back.

"What do you say, Samantha?" MacNamary asks.

"That original alpha tunnel was almost fully completed when we abandoned it," Grier muses. "But we have no blasting powder for the end of it. We'd have to drill straight into the magma."

"Who cares?" MacNamary says. "We'll be making one of these kids do it."

Grier looks at the three of us. I can't read her expression.

"We won't do it," Raquel says loudly. "We won't help you anymore."

"You will, or we'll kill you," Grier says.

"You were going to do that anyway," Raquel retorts.

"Do it and we won't kill your friends, then," MacNamary says instead. She turns to Grier. "See, Raquel isn't someone who cares about her own life all that much. At least, not in comparison to how much she cares about her friends. This is what I'm talking about—you have to get to know your team in order to manipulate them. When we get to our other supervolcano sites, keep that in mind."

"Shut up," Grier replies.

We all go silent, letting Grier and MacNamary draw their own conclusions about what we're "willing" to do. Something inside me seethes that MacNamary would make any assumptions about Raquel after what she's put her through.

I stare out the window at the ever-darkening park, my shoulders tense. We've at least got step one of our plan figured out, but how do we save ourselves from Grier and MacNamary and make sure neither of them actually makes one of us drill all the way into the magma?

Grier drives on for several minutes, while MacNamary radios the rest of their team to keep chasing down the rest of *our* team and then meet us at the original drilling site.

When we finally stop, the eruption looms closer than ever and everything around us is on fire. I can't see Yellowstone Lake from here, but there's the whole hazy smoke and ash situation, so visibility is really reduced in general.

Grier and MacNamary get out, shutting the doors and locking us in. Along with another truck, they start hauling out equipment, as they explain to the men what's going on.

It doesn't take long before another truck arrives. I spot Nolan and Kenzie in the backseat.

"Oh, no," I say.

"Do you think Todd and Eddie got away?" Wyatt asks.

"I hope so," Raquel says, her voice quiet. "Because the other option is that they're dead."

Nausea hits me, full force. I steady myself by clutching the door of the truck. *They're not dead. They must have gotten away.*

"So how are we doing this?" Wyatt asks. "Who's going down there?"

"I'm guessing they'll pick," I say, pulling myself together. "The rest of us up above just have to make sure we can get the person out in time, because we sure as heck know Grier and MacNamary won't do it."

"We should have a code word for the radio," Wyatt says, "when we're close to the magma tube."

"How about oatmeal?" I suggest. Not sure why that of all things popped into my head.

"That works," Raquel says. "But we can't leave it up to chance who's going. I'm not sending anyone else down there where Benny and Lucy died. I'm going."

"Raquel," I say, not wanting to cause an *actual* argument. "Wouldn't it make more sense if—?"

"No," Raquel cuts me off.

And there's no time to discuss, because then Dr. Grier opens up the door.

"Okay, out," she orders.

We do as she says. I wonder if we should at least act like we want to run, even though this is where we want to be.

They've got a pod jury-rigged up to a generator, and they're hauling it into a cabin. It's bigger than the ranger station we just came from. Its windows are all shuttered, and there's construction fencing around most of it with warning signs for the public to keep out.

"That's where the hole is that we were drilling into," Raquel tells us. I take in the building, impressed in spite of myself. Ms. MacNamary must have pulled some strings as park manager to get this place both built and kept locked away from prying eyes. I realize again just how far ahead she and Grier had planned.

Well, I think, a little bit smug. *They didn't plan for us.*

Men with guns nudge us forward, and we huddle up in a group with Nolan and Kenzie next to a sign pointing the directions to Yellowstone Lake and the Fishing Bridge.

"Careful with Nolan," Grier calls over.

"But get his ferrets before he tries anything with them," MacNamary orders.

Nolan takes a panicked step back, but not fast enough. One of the men wraps his arms through Nolan's, pinning them behind his back, while another man grabs for his ferrets from his sweatshirt pocket.

"*No!*" Nolan screams.

My heart tumbles over itself in my chest. "You leave them alone!" I shout.

"Ow!" the man exclaims, yanking his hand out. "One of them bit me!"

Buggy falls to the ground, shaking himself off. Ash flies around his white fur, settling on him and turning him gray.

The man that got bit raises one heavy boot up, as if to stomp down.

"No!" Nolan exclaims. "Run, Buggy!" I close my eyes—I can't watch.

"Get it!" MacNamary yells. I crack my eyes open, just in time to see a gray streak race away.

Meanwhile, the other man has gotten Baxter out and is squeezing him tightly.

"Let him go!" Nolan pleads, pulling against the man holding him.

We're all shouting now. But Baxter has it under control. He chomps down—hard. The man yelps, dropping the second ferret to the ground, who immediately races off after the first.

"Go, go, go!" Nolan shouts after them.

I'm both relieved and scared for them, all at the same time.

"Great," Grier says, marching over. "Now how are we going to run wires at our other sites?"

"You let him keep them, and he'll just have them do something to mess up our plans," MacNamary says. "They're slippery creatures."

"Yeah, and now they're *loose.*"

"They'll be dead soon." MacNamary gestures at the fires raging all around us. "Relax. We'll just make him train new ones."

Nolan hangs his head, his shoulders shaking. I think he's crying, and my heart breaks. "I hate you both," he says.

Grier's brow furrows, and I wonder if there's some part of her that's regretting her decisions. But given how many people she's already killed, I doubt she has much room in her heart for guilt.

"So what are we doing here?" Kenzie asks, coughing in the smoke. "Just wanted to bring us all together before you kill us, or what?"

Grier and MacNamary exchange glances. I wish I could reach out to Nolan, but I'm held tightly by one of the men.

"Actually, you can thank your friends that you're still alive," MacNamary says. "Despite your best efforts to *save the day*"—she makes air quotes—"there is another way to get the supervolcano to erupt. Even if people come to help you cool off our first pressure-releasing eruption, we're here to make a second one."

Kenzie stages a good, shocked reaction. I can't help but watch the eruption in the distance over her shoulder. It's as beastly as ever. Our plan sounded a lot more feasible from the safety of the ranger station. But seeing the smoke and ash again . . . helplessness overtakes me.

What were we thinking? We're just kids. Nolan sniffles next to me, trying to bring himself under control and punctuating my point. I hate that I have no idea if our plan can work. And I really hate that it's our only option.

I reach down deep inside, grabbing desperately for my resolve.

"We need a volunteer," MacNamary says. "If no one volunteers, then—"

"I'll go," both me and Raquel say at the same time.

MacNamary laughs. "Oh, my. Two volunteers! *Shocking* that it's you two."

"Which one goes in?" Grier asks. She looks tired, and also . . . disappointed? She locks eyes with me, and I flinch.

"I will," Wyatt says.

Both Raquel and I spin to stare at him.

"Go in for *what?*" Kenzie asks loudly, still keeping up her charade. My mind races.

"Three volunteers!" MacNamary exclaims.

"We only need one," Grier says.

I'd rather put myself in danger than anyone else, but Wyatt was the first one down in our tunnels, and he never steered us wrong. He was the fastest at drilling, the best at selecting locations . . .

"Me," Raquel insists. "I'm going to go."

I hesitate, looking between her and Wyatt. I know what this means to Raquel . . . but . . .

"What are you volunteering for?" Kenzie asks, flailing.

"They're making one of us go in to drill again," I explain to continue acting like this is news to Kenzie and Nolan. "To set off a second eruption, by connecting this old tunnel to the one under the first eruption site. Whoever goes is going to die, since they want us to drill straight into the magma."

"What the—no!" Kenzie sputters.

"It's the only way," Wyatt says. "They said they'll kill us all if one of us doesn't go."

"Raquel is more trouble." Grier turns to MacNamary. "Let's send her."

"No, see that's exactly why we can't send her," MacNamary says. "She'll try to pull something. Bri might, too, for that matter." She gives me a distrustful look.

I try to keep my expression neutral. Inwardly, I'm panicking. *She knows we're up to something. She knows.*

"Wyatt, on the other hand, will follow directions. Won't you, Wyatt?" MacNamary asks him.

Wyatt nods. "Yes, ma'am."

"I would, too!" Raquel says. "You have to send me! Please!" She grabs MacNamary's sleeve, her voice threatening to break.

"Nice try, but no," MacNamary says, shaking her off her arm.

"I just find it hard to believe that all three of you are willing to die," Grier comments. "So eager."

"We're probably going to die anyway," I say miserably. "We've figured that out by now. But if there's a chance we can save everyone . . ."

"Where's Todd and Eddie?" Wyatt asks. I stiffen.

One of the men grumbles. "Those two? Fee and Stiles are on the hunt."

Raquel lets out a sob of relief. *They're not dead.* The corners of my eyes sting, as a shudder runs through me. *For now.*

"I won't go if they kill them," Wyatt says.

"Oh, good lord . . ." the man says.

"Radio them, now," MacNamary snaps. The men step back from us, letting go of our shoulders while keeping a wall of muscle around the perimeter of the group. One speaks into his radio.

I beam at Wyatt, unable to stop myself.

"He's the one," Grier agrees.

"No!" Raquel protests.

Kenzie lunges at Wyatt, hugging him. "You're so brave!" she sobs dramatically. "You're an idiot for doing this, but you're so brave."

Raquel drops her head, defeated. I reach out and squeeze her shoulder, not knowing what else to do. "It'll be okay," I mouth at her, but she ignores me. I wish I could tell her how confident I am in Wyatt. I wish I could be that confident in the rest of us right now. It's going to be up to us to make sure he survives.

Kenzie releases him, wiping at her eyes.

"They what?!" the man who was ordered to ask about Todd and Eddie says into his radio. "Well, stop them!"

"We're trying!" the fuzzy radio call sounds back.

I can only hope that's more good news for Todd and Eddie. My heart leaps for a brief moment, but then I'm brought back to reality as the men start piling gear onto Wyatt.

"When you get to the edge of the magma tunnel, call us," Grier instructs, handing him a radio. "We'll need to complete our evacuation before you finish your job."

Perfect! I want to squeal. Grier and MacNamary fall into a conversation with the men once they're through loading up Wyatt, and I turn to my companions. Wyatt and Raquel are staring each other down.

"Raquel, I know what I'm able to do and what I'm not. And I can do this." Wyatt shifts his tool belt on his waist. "You have to stop treating me differently than the others. You think I haven't noticed, but I have."

"I know," she says. "I know, I'm sorry. I can't help it."

"Yeah. You can." His voice is flat.

I suck in a breath.

Raquel hugs her arms around herself again. "Wyatt—just, be careful. Benny and Lucy died in there."

Wyatt's expression softens.

"I don't want to lose anyone else," Raquel says.

Wyatt hesitates, then nods. "I'll be careful."

After Raquel nods in return, I hug Wyatt, squeezing him tightly. Dr. Grier turns around, and I don't dare say anything or I risk tears breaking through. I hope he knows that I trust him, and that I'm silently promising him I'll get him out again.

After I let go of Wyatt, Kenzie and I step closer together, something unspoken passing between us. Todd is missing. Wyatt is being taken away. We need to stick together, as best as we can.

"Let's go," Grier says.

MacNamary gives Wyatt a handshake. "You're one brave kid. If the world was made of people like you, we wouldn't have to do any of this."

Every word out of MacNamary's mouth makes me hate her more.

Nolan steps forward just before Wyatt goes. He hugs him, too. As he does, Nolan catches my eye over Wyatt's shoulder. I give him a nod, trying to reassure him that our plan will work. Nolan sighs, letting Wyatt go. A rumble goes through the ground, and I yelp. I can't help it. When the shaking stops, I clutch at my chest. If the supervolcano doesn't kill me, a heart attack will.

Next to me, Kenzie regains her footing, clutching my arm to steady herself. I hold onto her, even as the quake calms. Once the ground is steady, the men lock Wyatt into the pod.

I can't read Wyatt's expression under his mask and goggles, but he gives Kenzie and me one final thumbs-up before he and his pod are dragged into the cabin to go down an unseen tunnel.

We'll get you out, Wyatt. We will.

CHAPTER TWENTY-ONE

"Okay, take as much equipment away from here as possible." Dr. Grier turns to the men around us. "Only keep what is absolutely necessary for this project."

"What about the kids?" one of the men asks.

"We can't kill them until Wyatt's job is done," Grier says. "Load them up, too."

No! We have to stay! I look around desperately. Our entire plan rests on us staying here and somehow winning back control from Grier and MacNamary as we wait for help to arrive.

Several men move in to grab us. This is it. Oh god, this might be our only chance. I look to Kenzie. She's our time bomb—she could go off and do something that stops all of this. But she's staring upward. So is Nolan.

"Um . . ." Kenzie says, pointing.

Overhead, two small military jets are dropping out of the sky. Like, actually dropping. They're going to crash.

"What are those doing here?" MacNamary demands.

I have no idea. I've never seen jets like that so close. And I've certainly never seen any crash before.

"Idiots," Grier says. "Flying into a volcanic cloud. That ash is getting turned to ceramic in their engines."

I can't look away. I want to, but I can't. The planes continue to plummet.

Then—each pops out an ejected seat. Parachutes deploy, carrying the pilots safely to the ground as their jets continue to fall. The planes crash, exploding in the distance. Their flames just add to the smoke and fire that already engulfs most of the visible park.

I exhale, then start to cough.

"We have to move," Grier says, looking west. I follow her line of sight and gape at the flaming forest less than a football field's length away. I hadn't realized the fires had gotten so close.

One of the men grabs me by my shoulders, yanking me toward a truck. Instinctively, I struggle back.

"Do you want to be here when the next eruption happens?" Grier asks me.

"Let me go!" I shout, ignoring her. This is our only chance, and I'm not going to miss it. Clearly, neither is anyone else. Independently, Raquel, Kenzie, Nolan, and I all begin whaling on our would-be captors. I stomp on a foot, kick a shin, wince as my back gets punched, and scream as I twist to headbutt the man pushing me.

It's no use. The men aren't underestimating us anymore, and we're all quickly wrestled under control.

But then—another earthquake hits. The ground starts to shake.

"Wyatt!" I yell, spinning toward the cabin where Wyatt's long since disappeared.

"You don't think—no, he wouldn't have hit it yet," MacNamary says.

Grier shakes her head, and the ground stops moving. "No, we're still safe."

"What about Wyatt?" Kenzie demands. "He might not be!"

"Wyatt, status?" MacNamary asks into a radio.

There's a long pause as we all hold our breaths.

"I'm fine," Wyatt reports after a static pop.

"Keep moving," Grier orders the men, who grab us more tightly and continue to shove us toward the trucks.

"They're too much trouble," MacNamary says. "We should just tie them up here and leave them for the lava. Once Wyatt does his thing, they'll blow up with him."

"Oh, thanks," Kenzie says, her voice dripping sarcasm. "*Leave them for the lava.* I've never met two people as heroic as you guys. You're a true inspiration."

"I'm not leaving Nolan," Grier says.

"He's made his choice, Samantha," MacNamary replies. "I just don't get it. You're willing to kill the rest of your family, why not him?"

"He's useful. Bri would be useful, too," she says, not meeting

MacNamary's eyes. "For when we rebuild. She's smart."

"Listen to yourself!" MacNamary grabs Grier by her shoulders. "Sam, you aren't being logical. They aren't who you want them to be. They won't help us—*ever*. They're obstacles. That's all."

That triggers something in her. Grier's tall frame straightens, and the tiniest bit of hope I was feeling for her to redeem herself disappears. "I'm sorry," she says. "You're right. I've taken my eyes off the bigger goal."

"There's the Sam I know." MacNamary lets out a relieved breath. "Now come on." She steers her toward the trucks.

"Aunt Sam!" Nolan cries out, reaching for her. But then we're dragged to a tree, and men tie the four of us up around it—Raquel to the left of me, Kenzie to the right, and Nolan on the opposite side. The rope is so tight I can feel it bruising my arms.

MacNamary returns to check on us a couple of minutes later, once Grier is out of earshot. "I hate wasted effort," she sneers. In the distance, I can hear the crackling of a new set of trees going up in flames. "If only you four had—" But then, her phone rings. She answers it, turning from us. "Yes? . . . What? *Bulldozers?*"

I look up, and so does Raquel.

"Well, tell them to turn around and go home," MacNamary goes on to say. "We're under mandatory evacuation. It's for their own safety."

All of us are listening to the phone conversation now with rapt attention. *Please. Please be what we hope this is.*

"Fire trucks, too?! What do you mean, they're not listening to you?" She spins, glaring at the four of us on the ground around the tree. "Okay, I understand. Do what you can to stop them."

"What's going on?" Grier asks, jogging over from the trucks.

"Rangers are trying to turn people around at the park entrances. Seems like the kids weren't lying about calling for help."

If I wasn't tied up, I'd be leaping for joy. The video must have uploaded. Oh my god, the video *must have uploaded*!

"Bri!" Raquel almost inhales my name. "We . . . we . . ."

"We did it." I can barely believe my own words. Even if we die now, other people will know what to do. I relax against the tree, feeling my hair catch on the bark. *We did it.*

"*Hell* yes!" Kenzie cheers. "In your *stupid* faces!" Her eyes shine in the fire's light, blazing with victory. If I couldn't feel her secretly shaking next to me, I would think she was impossibly fearless.

"What if they come here?" Grier asks.

"Maybe we should just kill the kids now," MacNamary muses. "Though, then we run the risk of Wyatt asking to talk to them before he's done."

One of the men points a gun at Raquel. Kenzie cranes her neck to see what's happening, her shaking worsening but her attitude not betraying it.

"Don't you dare," Kenzie warns, her glare intensifying.

"Let's give your rangers a few minutes," Grier says. "They may be able to turn those people around. And even if they can't, they won't stop us here. They'll go to the first eruption site."

"Good point," MacNamary says. She waves a hand, and the man lowers his gun. Then she dials her phone and gives some orders, sounding for all the world like the sweet lady we met at the beginning of the summer.

We sit in silence for ages. Anticipation is as thick in the air as the ash at this point. I watch the eruption in the distance. From the other side of the tree, Nolan whistles for his ferrets whenever he thinks the men aren't paying attention. It hurts worse each time, because they never come. I wonder where they've run off to. If they've found someplace safe to hide. I can only hope so.

"Dr. Grier!" a voice shouts, ripping me away from my thoughts.

Out of the corner of my eye and just over Kenzie's head, I see two men running toward us from out of the haze.

It's Stiles and Fee.

"What is it?" Dr. Grier asks. "Where are the other kids? I thought you had them."

But whatever Fee and Stiles try to say in response gets cut off, because then the ground shakes again. Several rumbles move the earth underneath us, rattling us against the tree trunk we're tied to. A nearby tree, completely engulfed in flames, collapses into the construction fencing. The fence crunches in on itself, toppling.

And the cabin catches on fire.

"Wyatt!" Kenzie shrieks.

The large wooden cabin ignites within seconds. The hot ash

that's been falling all day must have already primed it. Two men run out of the building, patting down their clothes where sparks had leapt.

"Wyatt!" Kenzie shouts again. He's way down the tunnel by now, so the fire isn't the danger—but these quakes sure are.

I notice our bonds loosened slightly in all the recent shaking. I tug at them, trying to see if I can get them off, while watching Grier, MacNamary, and their men to make sure they don't notice.

But the adults are all yelling and pointing and not paying us any attention. The shaking of the ground slows to a stop, and I strain my neck in the other direction to see what all the commotion is about.

There—in the distance—a mismatched herd of vehicles speeds our way across the ash-covered landscape. There are semi-trucks with beds full of concrete barriers. Water tankers of every size imaginable. Fire trucks. Bulldozers, bringing up the rear, slow and steady.

Help has arrived.

"*Yes!*" Nolan exclaims in triumph.

"What?" Kenzie asks, tied to the only side of the tree not facing the arriving vehicles. "What is it?"

Raquel on the other side of me is rapidly whispering to herself too quietly for me to understand. Her shoulders have relaxed, and her head tilts forward. A tear stings a scrape on my cheek.

"Don't react!" MacNamary shouts. "No one react, don't let them know what we're doing here, and they'll pass by on their way to the eruption!"

"Fat chance!" Kenzie yells.

"You've got four kids tied up in plain sight—they'll see right away that you're up to something!" I add. Thunder rumbles in the distance. Lightning sparks through the clouds over the eruption, briefly lighting up the smoke-filled sky.

"And if they don't, I'll scream until they see us," Kenzie says. "And I'll tell them exactly what you're doing."

"Now should we shoot them?" one of the men asks Grier.

Grier is staring out at the arriving vehicles, blinking in disbelief, so MacNamary answers for her.

"We'll have to take that risk," she says. "Yes. Make it fast, so we have time to hide the bodies."

Before I can react, the man is already pointing his gun at me. Nolan yells behind me, and I squeeze my eyes shut.

"Watch out!" a voice shouts. *"Geyser!!!"*

My eyes fly back open as Kenzie screams. A massive blast of water slams into the man aiming the gun at me. The other men yell and run away, and I stare at the jets of water, trying to figure out how a geyser could blow sideways.

But then, Kenzie's scream abruptly stops, and instead she bursts out laughing. When I notice what she's laughing at, I want to applaud.

It's not a geyser at all—it's Todd and Eddie. And they've somehow got the slurry hose from one of Grier and MacNamary's trucks.

"Yeah! Get away from them!" Todd yells.

The man with the gun tries to get back up on his feet, caked solidly now in wet ash and mud. Eddie runs forward and kicks his gun far out of reach.

"Eddie!" Raquel exclaims.

Eddie and Todd together heave the slurry hose at the other men, blasting them with water next.

"Take that!" Eddie shouts.

I'm full-on laughing now. I can't believe it. How did they get *water*?

"Where have you guys *been*?!" Nolan calls. Kenzie lets out a whoop.

"We stole a truck!" Todd says proudly.

"The one with the pump!" Eddie adds.

"And drove it to Yellowstone Lake! And hooked it up and now we have water!"

They turn with the hose and aim it at the wooden cabin, which is nearly burnt to a crisp. They douse the building, and the fire calms within moments. I let out a relieved breath, knowing Wyatt won't be greeted by a raging inferno when he gets out of his tunnel.

"How did you get that pump into the lake?" Grier asks, stunned. The smoke billowing from the remains of the cabin makes her cough, and she barely gets her next sentence out. "It weighs hundreds of pounds." I turn, surprised to see her still nearby with all the hubbub.

Todd and Eddie exchange glances.

"Hope you don't want your truck back," Eddie says.

"We drove the whole thing into the lake," Todd adds.

"What?!" MacNamary yells from next to the drenched men, who are all trying to climb back to their feet, slipping on the wet ash left and right.

Then, there's a burst of static from her radio.

"Hello?" Wyatt calls. "Anyone there? I could sure use some oatmeal."

The signal. He's reached as far as we need for our plan to work!

"What does that mean?" Grier asks, still coughing.

"He's ready!" Kenzie exclaims. "We can do this, he's there, he's ready!"

"Ready for what?" Grier demands.

"Our plan to save the world!" Eddie cries.

Grier stares between the slurry hose and the hole Wyatt is down, and I can see she's piecing things together. "No."

There's no use hiding things from her now. "Yeah, those people coming?" I say. "They're coming to stop up the top of the eruption, while we stop it from below."

Todd and Eddie keep the hose aimed at her. Next to Grier, MacNamary sputters.

"You've lost," I say.

"Stiles!" MacNamary screeches, spinning toward him. "Take out that generator. Don't let that boy get back to the surface. We can't let them get down that tunnel with that hose!"

Fee and Stiles both race toward the hole Wyatt is down, climbing over the fallen fence and the collapsed walls of the smoldering cabin.

293

"*No!*" Raquel screams. Then she dives forward, flips under her loosened bonds, and breaks free.

With her ropes undone, it's easy for the rest of us to shake our own off and climb to our feet. Raquel leaps onto Fee just before he reaches the smoldering remains of the cabin. I tear after Stiles, but he gets to the generator before I can get to him.

A semitruck horn sounds in the distance.

"We have to go!" MacNamary shouts. "Load up!"

With a glance over my shoulder, I see the approaching trucks and construction vehicles are much closer now, and behind the initial group of them are dozens more.

Men race around us, piling into their own trucks. I spin back to Stiles, who is ripping apart the wiring of the generator.

"Wyatt!" I gasp. "No!"

Stiles kicks a hunk of burning wood in my direction, then runs off to get in a truck with the others.

I don't even see them all leave. My focus is on the generator and trying to piece it back together. Then, Nolan is next to me.

"What can we do?" I ask, distraught, staring down the hole in the floor of the blackened cabin. The cabling goes down it, leading to Wyatt. I wonder if we can pull him up manually. Maybe if it was only him. Unfortunately, he's inside a pod of heavy machinery.

"We can fix this, we can fix this," Nolan says on repeat, reaching for a wire, then pulling his hand back as the generator sparks. "They made me do a lot of electrical stuff with Buggy and Baxter. I can rewire this. We just need another power source. . . ."

I look back. The roar of the approaching vehicles grows, and with it comes the sounds of snapping trees and crashing bushes. I look forward at the forest fires drawing closer and closer.

"We'll have to hurry," I say, coughing.

Up ahead, Fee runs away from Raquel, scrambling to catch up with his departing friends. There's no time to give chase. Raquel races over to us, with Todd and Eddie close behind, still lugging the hose.

"What are we going to do?" Todd asks, leaning over the hole in the ground.

Nolan stares at all the trucks coming our way. "We're going to use a car battery," he says softly. "A *semitruck* battery."

Hope surges. Raquel wipes at her eyes.

"We'll get him out," I say, determined. "We've come this far. We're not losing anyone now."

A pickup truck drives straight up to us, its tires kicking muddy ash as it goes. We all turn as the door to the truck opens, and a woman in a firefighter suit jumps out. She looks familiar, somehow.

"You're all the kids from the video, right?" she asks. Her pale skin is half covered in freckles, and I can see strands of red hair poking out of her helmet.

"That's us," I say. We all stand up, gawking.

"Pauline Dobson sent it to us," the woman replies, gesturing to the trucks coming up behind her, including two fire engines. "We're from the volunteer firefighters of Jackson Hole. We were driving up to help with the evacuation when I got your email and one from Pauline not long after."

"You're the firefighters we interviewed last summer!" I realize.

"That's right! For your documentary," she replies, smiling. "It's good to see you, Bri. We're here to help, however you need us. And more of us are on the way."

Kenzie, returning from attempting to chase down MacNamary and Grier, juts out her hand. "Heck yes! Welcome to the apocalypse. I'm Kenzie."

The lady shakes her hand. "I'm Haley."

"We need to get our friend out of this tunnel," I say, spying the approaching Jackson Hole fire trucks. "Can we use one of your fire truck's batteries?"

Her eyes widen, looking down the hole. "Absolutely."

"Would that work, Nolan?" I ask.

Nolan nods, and he and Haley get to work, while my attention is torn away. Another truck pulls up—this one marked as the National Park Service. Immediately, I edge closer to my friends, preparing for MacNamary.

But the person who steps out isn't Ms. MacNamary.

"Okay, what needs to get done?" a dark-skinned man asks, adjusting his park ranger hat.

"Who are you?" Kenzie asks suspiciously.

"I'm the first of many," he says. "Dave Chaddha, Yellowstone park ranger, ready to put out this volcano."

"You aren't with Laura MacNamary, are you?" Todd asks.

"Absolutely not," he says, his face hardening. "We're all

horrified by what she's done. If we had known . . . well, there's no time for that now. Where do you need us?"

I open my mouth to answer, but then a third truck pulls up.

"Wow," a man in a hard hat says, climbing out and staring at the billowing smoke and exploding rock from the eruption in the distance. "We've got our work cut out for us, don't we?"

Next comes a cement mixer. Two people jump out of that. And then a bulldozer. Then two semitrucks. A water tanker pulls up behind them all.

I can't find my voice. It's choked up behind tears that won't fall.

We have *help*.

CHAPTER TWENTY-TWO

The adults form a makeshift circle around us. Flames from the tree line cause their shadows to dance on the charred ground, and I half wonder if I'm dreaming.

"Sounds like we'll have plenty to do," Dave says after we're done going over our plan.

"I'll take a team to the lake," Eddie says. "I've already hooked up one hose from there."

"And anyone who brought blockers and stuff to make my pool with, follow me!" Kenzie says, waving people to join her. She gives me a small salute, and I smile. There's zero way any of us could have predicted this is how our summer would turn out, but back at the beginning of July, Kenzie was my first clue that things would not go as expected. Seeing her dash off with dozens of rescue workers gives me hope that we may yet get out

298

of this, despite the odds.

While Eddie leads his own team off toward Yellowstone Lake, Raquel, Todd, and I rush back to Nolan, who is carefully moving wires from the cabling that's attached to Wyatt's pod.

I wish we had a way to communicate to Wyatt that we were working on saving him. I can't imagine being trapped down in a pod like that, without power, having no idea what was happening.

Haley directs one of her fire trucks to pull up as close to the tunnel entrance as possible. Todd and I step back, giving Nolan room as he motions for Haley to pop the hood. Raquel moves a few fallen, burnt chunks of cabin away from the hole in the floor, tossing the smaller pieces onto the pile of rubble Wyatt's drill has churned up out of the tunnel.

As I anxiously wait for Nolan and Haley to get power to the generator, my eyes continue to fall on the forest fire that's creeping closer and closer. We already had one incident with a flaming tree, and we don't need more when we've got all this other stuff to deal with.

"Hey," a voice calls. Dave jogs over, holding his radio. "Someone named Eddie is calling in from a ranger radio."

I stand up straight and he hands the radio to me.

I press the button on the side. "Eddie?"

"Bri!" he calls in response. "Is that you?"

"Yeah."

"We just got to the lake," his voice is fuzzy. "To get the new pumps set up from the—*kssssh*—but MacNamary and Grier are here! They—*ksssh*—stopping our pump! We need help!"

The tiny shred of hope I had moments ago sizzles away like the embers on the ground around us.

"MacNamary and Grier are still here?" Raquel asks, dropping a blackened chunk of wood.

"Of course," Todd says, shaking his head. "Of *course* they are!"

All of this will be for nothing if we can't get that water from Yellowstone Lake. "Can you drive us?" I turn to Dave, fighting back the sinking feeling in my stomach.

He nods. "Yes, of course."

"I'll stay here," Nolan says. Haley hands him an alligator clip, and he hooks it to the generator.

"I'll stay, too," Raquel says, unable to tear her eyes away from the tunnel. "You guys go. Bring Eddie back safe, okay?"

"And you two bring Wyatt back," Todd says.

"We will," Nolan promises.

Todd and I don't hesitate any longer than that. We follow Dave to his truck and jump in. He floors it, the tires spinning on the ash below. Several other trucks and jeeps follow us, each marked with the National Park Service logo.

"Don't worry, we'll stop them," Dave says. "I'll throw them into the volcano myself if it comes to it."

Yellowstone Lake, as it turns out, is only a couple of minutes' drive away from where we were—it is just so hazy, it was impossible to tell before. When we reach it, it's lined with other vehicles, hooking up hoses. Many of those are fire trucks, but I also spy a couple of large water tankers.

And then I see Grier and MacNamary's half-submerged truck with the pump from the cave. People are swarming it. There's a full-on brawl between Grier and MacNamary's men and a bunch of rescue workers. Water flies every which way, sparkling in the orange glow of the sky.

Amid the chaos, Eddie carries a section of the huge slurry hose over his head, trying to climb out of the lake. We come to a halt, and I leap out of the truck, not sure where to even begin.

"Get out of the water!" Eddie's screaming. "Get out, now!"

No one is listening to him. I can't even figure out why he's yelling, until Todd clues me in.

"Oh no," he whispers next to me. "The lake—it's heated by thermal vents."

I look closer and notice pockets of steam rising from the center of the lake—an eerie omen that sends terror straight through my gut.

With all the seismic activity going on, this lake could end up hot enough to boil.

"*Get out of the water!*" Todd yells, adding his voice to Eddie's.

"Tell everyone to get out!" I look to Dave, but he's already raced into action to help take out Grier and MacNamary's men.

"What do we do?" Todd asks me.

I glance down at the obsidian stones lining the edge of the lake. They start to hop up and down as another miniature quake rumbles through. I reach for one of the sharper obsidian pieces, the only weapon I can think of.

"We're getting everyone away from that pump," I say. Todd nods at me.

The lake must finally be getting hot enough for others to notice, because before we can move in, there's suddenly a *lot* more shouting and screaming.

People scramble over one another, splashing water left and right, trying to get to the shore. As they reach dry ground, they collapse, spreading their limbs out on the rocks and yelling in pain. Whether it's from the sharp stones or the burns on their skin, I don't know.

"Let's go," Todd says. We race toward the people. I'm not sure if we're running to help them or to fight them at this point. Honestly, things have been changing so fast, I'm sure we'll figure it out once we're there.

Meanwhile, Eddie has dragged the slurry hose out of the water with him.

"Guys!" he calls, waving at us from about twenty yards down the rocky shore.

"Eddie!" I yell. "We're coming!"

Todd and I are nearly to his side when suddenly Stiles is there, appearing almost magically out of the hazy, smoke-filled air and grabbing for the hose in Eddie's hands.

"Where did you *come* from?" Todd asks, exasperated. I chuck my rock at Stiles.

"Nice try," Stiles growls in response, easily dodging my throw.

Spinning, he sends a kick straight into Eddie's stomach, sending him sailing back into the lake with a massive splash.

"Eddie!" Todd shrieks.

"No!" I yell.

Grier pulls up next to us with a truck that kicks up obsidian stones with its tires like tiny glass missiles. We duck. MacNamary is in the passenger seat.

"Get in!" she directs.

Stiles jumps into the back of the truck and Fee helps him pull in the large end of the hose. They've given up on stopping the pump, it seems, and instead are carting the accordion-like hose somewhere else. It unwinds from its giant coil, lengthening more and more as they drive farther away.

"*Dave!*" I yell for the park ranger. "We have to catch them!"

He hears me and races back to his truck.

Meanwhile, Todd has waded into the steaming water to pull Eddie out. Dead fish start to wash ashore. Todd reaches Eddie, and they put an arm around each other, yelling and gritting their teeth as they make their way out of the lake together.

My heart is in my throat as they collapse on the shoreline. While the water might not be full-on boiling, I can't imagine how much pain they're in. Todd tears at his shoes and socks, pulling them off and crying out, while Eddie lays spread eagle, wheezing. I want to run and help them, but just at that moment, Dave pulls up to get me, and I have to make a choice.

I close my eyes. They're out. They'll be okay.

Sending a mental apology to Todd and Eddie, I climb into

Dave's truck. With a force that slams me back against my seat, Dave takes off after Grier, MacNamary, Fee, and Stiles.

What we're going to do, I don't know. What *they're* planning on doing, I don't know. In the rearview mirror, I see several people gather around Todd and Eddie, tending to them, and I relax back slightly in my seat.

They'll be okay, I repeat in my head.

"Oh no," Dave says.

I look forward again, through the makeshift parking lot of semitrucks and construction vehicles. Grier and MacNamary head straight toward the burnt cabin and the hole that Wyatt is down. Stiles and Fee still clutch the slurry hose, which trails behind the truck.

And then—another quake. The constant roaring explosion in the distance grows louder.

No. My heart seizes in my chest. *No, not yet!*

The billowing clouds from the eruption expand rapidly. Ash falls in larger and larger clumps on Dave's windshield.

"Is this the supervolcano?!" Dave asks over the horrifying noise.

"I don't know," I answer. "I don't think so, but I don't know!"

Grier pulls her truck to a stop as we swerve around a backhoe. The rumbling gets to be too much—we have to stop. Dave hits the brakes, and I brace myself from flying forward. I try to reach for the door handle, but the ground is moving too badly. I bounce up and down in my seat and have no choice but to use my hands to cover my head.

When the shaking finally calms, I warily look out through the ash-covered windshield. The farthest I can see is up ahead on the left, where there is a massive wall of concrete barriers getting lined up. Kenzie's tiny form points this way and that as huge bulldozers shove the blocks forward, slowly working their way around the perimeter of the eruption site. The latest quake may have stopped, but the ash is only getting thicker.

Thunk.

Thu-thunk. Thunk.

"Oh my god." Dave's knuckles have gone pale on the steering wheel.

Off the hood of his truck, we can both easily see bits of volcanic rock pinging, denting the metal. They're no larger than marbles, but I imagine they're only going to get bigger as the eruption continues.

"Help us!" I hear Nolan shout from up ahead.

Nolan is with Haley and the fire truck, and I see that they've got wires running to the generator, and that the cabling attached to Wyatt's pod is moving. My heart restarts itself. Wyatt is getting rescued!

I jump out of the truck and run through the ash field toward Nolan. I keep my hands over my head, in case any of the falling volcanic rocks hit me.

"What are you doing?" Dave shouts after me. "Get back!"

Reaching Nolan and Haley, I grab the edge of the pod as it emerges from the ground. The metal pinches against my palms and fingers, but I refuse to let go. Together, we heave. As we do, a thought hits me. "Where's Raquel?" I ask, looking around, squinting in the haze and smoke.

I get my answer in the form of a defiant roar from behind me.

Raquel has climbed on top of Grier and MacNamary's parked truck and is wrestling with Stiles for the slurry hose. He grips her tightly and swings her around, trying to grab for her neck.

"Raquel!" I let go of the pod to race to her side. More rocks fall around us: one hits me in the shoulder. Another, still molten, hits the ground behind Grier's truck. The grass ignites.

"Get the hose!" Nolan shouts.

But then Fee, coming out of nowhere, slams me violently to the ground.

My ears ring and my vision swims. The whirr of the generator sounds piercingly loud, and I cough, causing clouds of ash to roll across the dirt in front of me.

Fee climbs off of me, getting to his feet. I try to do the same, but the wind is still knocked out of me and I fall back to my knees.

A second truck pulls up, and a bunch of men jump out. I can hear Haley shouting. A brawl breaks out between the new truck of Grier's people and the handful of Haley's firefighters who aren't with Kenzie or at the lake. The chaos only grows. I clutch at my stomach, which still hurts.

"What's going on?" I hear a familiar voice ask.

Wyatt! I want to sob in relief.

"Wyatt, you're okay!" Nolan jerks open the bars to the drilling pod, which is now out of the tunnel and laying on the remains

306

of the cabin floor by the generator. Wyatt stumbles out, shaking himself off. He pulls off his safety goggles, and I can see his expression morph as he takes in everything that's happening.

I struggle to get up again, but Fee puts a foot on my back and kicks me down, face first into the dirt and ash once more.

Then Fee yelps, his foot leaving me in a flash. I turn to see Dave wrestling him. I crawl away from them both and scramble upright, glancing back at the truck bed for Raquel. She's still in Stiles's grip, and behind them, the brush fire grows closer.

MacNamary and Grier climb out of the truck. "Get that hose!" MacNamary commands. But Stiles's hands are full, and Raquel's grip on the hose is tight.

"Hold on, Raquel!" I yell. "I'm coming!"

Stiles flings Raquel around in the truck bed. She tries to aim a kick for his shins but misses. Then Fee is up and darting straight for them. I look back to see Dave rolling on the ground, clutching at his face, which is gushing blood.

I spin to run at Fee, but Nolan and Wyatt get to him first. Nolan tackles Fee to the ground in a poof of ash, and Wyatt delivers a sharp kick to his temple.

Fee doesn't get up this time.

Tiny, stinging rocks pelt us all. Reaching the truck, my feet slide on the hubcap of the back tire as I scramble to pull myself into its bed. A layer of ash makes everything slick.

But I make it in—and just in time. The fire behind the truck reaches the grass at the edge of the vehicle. The heat sears into my skin.

Planting my feet firmly on the steel bed of the truck, I shove Stiles with all my might, needing to get him away from Raquel. He stumbles, losing his grip on the hose. For a brief moment, Raquel has it all to herself.

At least, until MacNamary jumps up onto the truck with us. She grabs Raquel first, throwing her and the hose to the ground—thankfully over the side where the fire has yet to reach. Stiles slams his hands onto my shoulders and pushes me along the truck bed toward the flaming side. My boots slide on the metal.

"Bri!" Raquel screams. "*No!*"

"The hose!" I yell. I can feel the heat radiating as Stiles bends me backward toward it. My knees begin to buckle. Everything is glowing. Sizzling pops and hisses taunt me. "Don't let go of the hose!"

But Raquel has made her choice. She leaps back up onto the truck, grabbing Stiles around the waist. Startled, Stiles slips on the ash, and all three of us topple off the vehicle in a heap on the safe side. Everything hurts, but adrenaline keeps me going. I scamper up, sweat slick on my palms. Stiles tries to get up as well but is having a lot more trouble than me.

"It's too late!" MacNamary yells.

I turn.

She has the hose, and she's on the truck, holding it out over the fire.

"Laura, get down from there, the truck is going to blow!" Grier demands.

Stiles groans and tries to get up again, but Haley and her

firefighters have gotten the upper hand on the other men and now move in to take him and Fee away. Some of the firefighters turn to go after MacNamary next.

MacNamary hefts the hose out farther over the flames. "Come any closer, and I *will* drop this!" she warns.

Everyone stops in their tracks. Larger rocks start to fall, mixed in with the smaller ones. We all have a hand over our heads now, trying to protect ourselves.

"What do we do?" Raquel asks me.

"You're all going to back off," MacNamary says next. "Back off and let us leave."

"How can you do this?" Dave asks, stumbling to his feet and holding his sleeve against his nose, which is still bleeding profusely. "How can you betray everyone like this?"

"I'm not betraying anyone, *you* are!" MacNamary responds. Her curly hair flies around her head. "All of you! At this point, if you aren't actively working on taking out the human race, you are the problem!"

"You can't mean that!" Dave yells back, still in disbelief. "What about your park?"

Wyatt picks up the unhooked cabling from the pod, which was meant to latch onto one of us so we can go back down the tunnel. But there's no use doing that if we don't have the hose to take with us. He looks at me helplessly.

"Working at Yellowstone was just a means to an end," MacNamary replies. Sweat glistens on her forehead. "Now we're going to leave, and you're going to let us, or you'll have to come up here to get me and hope the gas tank in this thing doesn't blow when you do. Poetic justice if it does! Right, Samantha?" She laughs at that, looking to Dr. Grier.

Grier is as gray as the ash around us. "How did you get all these people to come help you?" she asks us, her quiet tone in stark contrast to MacNamary's. Nolan approaches her cautiously.

"I don't know," I say honestly. "We just asked."

"Aunt Sam," Nolan says, putting a tentative hand on her shoulder. "Please."

"Samantha!" MacNamary calls, demanding her attention.

Grier stares around numbly at the ever-growing crowds of people gathering. "There are so many."

"Samantha!" MacNamary repeats herself.

But Grier doesn't look at her. Nolan tugs at her shoulder.

MacNamary's eyes flash, reflecting the fire to her right. "Fine," she declares, widening her stance and challenging everyone around her. "I don't need her anymore, anyway." She goes to heave the hose into the fire, but then something catches my attention in the window of her truck.

Two somethings.

"Nolan!" I gasp. "Buggy and Baxter!"

"What?" MacNamary looks down at her feet, as if the ferrets could be up there on the truck bed with her.

Nolan cries out, letting go of his aunt. "Buggy! Baxter!" He whistles for them, and they hop out of the open driver's door. Buggy is dragging a bag of beef jerky with him, like a hard-won prize. They must've been hiding in there this entire time.

It's all the distraction we need.

Raquel runs straight at Grier. Wyatt darts forward and snatches at the hose MacNamary has dangling over the side of the truck. I take the cabling Wyatt dropped, wrapping it around myself like a harness. If we get that hose back even for a moment, I'm not wasting our chance.

"*No!*" MacNamary shouts, in a tug of war with Wyatt over the hose. A firefighter joins Raquel in hauling Dr. Grier away. She doesn't fight them. She just turns her head in all directions, lost and broken.

"Where were you all when we were trying to save our planet from climate change?" she asks, her eyes haunted. "Environmental destruction? Pollution?! Why now? Why *this*?"

"Samantha!" MacNamary yells again, stomping her foot. She yanks the hose from Wyatt, and he falls backward from the force. A firefighter moves to go after her and the hose next, but Haley shouts for him to stay away. She actually shouts for *everyone* to stay away, to get back from the ticking time-bomb truck, but most of us ignore her.

The ground shakes again under our feet, and in the distance, I see the eruption send out its highest burst of lava rocks yet. This is getting worse by the moment.

"How did you do it?" Grier asks me. Her captors are forced to stop to regain their footing. Nolan is with them, his ferrets back in his sweatshirt pocket. "How did you get them all to come?"

I shake my head. "I don't know," I honestly say once again. "I guess when all these people heard there was a way to save lives, they decided to do it."

There's more to it than that. There has to be. But too much is happening, and I can't sort out any more sense than that right now.

Tears fall down Dr. Grier's face as she's taken away. Then she whips her head up, as if thinking of something. "Be careful down there!" she yells back at me. "The quakes may have shifted things! Look for new signs of leaks in the bedrock!"

"*Samantha!*" MacNamary shrieks once more from the truck bed. She lets out a growl, glaring at us. "Well. I never thought I'd see the day that you managed to brainwash Samantha Grier against her life's work, but bravo."

There's a heart-stopping popping sound from the truck, like several gunshots going off at once. I shriek, ducking—but it was just the tires. Not the gas tank.

MacNamary almost loses her footing but manages to steady herself. She climbs up onto the roof of the truck, heaving the hose with her. The fire blazes behind her, a backdrop to her rage. "You think you're the heroes and we're the villains. But you can't even see that you're the same as us."

Wyatt and Raquel walk over to stand on either side of me by the tunnel entrance in what remains of the burnt cabin. Without speaking, we link arms.

"We're completely different than you," I retort, my harness shaking around me. "You say you want to save the world, but you're not. You're killing it!"

"Look at what you've done to Yellowstone!" MacNamary gestures out at the landscape. I don't want to, but I turn, unable to stop myself.

As far as the eye can see, giant vehicles roll around, churning up the ground and knocking down trees. The sky is filled with smoke. There are no animals. There is only mud and engines and hundreds of people, ripping apart the park.

"You made the same choice, Bri," MacNamary taunts. "You weighed destruction against destruction. Turn this hose on, and you'll only make it worse. You'll drain Yellowstone Lake. To save something, you have to kill something."

Horrified, I inch backward. "You're wrong," I say. Raquel and Wyatt squeeze closer to me, trying to steady me.

"Am I?" MacNamary asks.

"Yes! You are!" a shrill voice sounds. *"Now shut up!"*

Like the world's smallest but fiercest tornado, Kenzie comes tearing across the ground, leaping onto the truck and toppling MacNamary into its bed.

The horror in my gut freezes into spikes. *"Kenzie!"* I shout.

The hose falls from MacNamary's grip, and Wyatt and Raquel leave my side to race to grab it. They just manage to get their hands on it before it tumbles into the fire.

"Go, Bri, go!" Kenzie yells, rolling MacNamary toward the flames.

I hesitate, but only for a moment. Then I sit down on the floor of the destroyed cabin and drop into the tunnel.

CHAPTER TWENTY-THREE

"What is she doing?" someone shouts above ground.

"Get her out of there!"

"She's just a *child*!"

I realize too late the flaw in our plan. After all we've done, we're still kids to the people helping us—the firefighters, the park rangers. They'll never let us do what needs to be done.

"No," I whisper.

The cable I'm holding sways suddenly, jerking me to a stop. My headlamp dances along the wall, and I look up, prepared to argue as loud and obnoxiously as necessary.

But I don't need to.

"You'll have to get past me!" I hear Raquel say. I see her dangling on the cable inside the tunnel. The more I move down, the lower she sinks with me.

"And me!" I hear Wyatt next, and the cable goes even tighter.

"Guys!" I call up. "What are you doing?"

"Buying you time!" Wyatt shouts, dangling above Raquel. They drop the hose down to me, and I grab it.

My heart swells. They're blocking the tunnel. I wait in desperate hope for another body to jump in, because it would have to be Kenzie, and that would mean she was okay.

"Bri, I won't leave until you're out," Raquel promises me. "So you'd better come back, okay?"

"I'll try!" I say. "But if I don't—"

"Don't say that!"

"*If I don't,* I want you to get out, Raquel!" I shout up at her.

"Bri—"

But then there's a massive explosion, and the cable goes slack. I drop down the vertical part of the tunnel at super speed, dragging the hose with me. Looking up, I can see the tunnel entrance cloud over with smoke, and I scream.

"Wyatt! Raquel!"

They don't answer.

Oh no. Oh god, no. The truck must have blown up. If Kenzie was still on it, then . . .

I can't think about it. Fear grips me as fast as the bedrock flies past me.

A jagged edge juts out. I nearly slam into it, just managing to maneuver out of the way in time. Now I find myself glancing around wildly. That shouldn't be there. The drills make things smooth down our tunnels, not bumpy!

Shoot. Dr. Grier was right—all the quakes have shifted things down here.

I tense up, clutching the hose and cable. This was already a dangerous plan. When I turn this hose on, the water will hit the super-hot end of this tunnel and immediately turn to steam. That will trigger a massive explosion as the water vapor expands out, which should allow for the water still gushing from the hose to breach the magma tunnel and start solidifying it. But I have no idea if we can all get out in time. And with the tunnel even less stable than before . . .

Is this all worth it?

I realize in sick horror that I don't know. I can't know. If I go through with this, I might be sacrificing all our lives. And I'm definitely sacrificing Yellowstone Lake. By numbers, that's more than a fair trade, even if it makes me feel ill.

But trading lives for lives was MacNamary and Grier's logic, too, just on a bigger scale. It's exactly what MacNamary was talking about. It's what Aunt Pauline and I focused on in our documentary last year: regrowth after destruction.

The ground shakes around me, and I squeal. After a few terrifying seconds, it stops. I dangle there, not daring to move. Above me, I can hear Wyatt and Raquel shout. A small relief—for the moment, they're okay. Though that moment may be over soon, if I go through with this.

Is this really the right thing to do?

I . . . I think it is. I can hear my friends reassuring each other from hundreds of yards above me, their voices echoing. They chose to jump in here and help. To them, this was the right choice.

This doesn't feel right to me, though. It feels terrifying.

But I guess, when it comes down to it, what I feel isn't what matters. After all, my feelings have been wrong before. *Very* wrong.

I take a deep breath and then continue to lower myself in the tunnel.

No, this doesn't feel right at all.

But I know it *is* right.

Just before the tunnel makes its horizontal turn, I find red markings all over the walls. They're notes, from Wyatt. Written in . . . lipstick?

I laugh, smacking my head. Of course! That overly dramatic hug Kenzie gave him. She must've slipped him her tube of lipstick.

I read through the notes, which mark how much farther a person should go to lock in the hose to get it close enough to the magma for its job, while keeping enough distance for the person to conceivably get away in time. I wonder if he did all of this while waiting to be saved. Maybe he figured he wouldn't be and was leaving these notes for whoever took his place.

They're excellent notes, but Wyatt didn't calculate there being more than one person needing to escape the tunnel. Nor did he calculate the risks of groundwater releases from earthquake activity. And he certainly didn't account for the fact that the lake water was already going to be heated to scalding temperatures.

I'm going to need to make my own decisions about all of that.

I pause, trembling, even though I know this is no time to freeze up.

"Okay," I whisper to an imaginary audience. "This is it. I have to figure out how to hook up this hose as safely as possible. No big deal, right?"

I read through Wyatt's notes, wishing desperately that I had Earth Builder in front of me so I could test my ideas. I wonder what the superhero version of myself would do here. I think about the drawings Todd and I made back in our cabin all those weeks ago, and tears pinch my eyes.

"What we need is more time," I say, pulling myself together. I tap the edge of the hose against the rocky wall, watching the way the shadows play. The metal edging of it makes a satisfying clunking sound every time it hits the rock. "And a way to trigger the hose from a distance."

I stare at the metal edging where the lever is located to release the water. Then I look at the cable I'm holding. My thoughts start to spin into something tangible. Scary, but tangible.

"I might have an idea." The barest hint of courage reenters my trembling soul. "If it works, you may never see me again, though, viewers, so . . . thanks for watching."

My body tingles, knowing just how close I am now to the passageway of magma rising up to the surface. It's incredibly warm in here. The last of Wyatt's lipstick notes have melted into thin goo.

I'm flat on my stomach in the newest and most horizontal

section of this tunnel. Sweat pours off my head, and I lodge the hose into the narrowed end of the tunnel, packing it in tight with the bits of rubble I find. The rock is so hot it almost burns my hands.

Once I'm satisfied that it's in there well enough, I turn around in a small side passage that Wyatt must have dug, either on purpose or by accident, I don't know.

I begin my crawl back up the dark tunnel, wincing as my arms scrape on the rock and doing my best not to bump either the hose or the cable. I've tied the cable to the hose's lever. The moment someone pulls up on it, the water will release. I just have to hope people wait to tug on it until I'm back in the vertical tunnel, ready to be hauled out.

And that whoever is pulling me out can do it quickly.

In addition to the lever getting pulled, the hose will be yanked backward up the tunnel the more someone tugs on the cable. But if I did the math right, it shouldn't matter. The water will flood the tunnel at a rate that will make it okay for the hose to be positioned at any point along the path after the initial blast.

After many, many more grueling minutes of crawling, I can see the vertical turn ahead. Every muscle in my body aches, and my forearms won't stop bleeding. Just a little farther . . .

Then, the ground begins to shake. After all we've been through, I'm more than used to that sensation below my feet, but feeling it above my horizontal body is *entirely* different.

I shriek. I can't help it. My entire world is in motion, rumbling and rolling. I expect to be crushed at any moment.

319

The shaking gets worse. My body is thrown up and down now, slamming into the top and the bottom of the tunnel on repeat, the hose bouncing up and down next to me. I want to cover my head, but instead I grab for the cable. If I'm going to die, I at least need to release the water before the end.

But the moment my hand grips the cable, I'm jerked forward. Someone is pulling me out. I scream again, clutching at the cable with both hands now, my entire body scraping along the rock. My headlamp bounces light in front of me—I'm nearing the tunnel turn.

I hit it. My back slams into the top of the tunnel as I'm pulled upright. Stars burst in front of me—the pain is *blinding.* Whoever thinks they're saving me has *no* idea how close they just came to paralyzing me for life. I sob openly, flying upward, jerked unevenly every other moment.

Then—another quake.

No.

An *explosion.*

My sobs stop, horror overtaking me. If the cable's been pulled—that means the water was released.

"Oh no," I croak out.

The ground ripples in all directions, tearing itself apart. There's an ungodly deep rumble, like a giant fighting to break free of the bedrock. The tunnel cracks around me, and my eardrums vibrate so hard I'm sure they'll rupture. Chunks of falling rock rain down as I'm dragged up. I can't shield my head, or risk letting go of the cable. All I can do is hunch up and hope.

My shoulders and back get hit over and over, and my side scrapes up against the hose. One chunk of rock hits the top of my head and I see stars once again. They dance and prickle in my eyes, which I have squeezed shut.

My knuckles are bleeding, my hands clutching the rising cable. I can feel heat below me. A wave of steam washes over me in one massive blast. My skin screams, burning.

But as quickly as the steam hits, it's gone.

Instead, I hear a bubbling, popping noise. Shaking uncontrollably, I open one eye and look down.

I see my feet on either side of the hose. I see the walls of the tunnel, zipping past me. And I see water rising.

"Hurry!" I scream up at whoever is pulling me out of here, having no idea if they can hear me.

There's light above. Somewhere in my mind, I register that means my friends have made it out of the tunnel. But then, the edges of the tunnel exit start to crumble. Another batch of rocks shakes loose and falls toward me.

There are so *many*. They start to pile up on my shoulders, my back, wedging me into the tunnel and burying me alive. I close my eyes again.

I was so close . . . *so close.*

"Bri!"

My eyes snap open.

A hand lands on mine, pulling my grip off the cable and

yanking me upward, through the rubble and back onto the ground above.

It's Raquel. She grips my hand and won't let go, even as I lay safely on the dirt.

"She's out!" someone yells. "Let's move!"

My head swims. "Bri!" I can hear Wyatt say.

"She's alive!" Nolan exclaims. "Raquel, she's alive!"

Raquel collapses next to me, still clutching my hand and physically shaking.

"Look, guys, look!" Wyatt says next. "The eruption—it's shrinking!"

I want to look. I want to see. I want to believe what we just did really is working. But the world spins around me, and anything farther than three feet away might as well be in another dimension.

"Can you hear me?" some adult is asking me. "Can you move?"

"Kenzie?" I manage to ask. I blink my eyes at the man. He's in full military garb. Actually, glancing around, I realize there are soldiers everywhere now. Some part of me remembers the military jets earlier. Did the army get here while I was underground?

"Kenzie's okay!" Nolan says, kneeling down by my side. "But we need to get out of here in case this backfires."

"Todd? Eddie?" I manage next. Raquel lets go of my hand, climbs to her feet, and stares down the remains of the tunnel, every emotion in the world flashing across her face.

"They're okay, too," Nolan reassures me. Buggy and Baxter poke their head out of his pocket.

"We need a stretcher!" the soldier says, spinning away. "This girl's in no condition to stand on her own!" There's a lot of shouting, but I let the darkness overtake me. My friends are all alive. The eruption might be settling. From what's going on around me, it seems like the topside containment system is coming together.

I've done all I can.

Now I have to trust that everyone else will do the same.

When I next open my eyes, I'm on the back of a some kind of military truck, laying on the flat bed with several soldiers crouched next to me. We're speeding out of the park. The rear of the truck isn't closed, so I can watch out behind us.

I can see Yellowstone Lake.

Its water level has dropped dramatically. Pumps and hoses stick out of it in all directions. It's a disgusting, hissing muddy pit, overrun by people and trucks.

This park is never going to be the same.

I shut my eyes. Maybe it'd be better to be unconscious for this part. We've destroyed so much—both in starting and stopping the supervolcano. Our direct actions have turned this beautiful place into a land of nightmares. I try to find solace in the fact that from what Wyatt said the hose trick might have worked—the eruption might be shrinking, which means overall less destruction—but it's hard to block out the horror we've already caused.

"Bri, hey. Check it out."

I open my eyes again. Kenzie is next to me. I hadn't realized that. Was she there a moment ago? Or did more time really pass?

She's pointing. In the distance, by some trees that somehow aren't on fire, there's an elk. And with her, a baby. They're staring at us. Both are safe—both are alive.

The elk mother's eyes lock onto mine. And in that moment, I have the answer to my question from down in the tunnel.

I'm sure many didn't survive this disaster. But we've stopped a bigger one. Those that made it through this catastrophe won't have to face an all-out apocalypse.

It was worth it.

I lean my head back down at the urging of one of the soldiers. Once we're several miles out of the park, one of their radios sounds.

"Flooding is working like a charm. Going to take a while, but the volcano's already calmed way down. If we keep this up, we'll contain this sucker for good. And without the pressure release for that supervolcano, our scientists are telling us it should settle naturally over time. Those kids did it. If you're with them, tell them that. Tell them their stubbornness saved the planet."

"You hear that, Bri?" Kenzie says. I crack open my eyes to see her grinning. It's the first time I've seen her smile without any lipstick. "You better heal up fast. We're about to be extremely famous, and you don't want to spend all your interviews in a full body cast."

I laugh, which makes my chest scream in pain and my head feel woozy.

Famous, huh? Right now, I'd be happy enough to have a warm bed and about eighty fewer broken bones.

But more than that, I'd really love to find a way to restore Yellowstone.

CHAPTER TWENTY-FOUR

"You ready?" my mom asks me, straightening my shirt. The curtains near us blow in the breeze, and several leaves skitter by the outdoor stage.

"Of course she is," my dad says.

"I can't believe that our little girl is going to be on national television!" Mom gushes. "That's something even your aunt hasn't done!"

"Yeah, yeah." I brush them away with the arm that isn't in a sling. It's been over a month, and my concussion has finally settled enough that I am cleared to travel. Bed rest and some fantastic surgeons from my parents' hospital helped me recover from a lot of my injuries. My ribs are almost totally healed, and there's a metal plate holding two parts of my hip together where it fractured. Since I'm not fully grown yet, the doctors said I'll make a complete recovery.

"Aren't you excited?" my dad asks.

I look around the backstage area at my friends.

Kenzie is being fussed over by her grandma. She acts annoyed, but I know her well enough to see that she's absolutely loving the attention. Instead of lipstick, Kenzie now sports bright pink hair. She said she'd been wanting to dye it since the third grade, but her grandma refused to let her. I suppose now that she's saved the planet, she has some leverage to work with.

She catches my eye and makes a face, and I laugh.

Wyatt looks like he's getting last-minute tips from his dad. They sit together, talking a mile a minute. Wyatt never was quiet, I realize. He's an entirely different person than I had first thought. He's wearing a Volcanoes National Park hat, in honor of his mom. I wonder if he'd consider becoming a park ranger himself one day. He'd be really good at it.

Todd, his parents, and his younger brothers are all clustered together with Eddie's family. Todd's brothers are the polar opposite from him: loud, boisterous, and bouncy. I can see why they didn't first travel out with his parents when they dropped him off in Montana at the beginning of the summer. Eddie's sisters chase the younger boys around, and Todd and Eddie laugh together at them. I never would've guessed they'd become such good friends, but I'm pleased to see they have. And to add to the positive things, I found out today that Eddie recently rejoined a gymnastics program. He shows off with a handstand, which prompts one of the sound crew guys to dart over to check on Eddie's microphone pack.

Raquel sits some distance away, in a constant side-hug embrace with her mom. Raquel is the reason I'm here. She pulled me out of that tunnel. I owe her everything. Other than Kenzie, Raquel and I have kept in touch the most through the past several weeks. While she's not interested in joining in on my new YouTube channel, she does have a knack for helping me work through ideas for it. I've found that there isn't anyone whose opinion I value more than hers. I smile her way, but she's too busy laughing at Eddie's handstand to notice.

On the other side of my parents, Nolan sits with his family. His little sister is on his lap, bouncing on his knee. Nolan had said his parents weren't big fans of his ferrets, but his mom and dad are each holding one of them now, petting the critters as they all chat together. He does look a lot like his dad—they even have the same shy smile. Meanwhile, his mom looks like a younger version of Dr. Grier. It's hard for me to get past that, and I have to constantly remind myself that Dr. Grier is in custody. So is Ms. MacNamary. They can't do anything to hurt us now.

But I still can't bring myself to look at Nolan's mom too much.

I've been seeing a therapist to help with the nightmares. She says it is okay that I'm having trouble sleeping—that I feel like I'm haunted by MacNamary and Grier, that I still think I hear the roaring volcano on occasion or feel the weight of the rocks on my shoulders. She says we'll work to get through all that in time, and that I shouldn't feel bad for not overcoming every single one of the traumas immediately. It's strange how comforting it is to have permission to be upset. And for what it's worth, last night I slept for eight solid hours, even though we stayed in a hotel near Yellowstone, which I figured would make things scarier for me. But it didn't, so maybe there's some hope and progress there.

There's one piece of the whole . . . *ordeal* . . . that I'm having trouble setting aside more than the rest, though: Dr. Grier's shock at how people showed up to help us stop the supervolcano. I just can't figure that part out. What *happened* to her in her life to make her so surprised that people wanted to save the world? Who let her down so badly?

Nolan's mom lets out a laugh as Buggy gets tangled flipping around in her billowing skirt. I tense up as her all-too-familiar eyes crinkle at their corners. It's not a face I'm used to seeing happy.

From what I could understand of their stories, it sounded like both Dr. Grier and Ms. MacNamary's original intentions started out genuinely good earlier in their lives. They only got twisted after they encountered too many other people who had selfish goals. It's no excuse for what they did. They let themselves fall down a dark, murder-filled path—one that I'll never forgive them for as long as I live. But I can't help but wonder what they could have accomplished if they had been supported in their first attempts to save the world. Now that I've seen firsthand what people are capable of when we come together, I better understand their frustration. Not their solution—but their frustration.

I glance down at my arm cast, with the signatures of my friends all over it. Well, really, it's just a gigantic *Kenzie* with other signatures squeezed in at the edges. I inhale slowly, the way my therapist has taught me, and try to set thoughts of Grier and MacNamary aside.

"Bri?" my mom asks. "Your father asked you if you were excited."

I let out my breath, counting to five. The dull ache from my ribcage brings my focus back to reality. Honestly, right now I'm just glad to be with all my friends in a completely non-life-threatening situation. The television thing is just icing on the cake.

But I smile for my parents. "Yeah, I'm excited."

They beam.

Then my phone buzzes. It's a text from Aunt Pauline wishing me luck. A tingle of pride runs through me. She's been helping me set up my new YouTube channel, focusing on my plans for fixing up Yellowstone. Aunt Pauline wants me to jump on launching the channel, since I suddenly have quite the giant following online. It took a while to get over the guilt of being excited about how viral the videos I had sent her went, but I've decided that I can feel awesome about having an audience and still want to work to make the world a better place. Those aren't mutually exclusive. In fact, it's actually super helpful to have a lot of people care about what I have to say.

As I close my eyes, wind brushes past me, cool enough to signal that autumn is around the corner. There's still a smell of sulfur in the air. It threatens to throw me straight back into the horrors we went through weeks ago, but I tighten my fists. It's over now. Yellowstone is calming. Grier and MacNamary's other sites have been dismantled. Even James and Carlos were found alive. They're both recovering in a hospital in LA right now. Raquel sent me a picture of her and Eddie visiting them.

I open up my eyes to see a stagehand directing us toward the curtain.

"You guys ready?" Wyatt asks.

"Completely," Kenzie says. "Born ready. Almost died ready." She points at a burn on her arm. "Ready might as well be my middle name."

"And we're all in agreement about what we're going to say?" Raquel asks.

"We've been over this a million times," Eddie says.

"I'm just making sure," Raquel replies.

"We want people to not only help clean up Yellowstone, but push for the creation of more protected park lands and better technologies to reduce human impact on the planet," Todd recites from the pact we all made.

"We've done enough destroying," I say. "We want people to help us rebuild the natural world."

"But, you know, a little less violently than triggering every supervolcano on the planet to reset literally everything," Kenzie adds.

"Just a *touch* less violent than that, yes," Nolan agrees. We all laugh.

The stagehand motions for us to quiet down and come closer. All of us scoot toward the curtains. On the screen onstage, I can hear the host narrating clips from my videos, which now have view counts in the hundreds of millions.

"Now," the television host says from the other side of the curtain. "For the first time appearing together since stopping a *supervolcano*, we'd like to welcome the world's youngest heroes."

We all grin at each other, ready to hit the stage.

"The heroes who have already promised that they aren't done saving the planet."

Our grinning turns to ferocious nodding. We've made a promise. We have a voice, and we're going to use it.

"The heroes the internet has lovingly dubbed—*the Seismic Seven*!"

We step onto the stage set up at Yellowstone's park entrance. Media stretches out as far as the eye can see.

Waving, we greet the world we hope to change.

AUTHOR'S NOTE

Right off the bat, I'd like to point out something important: Yellowstone National Park *does* sit atop a supervolcano. Supervolcanoes are incredibly dangerous and have impacted the world many times in the past. But the odds of the Yellowstone Supervolcano erupting in any major way anytime soon are *minuscule*. Super slim. Next to nothing. Scientists monitor it closely, and there is no need for concern.

While the supervolcano isn't putting us in mortal peril at the moment, it does make the geology of the Yellowstone region absolutely fascinating. A decade ago, I was lucky enough to spend a summer doing a geology field course in the Yellowstone and Grand Teton area. Through the University of Michigan's Camp Davis experience, I gained a great deal of knowledge about the geology of that part of the world. I went on to study geology and paleontology much more in depth and thankfully had the opportunity to visit Yellowstone again a few years later.

This background certainly helped shape this book. But it didn't help with the biggest plot challenge of all: getting a volcano to erupt—and also getting it to stop.

At the end of chapter 17, there's an inside joke between me, myself, and anyone who reads this:

"We're not Googling 'how to stop a supervolcano."

Eddie

You see, when I first came up with the idea for this novel, that's exactly what I did. Seriously! Every book has to start somewhere, and mine started with a Google search. I researched online for how people might go about stopping a volcano, and this is what the internet told me: it's impossible. You can't.

So then I switched to the other major plot point of the novel—how to *trigger* a volcano. Google held the same answer for that question as for my first: it's not possible. You can't.

That presented a couple of problems to say the least. I always aim to keep the scientific aspects of my novels as accurate as possible. How could I write this book and have the science behind it be realistic if the larger plot points weren't?

To tackle this issue, I read through my old geology textbooks to re-familiarize myself with the basics, watched several documentaries on volcanoes for inspiration, and did a lot of academic research to make sure I was up to date with what current science had to say about human involvement in seismic activity. Most importantly, though, was the time I spent brainstorming with my friend and colleague Julia Sable, who is a real volcanologist.

With a little imagination and a lot of sketches and scribbles, Julia and I concocted the plan that Dr. Grier and Ms. MacNamary pursued in the book. And after that, we thought up how Bri and her friends could save the day. It took a lot of trial and error!

I owe a great deal to Julia's expertise, enthusiasm, and patience as we figured out how to make two of the biggest parts of the plot *work*. But I have to stress once again—what happens in this novel is not something that can happen in reality. It's a work of fiction. I stretched science into the realm of imagination to create this adventurous tale. In reality, humans can't set off the Yellowstone Supervolcano.

"But *what if?*" I hear some of you asking. Gosh, I love *what ifs*. They are what make science tick. They are what made this book possible. I encourage all the *what if* questions you have, but I also caution not to let yourself get carried away with worry about the Yellowstone Supervolcano or any other major potential natural disasters out there. Human ingenuity is a great thing, and with steady minds, compassion, and creativity, we can prepare for and pull ourselves out of nearly any situation, as long as we have the courage to take action.

That's what Bri and her friends do in this book. They see something terrifying happening that might cause others to give up or run away, but instead, they find a way to save the day. By working together, combining their strengths, and supporting one another, they refuse to back down and let the bad guys win. Even when the odds were seemingly impossible.

That's what I encourage every reader of this book to do. Dive into challenges. Explore new ideas. Take on responsibilities. Ask for help when you need it. And always try, try again, especially when you know your goal is important. No matter your interests—science, creative arts, sports, history, something else entirely, or if you're still searching—you can contribute to awesome things and can accomplish more than the world ever expects.

Sincerely,

Katie Slivensky

GLOSSARY

Aerosols: Tiny droplets of liquid or particles of solid suspended in a gas, such as in the air.

Augite: A dark-colored mineral, often found in igneous rocks.

Basalt: A common, fine-grained igneous rock formed by the rapid cooling of basaltic lava flow, mostly composed of the minerals feldspar and augite.

Basaltic magma: Magma made of molten basalt. It tends to be hotter than other types of magma and flows more easily. It is often found at hot spots.

Bedrock: The layer of unbroken rock underneath the soil that can reach miles into the Earth's crust.

Caldera: A crater formed by the explosion of a volcanic eruption or by the collapse of surface rock onto an emptied magma chamber.

Conduction: A type of heat transfer that is due to direct contact. When something at a higher temperature touches something at a lower temperature, heat will flow from the higher temperature substance or object into the lower temperature substance or object.

Convection: A type of heat transfer that relies on the movement of fluids. Higher temperature fluids rise and lower temperature fluids sink, due to higher temperature fluids being less dense than lower temperature fluids. This often creates a cycle or a current, especially when mixed with conduction.

Core: The innermost layer of the planet Earth. The outer portion of the core is liquid, while the inner portion is likely solid. The core is mostly made of iron mixed with some nickel.

Crevasse: A deep crack through a solid, such as ice or rock.

Crust: The outermost layer of the planet Earth. The thinner sections tend to be under the ocean and made of rock such as basalt. The thicker sections are continental and often made of granite.

Density: How much mass something has for the amount of space it takes up.

Earthquake: The shaking of planet Earth.

Eruption: When lava, gases, and ash are ejected from the ground. This can happen underwater or on land.

Fault: A fracture in the Earth's crust.

Feldspar: A common rock-forming mineral that, depending on the elements that make it up, can be different pale colors.

Fracking: A technique used by oil and gas companies to access natural gas thousands of feet underground. A specialized drill bit and drill pipe bore down through the ground, and pressurized fluid then creates cracks to get at the natural gas.

Geology: The study of Earth.

Geyser: A spring of water that's violently ejected from the ground, usually along with steam. This happens when water underground is in contact with hot rock—usually heated by magma—and comes to a boil. The pressurized, boiling water explodes out of available vents or cracks in the ground.

Grain size: How big the pieces of sediment are in a rock.

Granite: A type of igneous rock formed slowly underground by cooling magma. Usually made of quartz, feldspar, and a variety of other minerals that, depending on their mix, can make the granite look more pink, gray, or white.

Gypsum: A type of clear to white-colored mineral that can form as soft crystals where water evaporates.

Hot spot: A place on Earth where there is more volcanic activity than usual, possibly due to magma pockets closer to the surface and/or rising plumes of the mantle under the crust.

Hot springs: A spring formed by water that's been heated underground, often due to being near areas of volcanic activity.

Hydrothermal fluids: Mixtures of water, various elements, and gases that are heated naturally underground and bubble up through the mantle and through magma.

Igneous: A type of rock that is made from the cooling of magma or lava.

Lava: Molten rock that has escaped from the Earth's crust.

Magma: Molten rock that is underground.

Magma chamber: A large section of molten rock underground.

Mantle: The layer of planet Earth between the core and the crust. It is primarily solid but does flow slowly due to convection.

Mass: A measure of how much matter is in something.

Mass extinction: When a large percentage of species of life on Earth dies out in a relatively short amount of time.

Metamorphic: A type of rock that is made when other rock undergoes changes from heat or pressure.

Mica: A type of thin, flaky mineral.

Mineral: A solid substance that forms as crystals and is made of one type of chemical compound, rather than being a mix of many types of chemical compounds.

Nuclear winter: When small particles and aerosols enter the atmosphere, blocking sunlight from reaching the planet and resulting in the unnatural cooling of the climate. The term stems from the idea behind what would happen if there was to be nuclear war.

Obsidian: A type of dark, glassy igneous rock formed from lava that cools too quickly for large crystals to have time to grow.

Partial melt: When part of a solid is melted but not the full thing. This can happen if the solid is made of a mixture of different minerals or substances.

Plate tectonics: The slow movement of large, plate-like sections of the Earth's crust over the mantle underneath them.

Pumice: A type of igneous rock that cools from lava as it is still falling through the air after being ejected during an eruption. As a result, this rock is filled with holes.

Pyroclastic surge: A large amount of gas and pieces of rock that burst outward from a volcanic eruption.

Quartz: A type of mineral that is typically clear but can come in colored varieties. It is the most common type of mineral on the surface of planet Earth.

Rhyolite: A fine-grained igneous rock that is mostly composed of the minerals quartz and feldspar.

Rhyolitic magma: Magma made of molten rhyolite. It is slow moving and tends to pile up.

Richter scale: A scale that measures the size of an earthquake. The larger the number, the more severe the earthquake. The biggest earthquake ever measured came in at a 9.5 on the Richter scale and occurred in 1960 in Chile.

Rock: A solid that is made of one or more minerals.

Sedimentary: A type of rock formed by cementing together bits of minerals or organic materials that collect at the Earth's surface.

Seismic activity: The movement of the Earth as caused by vibrations, explosions, and earthquakes.

Spelunking: The exploration of caves.

Stalactite: An icicle-like structure that hangs from the roof of caves and is formed from mineral deposits from dripping water. Often paired with a stalagmite.

Stalagmite: A pointed structure rising from the floor of a cave, formed from minerals that drip from water from the roof of the cave. Often paired with a stalactite.

Sulfur: A chemical element that is often found in volcanic regions. Tends to be yellow in appearance, and many chemical compounds that include it have a strong odor.

Supervolcano: A nonscientific term for the biggest volcanoes on the planet.

Tuff: Rock made from cooled volcanic ash.

Volcanic ash: Bits of pulverized rock, minerals, and glass that come from volcanic eruptions.

Volcanic vent: An opening on the Earth's surface where lava flows out and pyroclastic material erupts.

Volcano: A break in the crust over a magma chamber, where gases, ash, and lava can escape.

ACKNOWLEDGMENTS

I want to start by thanking the National Park Service for all the work they do to protect unique landscapes, important ecosystems, and irreplaceable wonders. Yellowstone National Park holds a special place in my heart, as it was my first experience with nature on a grand scale. It gave me hope that people can and *will* save our planet. It won't be easy, and there will be setbacks, but we can *do* this.

Thank you to my entire editorial team at HarperCollins Children's. Erica Sussman—your insights are nothing short of magical in shaping my story and characters into a true book. I can't thank you enough, and I love that you love my cast of characters as much as I do! And Jocelyn Davies—without you, this manuscript never would have gotten past being a collection of cool ideas and rough scenes. Thank you both!

Endless thanks to my agent, Ammi-Joan Paquette, whose support remains invaluable. I'm one lucky author to get to work with you!

To my entire EMLA family: you have been key in helping me navigate my new path as a published author. I want to say thanks to each and every one of you, but we are a big family and that would take up far too many pages! So just know, if you're reading this—thanks!

All the thanks and love in the world to my critique partners and writing buddies: Tara Sullivan, Annie Cardi, Annie Gaughen, Lauren Barrett, Julia Maranan, and Lisa Palin. You made this entire life path possible for me.

Thank you to my sensitivity readers for your honesty and guidance. I am so grateful I had to opportunity to learn from each one of you.

Julia Sable, thank you for your time, thoughts, creativity, honesty, and interest in this project. I'm tremendously appreciative that we got to work together to concoct the awesome geological events that take place in this book. I had so much fun sketching and brainstorming with you!

To all the geologists who made their research available both to me and the greater public—thank you. The study of our planet and your outreach efforts have never been more important.

To my friends who saw me so rarely during the year I wrote this book—thank you for your patience and support. Kara Dowley, Breanne Cremean, Emily Lockwood, Carolyn Nishon, Marie van Staveren, Karen Powers, Donna Phillips, Emily Pease,

Maryanne Bradley, Greg Spiers, Andy Hall, George Pechmann, Jessica Pechmann, Christina Moscat, Fallon Durant, Liz Logan, Pam Scherl, Talia Sepersky, and so many others . . . To know you're all out there cheering me on means more than I can say.

To my whole family, for all your enthusiasm. And especially to Mom, Dad, and Jeannie: you are my foundation. Every book I write exists because of your support, encouragement, and love. Thank you. I love you.

And finally, thanks to all the kids out there. You know who you are. The brave ones who stick up for what is right. The stubborn ones who see a problem and vow to fix it, no matter what the adults say. The creative ones who do things a little bit differently and bring new ideas into the world. The kind ones who care for people, creatures, and problems others give up on. The curious ones who are always on the lookout for new and exciting things to discover. The determined ones who have a goal and chase it down. The hopeful ones who hold onto the light in the darkness. You're already all doing wonderful things, and I can't wait to see how you continue to change the world.

Don't miss these books by
KATIE SLIVENSKY!

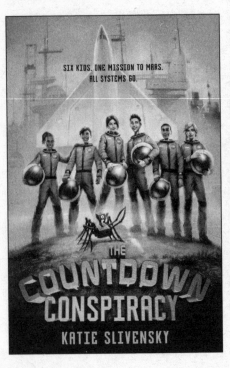

Action-packed, science-infused adventures that will have you on the edge of your seat!

HARPER
An Imprint of HarperCollinsPublishers

www.harpercollinschildrens.com